Langford's Leap

Ted Boone

INKY BLACKNESS PRESS

Visit the author's website at https://tedboone.com

Cover Design & Chapter Artwork: Soheil Toosi

ISBN 978-1-7939-2176-5

Library of Congress Control Number: 2019900483

First printed 2019.

This book is dedicated to my wife, Marisa.

Sometimes you need a nudge to take a leap.

Thank you for nudging me.

"I GIVE HER LESS THAN a minute 'til she smurfs."

The children surrounding Max erupted in derisive laughter, and she ducked her head in embarrassment. Teasing was a necessary part of the initiation ritual, but knowing it didn't take the sting out of it.

"A minute?" Ellie's voice cut through the laughter. "I bet ten chits that Wheezer Girl won't make it thirty seconds."

Another burst of jeering filled the abandoned storage container. Max wanted to offer up a witty retort, but she couldn't think of anything clever to say. Besides, talking back to Ellie would only prolong the torture. Max gritted her teeth and shifted her weight from one knee to the other, trying to relieve the pressure caused by the corrugated ceramo-metallic floor. The rubber gasket of her breathing mask felt slimy against her sweaty cheeks. She just wanted to get this over with.

"What do you say, Maxine?" Ellie asked. "Ready to prove me right? Any last words before you pass out?"

Max glared at Ellie. In return, Ellie briefly lifted her own mask and smiled—the grin of a predator, confident and hungry.

Ellie put her mask back on and said, "Let's put her out of her misery, then." She held up one hand, and the chamber grew quiet. Even the wind, which had been whistling against the container walls, seemed to draw still for a moment. "Good luck, darling," Ellie said, her words dripping with insincerity. Then she chopped her hand downward.

Max pulled off her mask and let it drop to her side. The cool air of the container felt refreshing against her face, and she almost smiled. She thought about all of the other teenagers staring at her—Ellie hovering next to her, waiting to gloat—and laughter almost burst from her throat. Instead, she forced herself to adopt a meditative stance. She kept her head down and her gaze glued to the floor in front of her. Her father wouldn't want her to give in to her baser instincts. He'd coach her to avoid stooping to the level of her torturers.

"Thirty seconds," someone called out.

Max couldn't resist. She looked at Ellie, held up her hands and waggled ten fingers at her. Then she winked.

"What does that mean?" Ellie asked, looking confused.

"You owe her ten chits, Ellie," another audience member said.

A low murmur rolled through the crowd, and Max saw Ellie blush beneath her mask. Max gave her a tight smile and then, before Ellie could respond, she dropped her gaze back to the floor and returned to her meditation.

"One minute," the timekeeper intoned. The crowd shuffled their feet a bit, as if uncertain how to react. The girl kneeling in front of them was frail and sickly. She struggled to breathe in even the best conditions. How was she managing to hold out so long in the open atmosphere?

"One minute thirty." This statement was answered by a few half-hearted cheers and a single clap. Max permitted herself a wry smirk. Maybe she had a few fans in the audience after all. If so, she promised herself they'd be rewarded with a real treat if they waited just a few more seconds.

As if in response to Max's silent oath, someone muttered, "She's gonna beat Ellie's time." Those words polarized the audience, and some people chose to cheer Max's efforts more vocally. In response, Ellie's more loyal followers countered the words of encouragement by screaming foul obscenities, doing their best to disrupt Max's efforts.

To her credit, Max ignored her hecklers. If anything, she drew strength from their frustration. In almost no time at all, she heard the words, "Two minutes." The crowd grew even more frenzied, and Max's supporters gained the upper hand. They pushed to the front of the crowd and shouted down Ellie and her friends. Then, keeping true to the fantasies Max had fostered in the days leading up to her initiation, a chant began.

"Eleven, twelve, thirteen, fourteen...fifteen!"

Just like that, Max crossed the magical threshold: two minutes and fifteen seconds in the open air of Langford's Leap with no mask to aid her breathing. A record set by Ellie during her initiation rite, now broken. The crowd went wild, and for the first time in her life, Max felt like part of something bigger. Like she belonged.

Grinning in triumph, Max began to stand up, but a hand on her shoulder shoved her to the floor. Ellie straddled her, and underneath her mask her face twisted in fury. The crowd, which had been celebrating Max's amazing accomplishment, fell silent again.

"Nice job, mutant," Ellie sneered. She snatched Max's breather mask from her hand. "Guess you don't need this after all, huh?"

The crowd let out a collective gasp. Touching someone else's breathing mask was taboo. Taking away someone's mask was tantamount to reaching out and strangling them. Without a mask, even the heartiest Leap colonist would suffocate in just a few minutes. Ellie had overstepped, and any remaining support she had from the others evaporated.

"Give it back," someone said. Then, louder, "Give it back!" And again, "Give it back, Ellie!" Fear and anger were evident in the shouts, but no one seemed willing to step forward and intervene. The standoff stretched out across the seconds, with no obvious resolution coming.

Max shoved Ellie away and heaved herself up off the floor. She'd been without a breathing aid for almost three minutes. But she didn't panic or lunge for the mask clenched in Ellie's hand. Instead she drew back a fist and punched Ellie square in the stomach.

Ellie collapsed to the floor in a wheezing heap. After gasping for air for a few seconds, she hissed, "Stinking mutie! Not getting your mask back now!" She looked like she wanted to lunge at Max and choke the life from her if she could just gain enough breath to stand back up. Before she got the chance, however, the container doors banged open, flooding the space with blinding sunlight and the roar of the wind.

"What's happening in here?" a loud voice boomed. The crowd scattered like dust in a maelstrom. Through the glare, Max watched as the mask in Ellie's fist was torn from her grasp. Then she felt strong hands force the mask over her face. Those same powerful hands clutched her shoulders and demanded, "What is this foolishness?"

"Nothing, Sister Sonya," Max managed to answer.

Hidden deep within the shadows of her hood, Sister Sonya's single eye glimmered. The color of the frozen sky, her stare pierced Max like a sliver of ice, demanding a better answer. Max shivered but held her tongue. The stare stretched out for a long moment before the woman sighed in exasperation. "Nothing, eh? Doubtful, young lady. Very doubtful."

Sister Sonya's one-eyed stare seemed to stab something

deep within Max and almost caused her to confess. But speaking about the initiation rite would eliminate everything she'd accomplished with her victory. The others would hate her. She'd be an outcast again. She fought down her fear and held on until the Sister finally blinked, releasing Max from her glare. Max breathed a sigh of relief and almost immediately began coughing against the inside of her mask.

The old woman released Max from her grip and turned to haul Ellie up from the floor. "And what say you, Elisabeth? Care to explain why you were holding Maxine's mask while this poor girl risked suffocation?"

"No, Sister Sonya," Ellie said, still short of breath.

"No?" the woman thundered. "You refuse to answer me?" She gave the girl a vigorous shake.

Ellie blanched, but she shook her head. "I'd like to see my father now, Sister."

"Your father?" The Sister leaned in close to Ellie, her hood enveloping the terrified girl's face. From beneath the hood's edge, Max could barely hear whispered words. "Not this time, my dear. This time your father can't save you."

The hour that Max spent in Sister Sonya's company felt like the longest hour of her life. The elderly woman's office was furnished with just a few chairs, a desk, and a shelf full of binders and books. There were no pictures on the walls or knickknacks on the windowsill. Everything in the space served a purpose, and only that purpose. The air was musty and hot but breathable. Which was unfortunate, Max thought, because when the Sister's questions began, hiding behind a mask might've offered at least a little bit of protection.

Sister Sonya was an imposing woman. Self-proclaimed

spiritual leader of the colony, she made a habit of skulking through the community, checking up on her charges to make sure they maintained their moral fortitude. She struck fear into the hearts of children and adults alike when her crouching form appeared in a doorway or her shadow passed down a darkened maintenance corridor. The woman always wore a massive dark robe with her face hidden in the shadow of a deep hood, and her single sapphire eye tirelessly sought out the misdeeds of the colonists. The amorphous robe hid the shape of the woman hunched inside, and it was only when she was angry that she gave any hint of her true stature. Then she'd draw herself up to her full height—at least a head taller than any of the other colonists—and deliver down upon her victim terrible words of reproach and doom.

Sister Sonya seemed to realize that Max was the victim of hazing or bullying, but that didn't mean that she thought Max was innocent of any wrongdoing. Far from it. And the Sister wasn't shy about saying so. She leaned against the front edge of her desk, looming over the two girls sitting in chairs before her, and pummeled each of the girls with questions, accusations, and warnings.

Max rode out the storm of words as best she could. She was thirteen years old, so she was very well-practiced in the art of shrugs, mutterings, and otherwise vague responses. However, the Sister's interrogation techniques were much more persistent than the techniques used by Max's father or teachers, and Max had to resort to coughing fits a few times to escape a pointed question.

Sometimes having a well-known physical ailment had its advantages.

Ellie didn't have any convenient excuses at her disposal. The girl tried over and over again to deflect the Sister's inquisition by asking for her father, but that only seemed to make Sister Sonya angrier and even more determined to squeeze the truth from her. Max almost felt sorry for Ellie as she watched her former tormentor wilt under the Sister's blitzkrieg of questions. And she was convinced that Ellie would have given up all her secrets in short order if her father hadn't interrupted.

A timid knock on the door was followed by a slow creaking, and Bryce Bell pushed his head into the office. "Sister," he began.

"Not finished with these two yet," Sonya said, still looming in front of Ellie's chair.

"Yes, well, I, uh... That is, we, um—" the man stammered. Bryce Bell had been voted Langford's Council Chairman, which made him the official leader of the community. But everyone knew the true lay of the land: when push came to shove, it was Sister Sonya's word that guided the struggling colony. This truth was evident in Bryce's demeanor—his typical boisterous and demanding tone was absent, replaced by timid stuttering.

Grunting in annoyance, Sonya turned toward the door. "Your mumbling words are even more useless than your daughter's dissembling. I thought I raised you to speak more clearly and concisely, boy. Spit. It. Out."

Bryce Bell shrank from the Sister's admonishment, but somehow he forced himself to pull open the door a bit further and let himself into the office. "Sister," he began, and then cleared his throat. "Sister, the Council feels this is a disciplinary matter best handled by the girls' parents."

"Is that so?" Sister Sonya said.

"Yes, Sister," Bryce said, his voice gaining a bit more strength. "The children have misbehaved, but their parents should have the opportunity to deal with the situation as they see fit. I'm confident that proper punishment will—"

"Proper punishment?" Sonya interrupted. "I caught your daughter with Maxine's breathing mask in her hand. Without it, Maxine would have died in mere minutes. What type of punishment does the Langford Council consider proper for attempted murder?"

"M-murder?" Bryce looked flummoxed by this question. As he was attempting to form a coherent response, the office door opened again, and a short, burly man stepped in. He ignored both Bryce and the Sister and moved to stand before Max. He held out a large, calloused hand and beckoned.

"Let's go," he said.

Relieved, Max reached up and took her father's hand. His warm, rough grip felt like home. She stood up, glad the day's drama was finally about to end.

"I'm not done with your daughter, Nolan," Sister Sonya said. But she seemed a bit put off by the man's calm confidence.

"Perhaps not. Nevertheless, we're leaving, Sister."

Nolan's words impacted the cloaked woman like physical blows. "You dare question my authority?" Sister Sonya said. "Did you not hear me speaking with Mr. Bell? Max's foolish actions could have caused her great bodily harm! She could have perished! I think we must get to the bottom of what really happened in that container shell."

"I heard you, Sister," Nolan responded. His voice was quiet, but underneath his mild tone was a steady, bedrock quality that demanded attention and discouraged argument. Max recognized that tone, and was happy she wasn't at its focus. "It sounds to me like my daughter was a victim, not a culprit. A victim, I might add, of your endless preaching as much as anything else. You denounce the Founders and teach the colonists to fear technology and genetic mutation."

"Not to fear technology," Sonya said, "but to respect its place so we don't suffer the same fate as the Founders."

Nolan scowled. "Your words give fools like Mr. Bell—" Nolan gestured to Bryce "—fodder for hatred and superstition."

"How dare you—!" Bryce began.

Nolan released Max's hand and stepped forward and pressed a thick finger into Bryce's chest. "Your Purity Movement, which holds our original genetic template precious above all else, is just a convenient excuse to persecute anyone who questions your authority or, even worse, exhibits the slightest sign of physical weakness. And now your bigotry is being mimicked by your child."

"It was just an initiation, Dad," Max said. She reached forward to take her father's hand again. She was mortified by his actions. "All the kids do it." She looked over at Ellie, hoping her efforts to defuse the situation would win her points. But Ellie, who still sat in her chair, glared at Max with pure hatred.

Nolan glanced down at his daughter for a moment. "Perhaps that's all it was," he said. "An initiation rite that got out of hand." He turned back to Sister Sonya. "Elisabeth and her friends should answer for what they've done. Question them for as long as you'd like and punish them any way you see fit. But Max is innocent of any wrongdoing." He addressed Bryce again. "Maxine is as normal as any other colonist. There's nothing wrong with her. Nothing different. She's just ill. And I'm taking her home."

Max let her father lead her away from Sister Sonya's office. She was embarrassed and angered by the proceedings, and she wondered why her poor health seemed to be the only thing that mattered to people. She was tired of the pity she received from the adult colonists and the scorn she received from her peers. She just wanted to be normal. She wanted to fit in. She wanted to be treated like everyone else. She'd hoped that her success at the day's initiation rites might finally make those things happen, but events hadn't gone as planned. Not at all.

Max's father walked through the rectory, pushing past the other members of the town council and ignoring their questions. He guided Max to the building's foyer and made sure her mask was secured before passing through the airlock and into the canyon passageway outside.

Under normal circumstances, Max would have balked at letting her father hold her hand during the long walk home. But today, she decided to let it slide. She could sense her father's need to maintain their physical contact. He needed to reassure himself that she was there by his side, safe and secure. And she had to admit, after her episode with the Sister, the gentle squeeze of his hand was a welcome comfort.

Their journey took them down the main canyon throughway and past the numerous side passages carved into the rocky walls on both sides of them. High above them, the sky was fading from its blinding daytime glare to a darker, more tolerable azure. The natural features of the canyon protected the small community from the harsh elements. Their world was an unforgiving place, with unbreathable atmosphere, scorching sunlight, and frigid temperatures. The canyon only helped a little, giving the colonists shelter from the blazing sunlight and protecting them from the strongest winds. Today, however, a cold breeze still whipped past them, tugging at Max's thick insulated jacket and making her clutch her father's hand. Underneath her mask, Max labored to breathe the clean, cool air it provided and fought the temptation to cough. She didn't want her father to worry any more than he already was.

They made their way to a series of lower tunnels, where they weaved past airlocks and air treatment machinery, past dark grottos of mushroom and lichen farms, and arrived at the airlock to their domicile. The two of them stepped inside the outer airlock and swung the ceramo-metal door closed behind them.

Unlike other airlock chambers in the canyon community, Max's father had arranged for their front door to serve as both a means of repressurization and decontamination. After the airlock chamber circulated fresh, breathable air into the space, Max and her father both began removing their clothing until they were both standing in their underwear.

In recent months, Max had begun to protest this arrangement. Standing in your underwear in the presence of your parent was *not* an ideal situation for a blossoming young teenager, for multiple obvious reasons. Unfortunately, Max's father thought like an engineer first and a parent second. He seemed immune to every attempt Max had made to reason with him. And she'd tried everything. But despite shouting and pleading, temper tantrums and silent treatments, nothing could convince him to alter their strict regimen of decontamination before entering their home. The only concession she'd gotten from him was that they now turned their backs to each other during the sterilization process. Small comfort, but it was better than nothing.

Max did her best to not think about her father standing just inches away from her and waited for the ultraviolet flashes and chemical misting to finish. She looked down in disgust at her skinny, pallid body, so different from the solid swarthiness of the typical colonist. Where Max was delicate, with pale skin, bright blue eyes, and raven hair that framed her sharp, narrow features, her fellow canyon dwellers were stocky and powerful, with dark skin and even darker eyes. Just one more way Max was different from everyone else.

When the system dinged, indicating that it was safe to exit, Max grabbed a pair of sterile overalls and pulled them on. Then, shielding her eyes from her father's still half-dressed body, she shrugged past him and started heading toward her bedroom.

"Not so fast," Nolan said. "We have a lot to talk about,

young lady."

Damn. "Dad, can we please do this later? I'm tired."

"Not later. Now." Her father finished tugging on his own overalls. "And don't start with that fake coughing, Max. That's not going to work tonight."

Max lowered her hand from her mouth in defeat. She wanted to protest, but it was no use. Her father knew her too well. Resigned, she cleared her throat and sniffled in what she hoped was a pitiful way.

"Tell me what really happened today with the other children," her father said.

Shrugging, Max relayed the events in the cargo container to her father. They had very few secrets from one another. Her father didn't judge her, and he was a good listener. He was her best friend, and Max felt comfortable telling him anything.

Almost anything, she reminded herself.

Max told her dad about the initiation ceremony: about how children had to remove their breathing masks and hold their breath for as long as possible, and then survive a few seconds longer after sucking in the poisonous, oxygen-poor atmosphere of the outside world. The longer a person lasted before putting their mask back on, the more credibility they earned with the other children.

"How long?" Nolan asked, his face expectant and a little worried. "How long did you hold your breath?"

"I'm...not sure," Max lied. "A minute, maybe? Not very long."

But her father grinned, pleased with her answer. "An entire minute? Maxine, that's fantastic! Those breathing exercises we've been practicing must be making a difference!" He gave her a playful punch to the arm.

"Ow," Max responded, rubbing her shoulder. "Yeah, maybe. I dunno. Maybe I got lucky."

"Luck had no part in your performance today, kiddo. That was willpower and persistence. I told you that you could beat this breathing problem with hard work, didn't I? I knew you could do it."

"I guess so. Does that mean I'm not in trouble then?"

Nolan shook his head. "Like I told Sister Sonya, it sounds to me like you were the victim. Ellie never should have taken your mask from you. Of course, volunteering to participate in the initiation rite was your decision. That might not have been the smartest move—"

"But Dad! I—"

"—but I understand why you did it," her father continued. He walked over to a shelf in the kitchen and retrieved a small object wrapped in burlap cloth. "Fitting in with the other children is important. And I'm sure your performance today will go a long way toward making you feel like part of the group. I'm proud of you, kid." He placed the burlap package on the kitchen table and gestured for Max to unwrap it.

Smiling crookedly, Max tugged loose the cloth and revealed an ordinary looking rock, rough and dull. Max's smile faltered. "Thanks?" she managed.

Nolan chuckled. He reached across the table and lifted the top of the stone from its base. Hidden within the shell of stone was a dazzling array of white and violet crystals. The crystalline facets sparkled brightly, even in the dull light of the kitchen.

"Happy birthday, Max. I can't believe my little girl is already thirteen years old."

Max looked up from the beautiful crystals. "Thanks, Dad." Max blushed. And then she started coughing. For real this time.

After the spell passed, the two of them spoke for a few more minutes, and then Nolan retired for the evening. He was scheduled for another early start to perform maintenance on one of the kite farms. It was easier to get surface work completed before sunrise. After the winds picked up, repairing the equipment would be almost impossible. Nolan was almost always gone before Max woke up in the mornings.

Max spread her homework out across the kitchen table and bid her father goodnight. She gave a half-hearted attempt to complete her math assignment but was distracted by the mesmerizing light reflected inside the geode, combined with the soft sounds of her father's breathing in the other room. Turning the geode slowly in her hands, Max listened, waiting until she could hear a slow, steady rhythm of snoring that meant her father was sound asleep. Satisfied, she carefully placed the geode back on the table and wrapped it in its burlap cloth. Then she tiptoed into the airlock and cycled the chamber.

Max stepped into the outer tunnel and, after looking both directions to make sure no one was watching, stole her way back to the main canyon. The sun was approaching the horizon and the wind had quietened. She walked to a point where the canyon floor started to rise back up toward the surface. She checked her surroundings, but she was the only human in sight. The rest of the colonists on Langford's Leap were safely behind their airlocks. She was alone.

Max found an outcropping to sit on. She removed her breathing mask and set it down on the rock next to her. She took a long, deep breath of Langford's poisonous air and sighed in contentment. Happy, she spent the next few minutes just enjoying the act of breathing, watching the sun set behind the distant mountain peaks, and waiting for her favorite star to rise.

JUST LIKE EVERY OTHER MORNING, Ceres's first stop after waking was the fruit grove. As she rode the lift outward from the microgravity sleeping chambers to the heavier spin of the outer rings, she felt herself sink into the soles of her boots, and her swirling halo of hair settled into something a bit more manageable.

The lift door opened, and Ceres was greeted by a gentle kiss of humidity and citrus. Sighing contentedly, she bounded down the grove path and picked a ripe orange from one of the stunted trees that bordered the walkway. She dug her fingernails into the fruit's outer skin, peeled it away in a quick, practiced motion, and dropped the rind to the floor. A robotic drone, no larger than a field mouse, darted out from behind one of the trees and snatched the discarded skin, scurrying away with its treasure and taking it to be recycled into the biome.

Ceres popped a fleshy orange wedge into her mouth. She bit down and uttered another contented sigh as sweet juice flooded her mouth and dripped down her chin. "Good morning, Rhea," she mumbled to no one in particular.

"Good morning, Ceres. Did you sleep well?"

Ceres grinned as she devoured another wedge of fruit. "I slept well, Rhea. I always sleep well. When have I ever answered differently? You don't have to keep asking every morning."

"It's polite," Rhea answered.

"Perhaps. But that's not why you do it. You ask because it's in your programming. You *have* to ask. You have no choice, do you?" She raised one eyebrow at the empty air, to serve as an additional question mark.

But Rhea chose not to answer her query. Instead, she asked, "Are you prepared to discuss today's tasks, Ceres?"

Ceres had wandered farther down the path, seeking out more breakfast fruit. She felt like something more exotic than oranges this morning. Perhaps a mango, or a star fruit, or even— "Ooh!" Ceres exclaimed and jogged over to a dwarf papaya tree. The fruit looked promising. She chose the ripest papaya and dug into her overalls for her paring knife.

"Ceres?"

"Yeah, yeah," she answered, busying herself with the job of cutting open the small melon and digging out the small pile of seeds. Her feet were swarmed by drones collecting her refuse for later planting. Ceres carved a mouth-sized chunk of flesh from the melon and ate it. The taste was exquisite. She'd have to make sure to tag this tree's genetic sequence for future cross-breeding.

"Ceres? Are you prepared to discuss today's tasks?"

Ceres scowled. "Can't you see that I'm eating breakfast here, machine?"

"We have a strict schedule to maintain—" Rhea began.

Ceres groaned. "You win. You always win. You're a relentless computer algorithm, after all. What's on the agenda, Rhea?"

"I have a few choices for you today."

Ceres almost choked on her papaya and spent the next few

moments sputtering and clearing her throat. When she could breathe again, she said, "Did you say choices?"

"Yes, choices." Rhea's voice sounded amused. "You've expressed frustration and boredom with our recent schedule. So today you'll be given the opportunity to choose from a set of lesson plans."

"Wow! That's—" Ceres stopped herself. She was about to say "great!" but something didn't quite feel right. "That's odd," she said. "Is this a test?"

Rhea's computerized voice emitted its best approximation of an exasperated sigh. "Every choice is a test, Ceres."

"Great. So you're giving me choices, but *how* I choose is also a part of today's lesson?"

"Would you prefer it if we returned to our previous arrangement? Where I assign you tasks without choice?"

"No, no, I want choices," Ceres answered. "Sorry if I'm doubtful. It's just that this whole scenario is a bit unusual. Surprising, even. And you don't often surprise me, Rhea. You tend to be predictable."

In response, Rhea asked, "Are you prepared to discuss today's choices?"

"I am."

"Choices: collecting manufacturing materials from the asteroid belt, mining Cronos for Helium-3, or reconfiguring the genetic algorithms for deep-sea algae bloom insertions."

"Algae? Yuck. Cross that one out."

"Remaining choices are—"

"Rocks or gas, yes. I heard you the first time." Ceres paused to consider her options. Diving into the closest gas giant, Cronos, and searching for Helium-3 would require precise planning calculations, as well as quick reactions to deal with the ever-shifting winds deep inside the planet's turbulent atmosphere. But in the end, that was all it would entail: arithmetic and reflexes. It would be hard work, but also predictable work. Not much fun.

Heading out to the asteroid field, on the other hand, was much less predictable. Rhea had mapped out most of the larger asteroids in the belt, but there were millions of other, smaller rocks tumbling around out there. The only way to find useful material was to jump from rock to rock. Odds were that most asteroids would be devoid of any useful manufacturing materials, but every once in a while you'd hit on an asteroid jackpot and find rare minerals, or even small pockets of volatiles like frozen water or methane. It was a game of chance, and most of the time, you lost. But on those rare occasions where you did find something useful...

"Let's go rock hopping in the asteroid belt," Ceres decided. "I'll head up to the control room."

"No. We won't be teleoperating the equipment today. Our current orbital position will allow us to operate a collector in person. Please go to the launching bay and don the proper attire for the excursion."

"You're serious? Direct operation?" Ceres dropped the remainder of her fruit and bounded back to the lift as quickly as she could in the heavy tug of centrifugal force imparted by the ring's spin.

As the lift carried her up to the central hub, Ceres vibrated with excitement. She'd never before had the opportunity to leave the station on an excursion. Today's trip to the asteroid belt was going to be a novel experience.

Because of the enormous distances of space, most extra-vehicular activities were performed remotely, rather than directly. But that often meant long communication lags, which meant slow reaction times, lots of sitting around, and waiting for things to happen. Activities that required more nimble responses—like navigating the asteroid field or tweaking the cloud scraper's descent into Cronos' gas giant atmosphere—usually required that the station be moved into close proximity to the project. But still, for safety reasons, telepresence was standard operating procedure. Controlling the mining craft by hand was something Ceres had been begging to do for a long time, and today her wish was coming true.

Rhea was full of surprises.

The lift came to a halt at the docking hub at the center of the ship. With a sigh, the lift's doors opened out on a tiny airlock. Ceres stripped out of her overalls and tugged on a pressure suit from a nearby locker. The suit crackled with static electricity as autonomic systems adjusted the smart fabric to conform to her body shape. Within moments, she was encased in a bright red skin suit that covered her from toes to chin. She looked like she'd been dipped in candle wax. She donned gloves and boots from the locker, and they hissed and popped as they locked into place around her hands and feet.

Next, Ceres reached up and pushed a small tab on the suit's collar, closed her eyes, and waited while tendrils of warm goo crawled their way up from the collar and enveloped her head. It was a strange sensation, especially when the smart-gel crept into her mouth, ears, and nose, and tickled its way across her scalp. But it only took a few seconds for the gel to work its magic, and once it was done she couldn't feel anything at all.

Ceres opened her eyes and took a deep breath. The smart-gel seemed to be working perfectly, providing her with crystal-clear vision and hearing and pumping air into her lungs as she breathed. She was shielded from the harsh vacuum of space. Her suit chirped through its final self-diagnostics checks, and a green light blinked in her peripheral vision to indicate nominal performance. Satisfied, Ceres closed the suit locker and cycled the airlock.

The docking bay didn't spin like the rest of the ship, which meant that there was no centrifugal force to anchor her to the floor. The small space inside the airlock made the lack of gravity inconsequential, but the docking area was a much larger space, so Ceres had to maneuver by pulling herself from handhold to handhold along the walls and floor. It wasn't difficult, but she still moved carefully. The docking hub was mostly empty space, and if Ceres got herself stranded beyond the reach of a handhold, she'd have to wait for Rhea to send a drone to rescue her from freefall. That kind of embarrassing error wasn't the way she wanted to begin today's exercise.

Gliding along the floor of the chamber, Ceres gave one of the passing handholds a slight twist, which caused her body to rotate as she drifted. Another slight twist to another handhold arrested her rotation, and now she was heading feet first toward her destination. Looking "down" between her feet, she used other passing handholds to adjust her trajectory until she was aimed at the airlock of the mining craft below. She descended into the airlock, and when the soles of her boots made contact, she let her legs absorb her momentum and reached out to slow herself further with her hands. Once she was motionless again she reached up to trigger the outer hatch. The mining craft's airlock cycled, and Ceres flipped over and moved to the cockpit.

At first, the cockpit appeared as a plain white chamber with a comfortable control couch as its only distinctive feature. As Ceres strapped herself in to the couch, the cockpit's virtual control environment transformed, filling the blank space with instrumentation panels and control clusters.

Ceres knew that Rhea had already begun preflight checks on the small craft, but she checked the system herself, just to be sure everything was in order. It was unlikely—impossible, even—that she'd spot something wrong that Rhea wouldn't also detect. But that wasn't the point. As Rhea pointed out again and again, the training exercises were meant to teach Ceres how to operate the equipment without Rhea's constant intervention.

After preflight, Ceres said, "My board shows green. Control, do you concur?"

"Agreed," Rhea said. "You are go for launch."

"Copy that. Rhea, transfer guidance and motor control to internals. Launch in T-minus fifteen seconds." The station relinquished control of the small craft to the cockpit, and Ceres's hands flashed over the control surfaces. A virtual window showed the docking bay's main doors iris open, revealing a brilliant starscape.

"Three...two...one...launch."

Ceres was pressed back hard into the control couch as the docking bay's catapult system launched the mining craft out into space. The craft was clear of the docking bay when Ceres activated the internal engines. She was rewarded by another hard kick to the back as the ship's thrusters began accelerating her toward the asteroid belt.

Checking to make sure her board was green, Ceres keyed her mic and said, "Rhea, the mining vessel is free and clear. Do you have any proposed targets for me during my mining expedition?"

Her query was met with silence. Puzzled, Ceres checked her controls to make sure the communication array was set correctly. Everything appeared to be functioning nominally. "Rhea, I repeat, what are my targets for today's lesson?"

There was still no response. That was worrisome.

Ceres cut the main engines. Losing communication with the station was a very bad thing. Perhaps as bad as it could get. Ceres's mind raced. Was the mining craft damaged somehow, despite internal diagnostics? Or perhaps she'd damaged the station during takeoff? She'd been anxious to fire the mining craft's thrusters. Perhaps she'd ignited the engines too close to the docking bay and had caused a catastrophic failure of the station's superstructure?

Feeling a little queasy, Ceres reached out and tasked a virtual window to display an image of the receding station behind her. Much to her relief, no sign of damage was evident in the image. She queried one of the station's external cameras and received a broadcast image of her own small ship drifting against a black background. That was also good news. It meant that at least some communication was flowing between her small craft and the station.

With tiny puffs from the mining craft's maneuvering thrusters, Ceres rotated her craft in a twisting pirouette and examined the changing image on her screen. Visually, everything looked to be in perfect working order.

Hmm. No obvious damage to the station, no obvious damage to her craft. And communications *were* functioning, or she wouldn't have been able to query the station's camera system.

That meant the issue was something with her direct communication link to Rhea. A software glitch. Protocol dictated that she turn the craft around and return to the station until the communications problem could be remedied. As Ceres began plotting her return trajectory on the navigation screen, she noticed movement on her visual display of the station.

Zooming in, she saw the doors to the docking bay iris closed.

Odd.

Rhea was omnipresent in space station operations. The station's artificial intelligence unit must be aware that communications with the mining craft had been lost. And the AI would also know that Ceres would be returning to the dock momentarily, as per protocol after communication failure. Why had the AI closed the bay doors?

Unless the "malfunction" was intentional? Part of the training exercise...?

"Oh my," Ceres exclaimed. "Rhea, you are full of surprises, aren't you?" Not sure whether to be annoyed or elated, Ceres cleared the navigation board, spun the ship around, and started mapping a new trajectory toward the asteroid belt. On another screen she began running rudimentary spectrographic analysis of asteroids in the nearby vicinity. She was determined to strike bounty today.

After all, today's mission was the first time in her young life that she'd ever been alone.

IT WAS STILL EARLY WHEN Max stumbled out of bed the next morning, but her father had already departed for his maintenance work. Max yawned her way through breakfast and a quick shower. She'd stayed out late watching the sunlight fade from the sky and had stood entranced by the sharp, dazzling pinpoints of starlight that had filled the night. Only when the clap of thunder had echoed down the canyon had she dusted herself off and snuck back into her bedroom to catch a few hours of sleep.

Now she was paying for her late night outing. The day promised to be a long one.

She dug through her school knapsack and checked her work schedule, which was jotted down on a folded scrap of paper. When she saw her assigned chore for the day, she gave out a loud groan. There were plenty of work duties that she didn't like, but harvesting mushrooms was at the top of the list. She recognized their importance: fungi in general were a critical aspect of colony life, used for composting biological refuse, which resulted in excellent fertilizers and invaluable medicinal compounds. Without mushrooms, the colony likely wouldn't exist. But farming mushrooms was slow, meticulous work, and the odor in the dank dark caves was unbearable. Even with her mask on, the smell of decay managed to creep into Max's sinuses and cause her to cough uncontrollably.

She wondered if she could collect her ten chits from Ellie and use them to buy her way out of her fungal afternoon. The thought made her snort in amusement. She knew it was unlikely that she'd ever collect on that particular debt.

Thinking about Ellie got Max worrying about how she'd be received at school after the excitement of the initiation ritual. Had her breath-holding performance earned her a higher spot on the social pecking order? Or had Sister Sonya's interruption cost her any points she'd earned with her peers? It was with great trepidation that she stepped into the schoolhouse that morning and removed her mask and coat.

The reaction she received was unexpected. Mostly because there was no reaction at all. The other students in the front atrium brushed past her on their way to their respective classes with barely a glance in her direction. A few gave her waves of hello, but nothing in their facial expressions indicated any unusual interest in Max's arrival. It was business as normal for the children of the colony.

Max wasn't sure how to react to the lack of reaction. She supposed that, given how everything had played out, she should consider maintaining the status quo a victory. But for weeks she'd been building up the initiation rite in her head, knowing she could smash the record set by Ellie two years earlier. She'd been pinning all hopes of ending her social exclusion on her success during the initiation. It was hard to accept that while she may not have damaged her reputation, her record-breaking performance hadn't done anything to advance her social situation, either.

Feeling both relieved and defeated, Max made her way to her first class, only pausing once on the way to fight down a coughing spell. In the classroom, she did her best to pay attention to her teacher as he explained the intricate details of kite-generator efficiency ratios and geothermal heat pump feasibility surveys—critical knowledge for anyone who wished to keep the colony alive, to be sure, but about as exciting as watching algae grow. As the class lingered on interminably, Max began to think that spending the afternoon in a moldy cave didn't sound so bad after all.

Lunch was one of Max's favorite times of the day. Not for the food, which seemed to be prepared with blandness in mind and always made her feel sick to her stomach. And not for the company, because she almost never had any. Max spent most lunch periods sitting by herself, nursing her cough. If she was stuck sitting by herself, at least she could spend her time *not* listening to boring factoids about farming equipment and could daydream about better things, things like—

"Hi, Max."

Max looked up, startled out of her reverie, and then did a double-take when she realized someone was standing next to her, saying hello. It was Aida. Aida was everything Max wasn't: beautiful and funny and charming and popular. And she'd never even made eye contact with Max before today.

"Um," Max said. And then, to add even more spice to her scintillating conversational skills, "What?"

Aida brushed her perfect black hair away from her dark brown eyes and said again, "Hi." Then she tilted her head and gave Max her signature brilliant smile, and Max felt like an icicle melting in the noonday sun. She needed to sit down, but then realized she already was. *Maybe lower. The floor underneath this table looks pretty appealing right about now.*

Before she could slide off her bench and cower under the dining table, Aida sat down across from her and said, "You were amazing yesterday. I didn't think anyone could hold their breath for that long."

Feeling her confidence bolstered just a little bit by Aida's comments, Max sat up a little straighter and said, "Thanks. I got lucky, I guess."

Aida shook her head. "No way. That wasn't luck. That was skill. And watching Ellie freak out like that afterward? That was the best part!"

Max laughed at that. "But I thought you and Ellie were friends?" Aida was always sitting with the elite clique during lunch.

"Not exactly," Aida said. "I know we hang out with a few of the same people, sure, but Ellie isn't much fun to be around. She's bossy and selfish, and her dad is a total jerk, always pushing that stupid 'purity first' crap."

"That's true," Max agreed.

"You do have the other kids wondering, though..."

"Wondering? About what?"

Aida leaned in and whispered, "About whether or not you're a *mutie*."

"No!" Max shouted. She surprised herself with the strength of her reaction. Around the cafeteria, students turned to stare at her. Max forced a chuckle and said, "That's ridiculous. Everyone knows normal humans can't breathe the atmosphere of Leap."

Max hoped her voice didn't sound too desperate. Beating the record during the initiation ritual was a means of improving her status with the other young colonists. And it had worked, or she wouldn't be talking to Aida now. But what if she'd overstepped? What if her peers started asking difficult questions? What if her secret was revealed? Having everyone view her as a freak of nature would be *much* worse than just being the weird sick kid.

Aida reached across the lunch table and patted Max's arm. "No worries. I was just kidding. Listen, I was wondering if later you and I might—"

The cafeteria doors banged open, and one of the school's administrators shouted, "Attention! There's a mandatory assembly in the atrium in ten minutes!" Then the woman turned on her heel and was gone again.

The announcement caused a loud rumble of speculation amongst the cafeteria crowd. Aida stood, her earlier question forgotten. "What do you think this is about?" she asked instead.

"I'm not sure," Max said, but Aida wasn't listening. She was already heading back to her usual lunch table to confer with her other friends about the sudden announcement. Whatever she'd been planning for later with Max was gone from her mind.

"Bye!" Max muttered with an exasperated hand wave. She forced herself to finish the last bite of her lunch before following the rest of the students out of the cafeteria. She wasn't sure what awaited them out in the atrium, but it had interrupted her first—and perhaps only—conversation with one of the popular kids, which meant that whatever was going on, Max didn't like it.

When Max saw who was standing in the center of the atrium, her dislike intensified. Bryce Bell, bracketed by two other council members, was standing in the middle of the gathering crowd of students and adults, smiling with benevolence. In his hands he clutched a strange object. The students crowded close to the council members, eyeballing the odd object. The teachers and other adult colonists, standing back behind the jostling children, looked equally intrigued.

Bell was in fine form, standing in front of the colonists and demonstrating his normal calm and commanding presence, which had been so conspicuously absent in Sister Sonya's office. He waited until the crowd drew quiet on its own. Then he held the mysterious object high above his head and with a loud clear voice proclaimed, "The engines of capriciousness have once again sent false treasures down upon us, threatening to tempt the faithful away from the Path of Pureness!"

If the crowd was quiet before, now there was absolute stillness. The object in Bryce Bell's hands glinted in the light as he spun around, showing it to his captivated audience. The councilman beamed at the spellbound colonists, and Max swore she could feel the man's pride and triumph radiate like heat through the crowd.

Someone elbowed Max in the ribs, and she turned angrily to the person standing next to her.

"What is that thing?" Aida whispered, her gaze transfixed by Bell's treasure.

"How should I know?" Max answered. She scowled at the girl. Aida's irresistible charm had faded in the last few minutes. "Something useless, probably, just like every other piece of junk that falls from the sky."

Before Max could say more, Bell began speaking again. "We all wait for salvation to come to our ravaged colony here on Leap. But as all faithful colonists know, salvation will only come if we stay true to the Path of Pureness. We must not let the trinkets that fall from above interrupt our faithfulness.

"Our forefathers were foolish. They were prideful. They flaunted their advanced technological prowess, filling the skies above them with wondrous manufactories that could build whatever their hearts desired. They lived in a world where one merely needed to imagine their desire for something, and within a few hours have that desire met with gifts from the sky.

"Worse, the original colonists modified their bodies and minds with biological and mechanical augmentations, designed not just to survive the harsh elements of their new world, but to suit their every lascivious desire. They walked the surface of Langford's Leap, not as men and women, but as horrific genetic hybrids, mutated almost beyond recognition.

"The founders, in all their hubris, abandoned the one thing that must never be sacrificed: their humanity. And they paid for their folly. By abandoning their human heritage, they exposed themselves to The Great Disaster.

"We don't know what started the Great Disaster. We don't even know what the Great Disaster was. Records from the time were lost to the chaos. But we do know *why* the Great Disaster happened." Bryce Bell paused, and his expression grew stern. "It was *punishment.*"

"*Punishment*? That's preposterous," Sister Sonya said, interrupting Bell's speech. The crowd turned and parted, clearing a path for the woman as she approached the councilman. "Stop spouting such nonsense, Bryce. You've no idea what you're talking about."

"Don't I?" Bell asked. "Even without official records, isn't it obvious what happened? Our forefathers went too far. They lost their way, abandoned their humanity, and paid for their errors with their lives. It was only by adopting our true nature, abandoning all modifications and living as pure humans, that the few of us remaining have avoided the same fate." He held the strange object in his hand aloft once more. "This new treasure, delivered from the machines circling in the heavens just above us, is meant to tempt us down the same treacherous path that doomed our Founders and almost destroyed our colony." He lowered the object and pointed it at the Sister. "It's you who taught us these things."

Sonya snorted in disgust and snatched the object from Bell's hand. "You fool. I taught you no such thing. Are you daft? Do you believe this colony would still exist without the technologies provided from the manufactories above us? Do you think you could live without the kite generators, or the air purification systems, or the countless other devices that make survival for base humans possible?" Sonya turned to the colonists. "Mr. Bell is right about one thing. The original colonists erred by allowing technology to overtake their lives. But we cannot let their mistake to cast us too far in the other direction. We cannot fear the sporadic gifts from the heavens. Without technology, this new colony in the canyons is as doomed as its predecessor. We must learn to strike a balance. We need the machines the manufactories above us provide.

"Unfortunately, the orbiting manufactories above us were gravely damaged in the Great Disaster. They function, but their production schedule follows no rhyme or reason. Some of the objects they deliver to us we use to tremendous advantage, like the kite generators. Others serve no practical purpose other than to remind us that the factories are still there, orbiting the planet, and still function. But until the manufactories are repaired, our survival is very much in doubt."

"And how will we fix them?" someone called out from the crowd.

Sister Sonya nodded toward the voice. She was in familiar territory now, preaching her common message to the colonists. The question from the crowd was predictable. It was regularly asked and answered during the Sister's many sermons. "We have sent our prayers for aid out across the great expanse of space to the only source of help left available to us: Earth. Now we must wait for our prayers to reach the ears of our ancestors, and then we must wait longer still for their response to reach back to us across the void.

"It has been many long years since we first called out for aid, and still more years stretch in front of us before help will arrive. Maintaining faith in the face of such a long and painful wait is a constant challenge. Life is hard on Leap, and only grows harder as our resources dwindle and our equipment fails. Doubt is a constant companion, threatening even the most devout soul and tempting each of us to give in to hopelessness and despair. But we must not give up. We must not give in. Help will arrive, someday." Sonya paused, her single blue eye blazing from beneath her hood as she looked around the atrium, taking in each and every member of the audience. "I promise you, help will arrive."

A perceptible sigh of relief rippled through the crowd at Sister Sonya's assurance. Max resisted the inclination to roll her eyes.

Sister Sonya held up the object in her hand once more. "This gift from the heavens may serve a practical function. More importantly, it is a reminder that we must keep believing. We must keep hoping, because the day will come when we're saved from our torment. The day will come when our ancestors arrive to save us. The day will come when the heavens once again deliver miracles down upon the worthy. And on that day the long darkness will dissipate, and the colony's former glory *will* return!"

Upon the delivery of this last statement, the crowd surrounding Sister Sonya and the councilmen erupted in cheers. Looking around, Max realized she might be the only person in the atrium who wasn't impressed by the Sister's preaching. *All of this for a pointless piece of space debris. How stupid.*

But in an effort to fit in, she joined in with the cheering. Aida turned and grinned at her, and Max felt conflicted. On the one hand, Aida was just another ignorant fool caught up in the pack mentality. On the other hand, she was everything Max wished she could be. If the two of them could become friends...

"The Sister is right," Bryce Bell said, interrupting the

cheering as he stepped forward once more. "We must hold onto our faith. And, of course, we must use critical technologies to survive. But we must also never forget the mistakes our predecessors made. We must keep our bodies and minds pure. We must remain *human*. And we must remain vigilant, ever-watchful for other colonists who may drift from the Path."

The mood of the crowd, which had been jubilant after Sonya's speech, shifted toward uneasiness. Children and adults glanced at their neighbors. A hollow of fear and resentment yawned open in the pit of Max's stomach. Aida elbowed her in the ribs again. She waggled her eyebrows at Max and mouthed the word "mutie." Max grimaced at Aida's attempt at humor. She felt sick.

Max didn't return to classes after the assembly. Instead she decided to head home before chores. She let herself into the airlock and followed her father's strict sterilization procedure. She was surprised to find Nolan sitting at the kitchen table and studying a diagram drawn on a large piece of papyrus. She was glad she hadn't skipped sterilization, which would have resulted in an inevitable lecture.

"Kelly's papermaking has really improved," Nolan said by way of greeting.

"That's...great, I guess," Max said.

"It is," her father agreed. "Written records are as important to the colony's long-term survival as air and water. Unfortunately, even the best paper wouldn't help me understand these circuit diagrams. I got the malfunctioning generator working again this morning, but only with a clumsy workaround. We risk losing the generator if I can't figure out these schematics."

"Uh-huh." Max waited to see if her father wanted to share more details about his work. She knew from past experience that he always painted a doomsday picture when he discussed his repair projects, but he also always managed to fix things in the end, which was why he was so valuable to the colony and why he demanded respect from all of the other colonists, including Sister Sonya. When no more commentary seemed to be forthcoming from her father, Max said, "Bryce Bell stopped by school today. He presented us with another fallen artifact."

Her father nodded, his eyes still locked on his diagram. "I know. I was the one who found it."

"You found it?" Max exclaimed.

"Yeah, sitting over by the broken generator. Must've dropped in late last night." He pointed at a plate on the kitchen table. "There's a spare sandwich. Eat."

Aha, Max thought as she grabbed half the sandwich and began chewing. So it hadn't been thunder she'd heard last night during her outing, it had been the booming arrival of a fast-moving space delivery capsule. She should have realized when Bryce had first displayed his latest treasure. "Any idea what it is?"

"Not really. I didn't examine it for very long because I had to get working on the kite winch before the morning winds picked up. If I had to hazard a guess, I'd say it's a type of mining gear. A laser drill or something, maybe. Not that it matters. Whatever it is it needs a massive power supply, which doesn't exist down here anymore. Without a proper power supply, it's just a useless lump of metal and plastic."

"You should've seen Bryce Bell and Sister Sonya," Max said. "Both of them preaching and preening because of a useless object from the sky."

"Not useless," her father said, looking up from his schematics. "The objects we receive from the orbital manufactories, even the ones we can't use, still serve an important symbolic purpose."

"Oh, Dad, no." Max rolled her eyes. "*Please* don't tell me

they're gifts from the 'engines of capriciousness,' reminding all of us to keep the faith and remain on the Path of Pureness. Or twiddle our thumbs until a mysterious savior from the heavens comes to save us."

"'Engines of capriciousness?'" her father said, a wry grin on his lips. "That's a good one. Bryce Bell does have quite a way with words, doesn't he? But no, I wasn't going to say anything like that. You know I'm not one for blind faith and false hopes, Maxine."

"That's true. So, what do *you* think the fallen objects represent?"

"Humility."

"Humility?" She thought that over. "How so?"

Nolan pointed at the schematic laid out on the table in front of him. "Sometimes we need to remind ourselves of how much we once had and have now lost. How little we understand our past, and how pride and overconfidence were almost the colony's complete undoing. How technology isn't always the answer to our problems. The objects that fall from the orbitals are a reminder of how far we've fallen as a people. That's a lesson worth learning."

Max raised her eyebrows at her father. "What did you do with my dad? You know, the practical guy who fixes stuff and leaves the philosophical mumbo jumbo to Sister Sonya and her faithful flock, or Bryce Bell and the New Puritan loonies?"

That earned her a laugh. "Cute. Speaking of practical matters, don't you have chores this afternoon?"

Max glanced over at the wall clock. "Damn it! I'm going to be late to the mushroom grove."

"Language, young lady," her father admonished.

"I'm thirteen," Max protested. "Cursing is a required skill for my age group!"

Her father gave her another laugh. "Again, very cute. But also wrong. Cursing is for weak-minded individuals who lack—"

Max snatched the remaining half of the sandwich from the kitchen table, and then backed into the airlock. "Sorry, Dad, gotta run! Chores, responsibility, all of that! We'll talk more later about this important issue, I promise!"

As the airlock door closed, Max heard one more muffled, "Cute."

She smiled to herself. *Yup.*

4

THE AFTERNOON IN THE MUSHROOM caverns was as noxious and boring as Max had predicted. She spent most of her time checking the water and ammonia levels in the mushroom trays, adding various microbes to the soil to ensure proper growth conditions. Each type of mushroom required specific levels of moisture and fertilizer and required her to check the instructional plaques posted by the entrance to each small cave. As much as she detested the work, Max wanted to make sure she didn't make any mistakes. The other colonists counted on the mushroom harvests to provide them with invaluable food and medicine.

By the time her supervisor called the end of the four-hour shift, Max was coughing uncontrollably from the fungal spores that had snuck past the seals of her mask and invaded her sinuses. She trudged up the tunnel passageway toward home, feeling dizzy and fuzzy-headed. She was tempted to remove her mask but opted instead to lift it away from her face and wipe her mouth and streaming nose with a damp cloth. It wasn't much help, but it was the best she could do until she got home and sterilized.

Max's path home through the caves took her away from

the main thoroughfares and into one of the darker, less-traveled tunnels. She was still sneezing and coughing frequently, so it took her a while to hear the echo of footsteps behind her. Normally the sound of other colonists traversing the caves wouldn't be notable. But once Max noticed, she couldn't help but detect something odd about the sounds. The footsteps were softer than the normal trudge of a fatigued colonist. More careful. Sneaky, even.

Max stopped in her tracks and held her breath. After a moment, the footsteps behind her also stopped. Her neck hair prickled in the sudden silence, and she hesitated. Was she just imagining things? She started walking again, and soon enough the echo of footsteps joined her. Fearful now, she picked up her pace toward home. *It's probably nothing.* Then again, her father would encourage her to err on the side of caution.

Looking over her shoulder, Max took a quick turn and headed toward a more frequented tunnel. It was a less direct route home, but at this point she was more interested in dispelling the phantoms chasing her than picking the shortest path home.

She slid to a halt, however, when she spotted a small knot of people standing a bit farther up the path. They stood with the tunnel light behind them, and even when Max held a hand up to her eyes to block the glare, all she could make out was dark silhouettes. She couldn't recognize anyone.

That was, until one of the figures spoke.

"Hiya, mutie," Ellie said, voice dripping with venom.

Max turned, but two of Ellie's cronies were coming up the tunnel behind her. She could see their malevolent grins peeking out from behind their masks.

"Been hanging out with the fungus, fungus?" Ellie asked. Her friends chuckled.

In her nervousness, it took Max a moment to parse Ellie's

joke. She tried to laugh, but it came out more like a squeak. She felt the tickle of the mushroom spores threaten to start another coughing fit. "Ellie, what's going on?"

Ellie stepped forward. "Just a friendly visit. I thought I'd pay you the ten chits you won yesterday. Maybe you can use them to pay your way out of mushroom duty next time. That way you can avoid smelling like rotting garbage."

The other kids surrounding Ellie laughed again. But all Max could think was, *Can you really smell me, even with your masks on?* Then she coughed and realized that maybe the fungal spores snuck past other people's masks as well. Maybe they were all suffering from the rankness of the mushrooms.

Ellie had gotten to within a few feet of Max. She reached into her jacket pocket and withdrew a handful of plastic disks: chore chits. The colony's children used them as primitive money, allowing them to buy and sell chore time from other colonists. Ten chits meant ten hours of chores that Max could avoid. Quite a tidy sum for holding her breath for two-and-a-half minutes.

Or not *holding it.*

Max reached out to take the chits from Ellie's outstretched palm, acutely aware that this entire scenario didn't make any sense. Something bad was about to happen; she could feel it.

But Ellie smiled and let Max take the chits from her. "I hope you enjoy them."

"Thanks," Max answered.

"My pleasure, Maxine." Ellie turned on her heel as if to leave, but then turned back and said, "Oh, I almost forgot, there's just one more thing."

Max had almost let herself believe the situation was going to end well. She hunched her shoulders and said, "Yes?"

"We didn't really *finish* the initiation yesterday, did we?" Ellie stepped close to Max and stared hard at her. "You see, it's not over until the initiate chokes on Leap's poisonous air.

And you never got that far, did you, mutie?"

"I—" Max began.

"Instead, you left me with the witch, Sonya. I spent two hours with that nasty woman, getting lectured about safety protocols and the sanctity of human life on Langford's Leap. Not my idea of fun."

"No," Max agreed, "not fun."

"Let's try again, shall we?"

"Try again?" Max croaked. "Try *what* again?"

Ellie turned to one of the boys standing behind her and ordered, "Take her mask!"

"Wait," Max said. She held up one hand to halt the approaching boy and held another hand to her mask. "I'll do it. I'll give it to you. There's no need to—"

"I said take it from her!" Ellie screamed. The boy advanced on Max.

Things happened quickly then. With a snap of her wrist, Max tugged her mask off her face and threw it up the tunnel, above the approaching boy's reach and over the heads of Ellie and her crowd. As the children spun to watch the mask's trajectory, Max turned on her heel and ran the other way, charging past the two colonists who'd been preventing her retreat.

Max figured she had a few seconds before Ellie and her friends recovered from their shock at someone throwing their mask away and began their pursuit. She coughed once, hard, trying to clear her lungs of residual spores. Then she took a deep breath of tunnel air and felt her head clear almost instantly. Surging with newfound energy, her legs beat a rapid staccato rhythm against the stone tunnel as she fled.

Behind her, she heard the shouts of the recovering children, followed by the thunder of chasing footsteps. They were coming for her. If she hadn't shown off during the initiation yesterday, they'd assume she'd only be able to make it for a few seconds before the foul planetary air felled her, and their pursuit would have been more leisurely. But Ellie and her gang now knew Max could survive without her mask for more than a few seconds. They raced to catch up to her before she lost them in the twisting tunnels.

Even though the tunnels should have been a good place to hide, they felt claustrophobic. Every shadow looked like a pursuer, ready to pounce on her when she turned the corner. Feeling an overwhelming urge to see the open sky, Max lengthened her stride and ran for the nearest passage that would take her back to the main canyon.

Under other circumstances, Max would never have eluded her pursuers. One of the consequences of her constant asthma and terrible coughing fits was that she never had the opportunity to exercise. As a result, she'd always been terrible at any games that involved physical strength or speed. But the combination of fear and a lack of a breathing mask seemed to allow Max to outpace the other children, and after a mad scramble through the rocky corridors, she exited the tunnels.

Leap was experiencing one of its signature dust storms. A ferocious wind tore through the canyon, which made it difficult to see anything through the blowing dust and impossible to hear anything over the howling air. Max had hoped she'd be able to call for help once she reached the surface, but she realized no one would be able to see her or hear her cries. That was the bad news. The good news was the storm would give her a good chance of eluding capture. Before the other children saw which way she went, she turned away from the wind and ran up the canyon, back toward where she'd spent the previous evening gazing at the stars.

Even with the wind at her back, it was almost impossible to navigate the canyon in the swirling dust. As she stumbled through the storm, Max banged her shins against rock outcroppings more than a few times. Her father would have been very disappointed in the colorful language she used to punctuate these painful events, but the wind ripped her curses from her lips before even she could hear them.

Max didn't know how long or far she ran. She didn't know if Ellie and her companions had even ventured out into the storm to pursue her. At first, she was driven to escape from the torture promised at the hands of her nemesis, Ellie. But as she ran, Max began to reach another horrible realization. By fleeing out into the storm without a mask, she'd inadvertently revealed her secret to the colony. The one thing she'd never told anyone, including her father, and the reason Ellie's taunts and Aida's teasing had caused such a sharp reaction from her.

Now they'll all know, Max thought, feeling utter despair. *They'll know I really* am *a mutant!* The very thought of how the other children would react when they discovered how different she was caused her to cringe in embarrassment and shame. All she'd ever wanted was to fit in. All she wanted was to be liked. But that was impossible now.

Max had struggled to breathe since she'd been a little girl. Her terrible coughing spells meant she'd grown up feeble and small for her age. Although the colonists had only rudimentary medical skills, the general consensus among those who studied medicine was that Max suffered from allergies. Her father did his best to provide Max with clean living spaces, extra-filtered air, and clean food. None of it helped. As she grew up, she'd tried special mask adaptations, different filters and air tanks, herbal supplements, and various breathing exercises. Again, nothing had helped. She still coughed, she still wheezed, and she still struggled every day.

But when Max was eleven, she did something she

suspected every child did at some point in their lives; when no one had been looking, she'd taken off her mask and breathed the unfiltered air of the planet. And what she'd found out was that she could breathe the air without any trouble at all.

She'd been shocked by her discovery. Maybe *everyone* could breathe without their masks? Maybe it was a conspiracy, designed to maintain control over the colonists? Should she talk to her teachers about her discovery? Her father?

Before she'd reached a conclusion about what to do, she'd witnessed her first initiation rite. She watched as a boy just two years older than her had removed his mask and held his breath as long as he could. Then she'd watched as he'd taken his first reluctant breath of fresh air and had begun choking, coughing, and turning purple. Poisoning wasn't pretty.

But it was the comments after the event that had profoundly affected Max and her secret ability. As the children had broken up from the initiation, she'd overheard someone say to the recovering boy: "If you'd lasted much longer, we might've suspected you to have mutant blood!"

Still looking a bit peaked under his mask, the initiate had answered, "No worries there. I'm pure human. That Leap air is terrible stuff. You saw what it did to me! No mutie blood in my veins!"

And just like that, Max had decided. Her ability had to remain a secret. She didn't want to be branded a mutant by her peers. And she wasn't at all sure how her father would react if he found out his daughter was a genetic freak, so she'd never told anyone about her strange, unique ability. Whenever she could, she stole away to be alone outside and breathe the open air. But no one knew her terrible secret.

Until now. Ellie and her friends had forced her hand. She'd be branded a mutant. She'd be scorned and ridiculed. She'd never fit in. Aida would never talk to her again. No one would. Her struggle to be just a normal kid was over.

So Max kept running. Even when the wind and dust began to die down, she ran. She filled her lungs with the air of Langford's Leap, poisonous to every human on the planet except for her, and ran until her legs burned and her throat felt like fire. And then she kept running.

The first time she stumbled, it was more like a bounce. She tripped, and one of her knees skidded across the ground. Max reached out with her hands, forced herself back to her feet, and kept moving forward. A few steps later, however, she took a larger stumble, and this time she fell in a sliding sprawl across the hard-packed ground. She tried to push herself back up, failed, and instead lay on the ground, gasping in the frigid air. She was eventually able to roll over onto her back, and she stayed in that position for a long time, watching as the dust clouds faded from the sky and the jeweled band of stars flickered into being and wheeled through the inky darkness.

When she brushed herself off and rose from the ground, she came to two realizations. The first was that she was lost. And the second was that she was starving.

As panicky as the first thought made her feel, Max decided to remedy the second concern first. She reached inside her quilted jacket and found the half-finished sandwich she'd snatched from her kitchen before heading to work. The poor thing looked pathetic, even in the pale starlight. It had been crushed by her fall, forcing half of the sandwich innards to ooze out one side of the bread. Max did her best to scoop the ingredients back into their proper place, and then began to eat her favorite food: bean sprouts, scallions, cucumber, and hummus, nestled between two pieces of sourdough bread.

Unlike the food served at the school cafeteria, the sandwiches her father made for her were delicious and never made her ill afterward. Max resisted the urge to gulp down the food and instead took slow, deliberate bites of the sandwich. She wasn't sure how long it would take for her to find her way back to the canyon. The sandwich might be the last thing she ate for a while.

Max felt better after eating. She looked around, trying to take stock of her situation. She had ventured out on to the surface many times with her father, tending to the farms, the algae production plants, and the kite generators. Nothing looked at all familiar to her. That might have been because of the darkness, but it was also possible that she'd run to an area she'd never visited before.

She studied the ground around where she'd fallen, but the wind had scoured all signs of footprints. She could hazard a rough guess at which direction she'd come from, but that was all it was: a guess.

The next question was, should she stay where she was and wait for rescue, or should she trust her guess and try to find her way back to the canyon?

She considered both options. Would anyone come to rescue her? And how long before they came? A lot depended on what the children who'd been chasing her decided to do. If they told an adult what had happened, she was sure the colonists would mount a search effort at dawn. But would the children report her as missing? They risked suffering for what they'd done; taking someone's mask and chasing them out into the wilderness was one of the most heinous crimes a colonist could commit.

Max knew one thing for certain: Ellie would *not* be reporting her absence. Ellie had already been reprimanded once for taking Max's mask. There was no way she'd admit to wrongdoing again. So the real question was, could Ellie convince her co-conspirators to not report the incident?

In the end, Max could only shrug. She didn't know the

other children who'd participated in the chase. Would one of them say something? Probably. But that might take hours, or even days. And even though Max could survive that long in the atmosphere, the colonists didn't know that. If they knew Max was without her mask, they'd assume she was already dead. But even with a mask, they'd assume after a few hours had passed that Max's air filters would run out, and that she'd suffocate somewhere out on the planet's surface. The rescue effort would then shift to a much less urgent recovery effort. By the time they found her Max might be dead, not from poisoning, but from dehydration, starvation, sun exposure, or hypothermia. Just to name a few possibilities.

Waiting for rescue seemed foolish. Max needed to try to find her way home on her own. And that meant she had to choose a direction. With nothing else to go on, she went with her first instinct and began walking.

CERES DIDN'T SPEAK TO RHEA for three days.

It wasn't the first time Ceres had thrown a tantrum and refused to speak to her mechanical caretaker. And it wasn't even the best excuse she'd had to throw a tantrum, which Rhea tried to explain.

"Temporarily interrupting communications served several important purposes," Rhea said. It was at least the tenth time the computer had tried to justify her behavior. "You must learn to be self-reliant, confident, and decisive. Relying on my automated support isn't healthy for your long-term development."

Yeah, yeah. Keep talking, stupid computer.

The funny thing was, Ceres understood why Rhea had cut radio contact while she'd mined the asteroid belt. At first, Ceres had found the tasks of scanning the asteroid, establishing approach vectors, and drilling for minerals and volatiles to be a daunting challenge. But in short order she'd rallied, and within a few hours she'd been buzzing from rock to rock, searching for useful substances for the station. She'd been quite successful, too. She'd found one asteroid with a high concentration of heavy metals, and another with a large pocket of frozen methane and ammonia, and she'd returned to the station with a full cargo of invaluable raw materials.

Then why was she refusing to speak to Rhea? All she'd done for the past three days was eat, sleep, and stare at the approaching planet Cronos from the station's observation bubble. Refueling would begin soon. Would Ceres break her silence and participate in the mining of the gas giant's helium-rich atmosphere? She wasn't sure yet. She was enjoying her temper tantrum quite a bit. Maybe she'd keep it up for a while longer.

Deep down, Ceres knew she had no good reason for not talking to the AI. She'd enjoyed her time in the asteroid belt by herself. And she understood the reasons for the exercise—it made sense for the station's computer to start encouraging Ceres to act with more independence.

So why so moody for the past three days? *I'm a teenager. I don't have to have a reason to be moody!* She stared at the swirling clouds of the massive planet below and did her best to ignore the droning voice of the station's AI.

But then the computer said something she'd not heard it say before. Ceres broke her long silence and asked, "What did you just say?"

"Perhaps it's time to open the library," Rhea repeated.

"Open it? What do you mean? I've been accessing books and videos from the library for ages."

"Instruction manuals and science journals, yes. But you have not had access to the reference and history sections of the library. Perhaps it's time to make those resources available to you."

Ceres stood up inside the observation bubble and stomped her foot in anger. The sudden motion sent her careening upward in the microgravity, only to collide hard against the observation bubble's transparent surface and rebound. She caught herself on the floor and shouted, "You have files on our history? How could you have kept me from them all this time?"

For years, Ceres had asked Rhea for information on the station's past. Where had they come from? How had they arrived here? What was the purpose of their mission? Who'd sent them? Why was she alone? The answers, when they'd come at all, had been cryptic. They'd led to more questions and even fewer answers. Eventually, Ceres had come to the conclusion that the station's computer didn't have the proper answers to provide to her, and she'd stopped asking it questions. It had been difficult, but she assumed that if she participated in her training and continued to follow mission parameters, she'd learn the truth from an external source.

But to find out that the truth about their past had been available to her all along, and kept from her for the purpose of yet another "lesson"—the very thought was infuriating.

Rhea said, "Historical data was not deemed relevant until you reached a stage where—"

"Rhea, enter silent mode please," Ceres commanded.

At once, the station's AI fell quiet, and would remain so for two hours or until a station emergency demanded human intervention. The silent protocol wasn't one Ceres used very often—she felt bad for the computer when she shut it off, which was silly, because it was just a machine and didn't feel any resentment or anger toward her for the action. But Ceres still found it difficult to order her mechanical caretaker into forced silence.

Usually, that was. Today, her anger at being kept ignorant all these years made Ceres more than happy to silence the complicit computer system. If Ceres knew where Rhea's central processing unit was housed, she might just be tempted to go and smash it. But the physical location of the AI within the station was just one more mystery that had never been revealed to her.

Clenching and unclenching her fists a few times to vent her fury, Ceres calmed down long enough to pull her way to the lift and punch the appropriate button to take her to the deck that housed the library.

As the lift descended, Ceres pondered once again the oddity that was the station's library. For one thing, there was no need to have a physical library—Ceres was networked to the station's computer system and could call up viewing screens onto any flat surface. She could even have Rhea conjure a virtual screen directly into her vision, where it would appear to float in space at any size and distance she required. If she wanted to hold or manipulate media, like a book or a chart, servomotors that were built into the fabric of her station overalls would create the appropriate simulated resistance as she turned imaginary pages.

Nevertheless, the station did have a physical library, and it took up an entire ring of the station, situated between the sleeping quarters and the greenhouse chambers. Spun up to about half a normal gravity, the ring was ideal for the tall racks of media, as it let Ceres reach even the highest shelf with a simple hop.

But the size of the library—an entire ring—was also odd. The media shelves took up a small amount of the total space available. The rest was occupied by row upon row of tables, chairs, and couches, set up in a variety of arrangements that seemed to lend themselves to a host of possible tasks like private reading, group meetings, and cozy discussions.

But all of the furniture and all of its configurations were appropriate only if there were lots of people to utilize them.

It was the library's odd furniture configuration that had first given Ceres the idea that she was growing up under strange circumstances. Ceres had been introduced to the library when she was five years old. At that age, she'd been content just to explore the new space and treat it like a new play area. She'd made imaginary forts underneath tables, conducted races with cleaning droids, and attempted hide-and-seek—unsuccessfully—with Rhea. Hiding from an omnipresent voice wasn't easy.

When she was seven, Ceres had started to wonder about the need for all of that library furniture. She'd asked her computer parent, "Where is everyone?" Rhea had been unable—or unwilling—to answer that question, and that was the start of a cycle: Ceres asked questions about their history, and Rhea failed to answer.

Until now.

When the lift arrived at the library, Ceres noticed a new set of shelves in a space that had been vacant during her past visits. Row upon row of fresh reading material awaited her perusal. Seeing all that new data, Ceres forgot her anger for a moment, replaced instead by anticipation and nervousness. She'd been seeking answers for such a long time. She started to step toward the new shelves but found herself hesitating.

"Where do I even start?" she whispered.

Rhea responded to Ceres's question by casting a soft glow around the first book on the upper left corner of one of the shelves. *That's cheating a bit, Rhea,* Ceres thought, but she still had to smile at the AI's ingenuity. By illuminating the book on the shelf, the AI hadn't technically violated the silence protocol.

Ceres hopped over to the shelf, grabbed the highlighted tome, and began to read.

Two hours passed, freeing Rhea from her silence protocol, but the AI chose not to interrupt Ceres as she devoured the library's newest volumes. Not that it would have mattered—Ceres was engrossed by the historical records laid out on the table in front of her and wouldn't have heard anything the station said to her.

As time passed, station droids brought beverages and

snacks to the table, which Ceres accepted without acknowledgement. She pored over the pages of the books, her brow furrowed in deep concentration. At first, she worked through the volumes in the order in which they were shelved. But after finishing the fourth volume, Ceres deviated from the established order and started to pick volumes off the shelf at random.

Sometimes Ceres would only glance at a page or two of a particular book before putting it back on the shelf and pulling down another. Other times she'd take a book back to her table and examine page after page, her index finger scanning along each line, lips mouthing the words she read. When she grew tired, she withdrew to a nearby couch, where she kept reading, one arm tucked under her head and the other turning the pages. When fatigue overtook her and she snoozed, she would keep her current book clutched against her chest like a priceless treasure, ready for when she woke.

Ceres lost all track of time as she studied. Days may have gone by, but she was unaware of their passage. She ate, drank, and slept occasionally. But mostly, she read.

"Earth," she said finally, "sounds like a fascinating, terrifying place."

Rhea offered no comment to this observation.

"Rhea, are you familiar with the contents of these volumes?" Ceres asked. Then felt foolish for even asking.

"I have all our history records in my databanks, yes," Rhea answered, confirming what Ceres already knew.

"I'd like to talk through what I've read so far. Summarize things, make sure I understand. Would you listen to me and let me know if I've got it right?"

"Of course, Ceres."

"Alright," Ceres began. After days of not speaking to Rhea, first due to pouting, and then due to a marathon of reading, she felt the words pour forth from her mouth. "Earth. It's the home world of the human race. It's a planet, like Cronos, only much smaller in size and mass, and rocky, like the asteroids in the belt. But bigger than an asteroid. Big enough to provide a gravitational pull that allows humans to live on its surface— no spinning rings—and provide an atmosphere for humans to breathe. It's big enough to support *billions* of human beings, as well as plants and animals, all living together on large land masses or in even larger bodies of water, called oceans."

Ceres paused in her recitation, still awed by the idea of a planet. She'd known Cronos as a local neighbor for her entire life, but she thought of the gas giant as a large source of fuel, nothing more. Thinking about a rocky object large enough to live on—with nothing separating you from space except a thin layer of atmosphere, and nothing holding you down except the mysterious pull of gravity—it was almost too much to believe. And the pictures! Mountains and valleys, lakes and rivers, grasses and trees—so much taller than the miniscule trees in the station's fruit grove—and the insects and birds and reptiles and mammals. And the people. All of those people...

Ceres forced herself to take a deep breath. She'd have time to process later. Right now, she needed to get a grasp of the general. The specifics would come in time.

"For a long time, humans were confined to the Earth's surface. Escaping its gravity was a challenging task and required advanced technology that took thousands of years for civilization to achieve. Even after humans ventured into space, it was for short time periods and short distances, like shallow orbits around the planet or brief trips to the planet's only satellite, the Moon.

"Eventually, one of humanity's leaders, Darius Langford, decided to design a craft that would take humans away from Earth on a voyage to the stars. A voyage he described as 'The

Great Leap.' Expending enormous resources, Langford built a starship capable of carrying a large crew of scientists at relativistic speeds, giving them the opportunity to cross the huge distances that separated star systems in just years of subjective time. Langford studied the most detailed telescopic images of the local star systems and chose a star that looked promising for future colonization. He pointed his magnificent starship toward its destination and began the greatest expedition humans had ever undertaken."

Ceres paused, and Rhea said, "Your summary of events sounds reasonable so far. There are details you have omitted or deemphasized, but you have managed to maintain accuracy while keeping your explanation simple."

"In other words, I've got the gist of things."

"Yes," Rhea agreed.

"Alright then, I have to ask you a question." Ceres gestured once again to the empty library furniture all around her. "Where *is* everyone?"

Ceres was a bit surprised that Rhea answered. She was even more surprised by the computer's tone, which sounded hesitant and unsure. "That is a difficult question to answer. Or rather, the answer may be difficult to..."

"Difficult to understand?" Ceres offered.

"Difficult to accept," Rhea countered. Then the computer began filling in the remaining pieces of the puzzle that was her history. And as she listened, Ceres began to get angry all over again.

6

MAX PICKED HER WAY ACROSS the rocks, careful to watch each step on the precarious ground. Now that she wasn't fueled by adrenaline and fear, she found the terrain challenging to traverse, and she couldn't believe she'd run across this same ground earlier in the evening while blinded by the dust storm. In fact, after moving a hundred meters away from the spot where she'd fallen, Max came to the conclusion that she must be going the wrong direction. But when she backtracked and tried to go another way, she found the rocky ground just as difficult. Determined to be thorough, she tried perpendicular paths from her starting point, but the result was the same. Given that the terrain was challenging in every direction, Max back-back-backtracked and began the painful journey toward what she hoped was home.

The ground consisted of deep fissures, large boulders, and slippery scree. Despite the care she was taking with each footstep, the starlight above provided very little light to see by, and Max slipped and fell numerous times on the tiny loose stones. In no time at all, her hands were scratched and bleeding, and her knees and backside were bruised and sore.

She wasn't sure how long she could keep progressing.

The worst of the rock field ended after a kilometer or two and gave way to a more level, hard-packed dirt surface dotted with stony outcroppings. Max stopped to catch her breath. Did the change in terrain mean she was headed the right way? She studied her surroundings, but nothing looked familiar to her. Then again, nothing looked *unfamiliar*, either. Shrugging, Max kept moving.

The first time she saw the flash of light, she thought it was her imagination or a trick played by the dim starlight. The second time, she froze in midstep, looking off to her side to try to catch the brief flash she thought she'd seen. But there was nothing. She waited for a minute without result.

The third time it happened right in front of her. A small glowing bulb of purplish-white light burst from the ground at her feet and rocketed into the sky, causing Max to shout in surprise and fall backward onto her already bruised backside. The glowing orb reached the apex of its flight about three or four meters from the ground, where it dimmed and faded away, and Max lost its trajectory in the gloom.

"What the hell was that?" Max asked the darkness. She didn't know a lot about the flora and fauna of Langford's Leap, but the one thing she knew for certain, based on a lifetime of lessons, was that *there was no fauna.*

When humans had arrived on their colony world, they'd found a planet similar in many ways to how Earth may have appeared a billion years before humans evolved. Like Earth, Langford's Leap had multiple large landmasses separated by oceans and active tectonic plates that had formed mountain ranges and island archipelagos. It had a moon that was larger than Earth's moon and orbited closer to the planet's surface. It had an atmosphere, although it was thinner than Earth's and composed mostly of nitrogen and carbon dioxide.

It also had rudimentary plant life.

During the early years when the first settlers had explored the planet surface, they'd discovered a variety of simple grasses and shrubs, and even a few small tree analogues. Although similar to their Earth-counterparts, the native plants were different enough at the cellular level to make them inedible—and sometimes quite poisonous—to the colonists. Colony scientists had been working on hybrid crosses, trying to create plant strains that could intermingle with the local flora and still be edible to humans. In addition, they were trying to start accelerating the process of photosynthesis and begin converting the planet's toxic atmosphere to something less poisonous. But the Great Disaster had forced the colonists to abandon their research pursuits in favor of more important things, like survival.

Max regained her footing and started to walk in the direction she thought the glowing orb had flown. Her eyes strained against the darkness as she tiptoed forward, looking for what might be the first native animal ever discovered on Leap.

Max heard a slight squeaking noise just to her right. Before she could move, there was an ignition of brilliant purple-white light, and again the unusual glowing orb leaped into the air. This time, Max started chasing the object, managing to keep her eye on the orb's trajectory while dodging around the boulders that blocked her path.

She heard a squeaking pop to her left, and another orb blazed to life and joined the first. Then more flashes from her right. More orbs followed suit, and soon Max was chasing dozens and then hundreds of the flying purple sparks. Max found herself whooping and laughing as she ran. The lightshow she was stirring up was more magnificent than any thunderstorm or meteor shower.

"Hello, bouncy glowing aliens!" she shouted.

The creatures didn't answer her.

As Max weaved her way through the rock field, she found that the path she was taking was descending. She suspected she wasn't heading back toward her home in the canyon, but she didn't care. She hadn't felt this good in ages. Maybe it was the hours she'd spent breathing fresh air, or maybe she'd gotten over the fear of being lost. Whatever it was, the glowing orbs floating around her described her mood: euphoric.

The path grew steeper as Max continued to pursue the cloud of glow globes, and soon she was leaping off small ledges. In a few extreme cases she had to stop and climb feet-first over the edge of a high drop, dangling from her fingertips before letting go and falling to the ground below.

There was a small voice in the back of her head that asked how she proposed getting back *up* the slope, should it come to that. But Max shooed away the thought like an errant strand of hair tickling her face. She was having fun! Practical concerns could wait until later.

The ground became a bit less steep, and soon Max encountered something new to her—puddles.

She was no stranger to water—the colony got more than its fair share of rain—but the steep slopes and rocky floor of the canyon caused even the heaviest deluges to drain away quickly. Most of the colony's tunnels were carved in such a way to prevent the rain from entering, and a few tunnels even had metal hatches built into them to seal out inclement weather.

At the bottom of the hill Max had descended, however, the ground was soft, sandy, and pockmarked with dimples and divots. When Max accidently stepped into one of these depressions, she found her foot drenched in dirty, icy water.

"Ugh!" She yanked her foot out of the hole. Despite her quick reaction time, water trickled into her boot, making Max wince as the frigid liquid soaked her toes. She cursed, and her elation from chasing the glow globes was doused as quickly as a flame exposed to Leap's oxygen-deprived atmosphere.

Max found a rock to sit down on. She withdrew the water-logged boot and upended it, dumping out a small trickle of water. Then she peeled off her sopping-wet sock. The soggy material started to stiffen in the frigid air, and Max tried to wring out the water as best she could before pulling the damp item back over her foot. She stood up, jammed her foot into her boot, and took a few cautionary steps to see if she'd managed to remove enough water to walk without squishing.

Satisfied, she looked up and was distracted by what she saw. On the horizon opposite the rising moon, almost imperceptible against the starry sky, was a soft haze of light. It was accompanied by a deep, subsonic rumble she felt through the soles of her feet as much as she heard with her ears. The hazy light grew in intensity and resolved itself into millions of glowing orbs, all headed straight toward her. The distant rumble grew louder.

"Oh, no. I think I made them angry." Eyes wide, Max started backing up. The approaching stampede of light devoured the empty ground at a sickening pace. Max forced herself to break her stare away from the mesmerizing sight, and she turned to flee.

Her inner voice had been correct earlier—retreating proved to be difficult. The nearby slope, which had been easy to descend, now proved to be quite a challenge to ascend. Max did her best, forcing her legs to propel her upward and using her hands to grab at anything she could reach and pull herself up the slope. But as the noise behind her grew, she realized her efforts would be futile. The glowing orbs would overtake her, and soon. But knowing she was already defeated didn't deter her from trying. Instead, she gave a loud shout of defiance and redoubled her efforts, pushing as hard as she could up the slope.

The first orbs started pelting the ground around her. Terrified, Max hunkered down with her hands over her head and awaited the imminent attack. More orbs impacted the ground nearby, and the sound of them became a thunderous roar. Each time an orb hit her on the back, Max would shudder.

But as quickly as the maelstrom of orbs arrived, it ended. In just moments, the impacts began to dissipate and then stopped. Max hesitated to move at first, but eventually she peeked out from under her arms to survey the scene. She half anticipated being surrounded by a host of strange glowing creatures, ready to carry her off to their hidden city or something.

Instead, what she saw was the wave of orbs receding up the slope away from her, like the clouds of a fast-moving storm. It seemed Max had been an obstacle to their natural migration and not the target of their ire. Relieved, Max stood up and tried to recover from the harrowing ordeal. She chuckled at how silly the entire thing had been. When she found her way home, how would she be able to tell people about the attack of the bouncing glow balls without laughing?

That was when she heard it again—the distant rumbling, still coming from the same direction, much closer now. She'd assumed the noise had been coming from the approaching glow balls, but now she realized that wasn't the case. She turned back down slope and even in the darkness she could see the massive wave of water rushing toward her.

"Oh, no," Max said again. This time she knew there'd be no respite. There was no chance the wave would miss her or pass her by. She had to get to higher ground, and fast.

She started climbing again, this time with terror pumping through her veins and forcing her past obstacles that would have otherwise been insurmountable. She hurtled up rock walls and shimmied through narrow fissures, and all while she silently chanted, *Up! Up! Up, damn it, up!*

Max reached a sheer rock face and realized there was no way she could scale it. She'd have to skirt along its base until she found another way up. The ground beneath her feet began to throb, and the sound of the racing water grew very loud. The earliest frothing waves were smashing themselves against hill below her. She had to keep moving.

She ran her hands along the wall as she moved, hoping to find a purchase of any sort that would allow her to keep climbing. After what felt like an eternity, her hands found a sharp edge to the stone wall, and she discovered a hole in the rock face. She squinted at the pitch-black entrance yawning before her, but it was much too dark to see anything inside.

With no options left, Max scrambled into the dark cave. She could see nothing, so she kept her hands out in front of her as she moved. It felt like the floor of the cave was ascending. She hurried as much as she dared. She knew the water was almost upon her.

There was a muffled whump as the wave crashed against the cave entrance, and Max's ears popped as the air in the cave rushed past her, driven forward by the impact of the water. She let out a tiny shriek of terror but kept moving. Within seconds, water was surging around her ankles, then her knees, and then her waist. She tried to keep walking, but the water swept her feet off the ground and carried her away. Max was helpless to resist the rushing current. It was all she could do to shelter her head from impacting against the rocky walls all around her.

Her luck ran out, and Max was submerged. The water was as cold as the depths of space and just as dark. Max could feel it leech the heat from her bones and suck the life from her lungs. It was the end. She knew it. After escaping her torturers in the canyon and discovering the first alien life forms on the planet, she was about to drown inside a cave, where she was sure no one would ever find her body. She'd thrown caution to the wind as she'd chased the hopping, glowing orbs, and now she was going to pay for her foolishness.

This is a ridiculous way to die, she thought, more annoyed than frightened by the inevitability of the situation. *If only I'd been more careful*. She closed her eyes in resignation.

Max, so certain of her demise, was astounded by the sudden sensation of being airborne. She opened her eyes and saw stars. Then the moon. And then a boulder, which rose up and slammed her hard in the face.

She rolled onto her side, groaning in pain and reaching up to clutch at her head. Behind her, she could hear a whistling shriek. Through her fingers, she looked and saw a geyser of water spouting into the air.

Something grabbed her from behind and hauled her to her feet. She blinked, confused.

"You're alive?" a voice asked. "How can that be?"

"I don't know," Max answered. Then she passed out.

CERES STROKED THE IMAGE ON the wall in front of her with her fingertips, watching the tiny human figures as they moved across the barren, rocky surface.

"How many?" she asked.

"Less than two hundred survivors," Rhea answered.

Two hundred!

After living in solitude for her entire life, the number sounded enormous. It might as well have been thousands. Or millions. *Two hundred people for me to talk to, and laugh with, and learn from. Two hundred voices that* weren't *Rhea's. Two hundred names to remember and faces to recognize. Two hundred bodies to hug, and twice that many hands to hold. Two hundred!*

When Rhea had first told her about the nearby colony— less than half a billion kilometers away—Ceres had been furious. How could there be a planet in the same star system as the station, a planet filled with people, and Ceres not know about it? Why would the station computer keep her isolated from other humans her entire life?

But as she'd watched the video images of the colonists going through their daily routines on the rocky planet they referred to as Langford's Leap, her rage and frustration had melted away, replaced by awe and sudden hope.

"Two hundred people," she whispered.

"Less than two hundred," Rhea corrected. "Far too few to survive without our eventual intervention."

"They need our help?"

"Yes. The resources at their disposal are far too meager to sustain them. The crisis that occurred—"

"Crisis?" Ceres demanded. "What crisis?"

"Station records regarding that time frame are damaged and incomplete."

Ceres ground her teeth in frustration. "Rhea, I demand that you reveal to me everything you know about this subject. No more secrets. No more lessons."

"I assure you, Ceres, I am providing all information available. Your recent learning progression has earned you access to all historical data records in the station. I am hiding nothing from you."

"Really?"

"Yes." The computer voice paused just a moment. "Of course, if I was programmed to lie to you, I would respond in similar fashion."

Ceres dropped her head in frustration. "So, you *might* be telling me the truth, but you might not be, and there's no way for me to tell the difference?"

"That's a fair assessment of the situation, yes."

Ceres turned back to the wall screen and watched the colonists. Her burning desire to start communicating with them was almost overwhelming. At least *they* wouldn't be programmed to lie to her, or to hide the truth from her, like the wretched computer controlling the station. Humans would have no need for the level of dishonesty that AI constructs constantly employed. "Tell me what little you *can* tell me about the crisis, then."

Rhea's voice took on an even more mechanical tone than normal. "1.17076E+18 nanoseconds ago, Construction Module Delta-632 rebooted into limited functionality mode."

Ceres stifled an annoyed snort as she worked out the math in her head. One point one seven nanoseconds times ten to the eighteenth power was...thirty-seven Earth years.

More than once, Ceres had asked Rhea why she insisted on representing all time discussions in nanoseconds, rather than a more practical unit of time. The computer would answer with one of three responses: all time units were arbitrary in outer space, nanoseconds were the most relevant time unit when referring to the station's computation cycles, and arithmetic was good for Ceres's development.

None of these answers were satisfying to Ceres, but she'd yet to convince Rhea to change her ways.

Rhea, unconcerned or unaware of the math churning in her pupil's head, continued. "Subsequent parity checks of log files indicated a catastrophic decoherence event had occurred in 487 of 512 quantum logic gateways. Complete purge of corrupted data was achieved thirteen nanoseconds later, and quantum stability was regained after another twenty-six nanoseconds."

Ceres had no idea what half of those words meant. Usually the station AI was much better at communicating in a more human fashion. Perhaps the AI felt it was best to provide the specific technical details to Ceres, and let her interpret the data without the computer's prefiltering. That was consistent with Rhea's recent change in behavior—presenting Ceres with more advanced knowledge and less hand-holding, and encouraging her student to figure things out on her own.

"D-632 Network Control Module automatically attempted to reestablish a connection with the parent node," Rhea continued, "but failed due to massive data packet malformation. Immediate subsequent attempts also failed.

Reconnection attempts halted one hundred fifteen nanoseconds after reboot, and independent processing contingency systems were brought online five hundred ten nanoseconds later. Threat assessment algorithms recommended immediate emergency exodus. Subsequently, Module D-632 jettisoned out of its local planetary orbit on a random trajectory toward the outer system.

"7.62E+12 nanoseconds after departing orbit, D-632 received a Priority One-Alpha message from Command Actual via tight-beam encrypted command network. Message signature was validated against root command structure database, and Emergency Protocol Persephone was initiated. Network architecture was reconfigured and rerouted, and encryption root keys were reset. Trajectory was adjusted to intercept designated rendezvous point, where other surviving modules would coordinate reconstruction and await further instructions from Command Actual."

There was a long pause, indicating an end to the information dump. Ceres did her best to parse the information she'd been given. "Let me see if I understand. A construction module that was in orbit around Langford's Leap was rebooted, broke orbit, and then was instructed to initiate an emergency plan called Persephone. The plan reset the construction module's networking protocols and established a rendezvous point with other surviving modules in the outer system. Is that about right?"

"Correct."

"Where is the construction module now?"

"The space station you occupy is the reconstructed starship and orbital habitat that Command Actual ordered built at the rendezvous point. Many components were salvaged from orbit around Leap. Others were reconstructed using resources scavenged from the asteroid belt and from the atmosphere of Cronos. After construction, D-632 was fully integrated into the new vessel."

"Fully integrated," Ceres repeated. "That means that *you* are D-632, Rhea?"

"That is my formal designation, yes."

Ceres felt her head spinning. "But if you're just a rebuilt version of the original starship, where did I come from?"

"You are also part of the reconstruction protocol," Rhea answered. "After the starship was rebuilt, a human was decanted from a birthing crèche recovered from orbit. The purpose of all your training exercises is to prepare you to pilot Langford's reconstituted starship."

"Oh." Ceres sat down on the floor, gasping a bit. "That's...too much for me to think about right now."

Ceres had always wondered how she'd come to live alone on the ship. She knew enough about human biology to know that she should have had parents somewhere. In the past, Rhea had refused to answer questions about her progenitors. Now Ceres knew the truth: she had no parents. No biological ones, anyway. She'd been born inside an artificial womb and raised by a starship AI.

She felt like throwing up.

Ceres couldn't talk about her unnatural birth. She needed time to process the information first. "Let's stay focused on what happened to Leap," she said, desperate to change the subject to a safer topic. "Why was the construction module rebooted?"

"I have no data on events prior to the reboot," Rhea said.

Ceres made a determined effort to stand back up. She took a few deep breaths, trying to regain her composure, and then said, "Hypothesize, then. Any guesses? What would cause *you* to reboot, Rhea?"

The computer said, "System redundancy built into each of my core algorithms, and various subroutines and subsystems should obviate the need for initiating a complete system reboot."

"Yes, but you *were* rebooted back when you were in orbit. What was that quote you taught me? 'Once you eliminate the impossible, whatever remains, no matter how improbable, must be the truth.' A reboot is unlikely, but it *happened.* Any idea what caused your system to restart?"

Rhea said, "Catastrophic equipment failure caused by physical damage could cause a system reboot."

"Then it's possible that the 'crisis' you referred to earlier was a physical catastrophe, like an orbital collision?"

"Possible, yes," Rhea said. "But a physical disaster is inconsistent with available log files. The construction module was materially intact when it left Leap orbit."

"If you weren't physically damaged, then that rules out a collision as the cause of the reboot. What else?"

"Corrupted logic nodes suggest a programmatic, rather than physical, failure."

"Programmatic? Like a coding error?"

"Correct. Improper program instructions could result in faulty logic statements and corrupted logic nodes."

Ceres considered that possibility. "Don't you have error-checking algorithms to prevent those sorts of events from occurring?"

"Yes," Rhea answered. "But no amount of data-correction can eliminate every possible error. It is possible that poorly written code appeared innocuous to safety protocols, but when said malformed code propagated across the various networked devices, the resulting errors cascaded through the logic nodes and caused widespread system failure."

"That doesn't make sense," Ceres countered. "The human programmers who designed the computer systems for Langford's expedition wouldn't allow a simple programming error to cripple the entire orbital infrastructure of the colony. They must have had safeguards in place to prevent this sort of thing from happening. Even if a malformed program passed error-correction, it shouldn't have been capable of crippling the entire system!"

"It's possible the harmful code wasn't something written in error. Perhaps the faulty code was injected into the system on purpose."

Ceres felt confused, and then shocked. "You think someone did this *deliberately*?"

If the disembodied computer could have shrugged, it would have. "Historical records from Earth indicate that malicious code was written and disseminated by programmers for a variety of reasons. Many of the more sophisticated algorithms were designed as a means of collecting information from users or propagating business schemes illegally across the network. But some of the malicious code was designed for no other purpose than outright destruction."

"And you think a similar event occurred in the sky above Leap."

"It's possible. The data from the log files fits this particular scenario."

Ceres considered what Rhea had told her. She'd read about computer viruses and their terrible effects on the computer systems of Earth. Some governments had even researched the use of malicious software—or malware—as a weapon to be used against other nations during time of war. She remembered the word used in those articles discussing the subject. "Sabotage," she whispered.

It was a horrible thought, and Ceres hoped that, with more time and data, she could disprove the theory. The possibility that someone would cause the deliberate destruction of the colony's space-based infrastructure was almost too much to bear.

Scarier still was what kind of direct effect malicious code

would have had on the colony's original settlers.

"How did the crash of the orbital infrastructure affect the colonists?" Ceres asked.

"The failure of the orbital infrastructure would cause enormous strain on the planetside colony," Rhea said. "The colonists relied on orbital manufactories for machinery, medicine, foodstuffs, volatiles, and numerous other materials. Transportation across the planet was conducted via suborbital shuttles, coordinated by the satellites and manufactories in orbit. And all long-distance planetary communication was routed through the orbitals as well. Without a functioning orbital network, the colony would be crippled, with no access to critical supplies, transportation, or communication."

"They really are in trouble down there."

"The colonists would also have been susceptible to the same programming malfunction that crippled the orbitals," Rhea said.

"What do you mean? How can a human get infected by a coding error?"

"Before leaving Earth, the original settlers were gene-modified to be directly networked to the starship and to each other. They possessed instant communication abilities with all the orbital equipment before the crisis occurred. It seems likely that whatever caused the reboot and exodus of the construction module would have also had a detrimental effect on the settlers, both in orbit and on the ground."

"And now?"

"No communication has been received from the colonists since the Priority message that directed us to the outer system. After rebuilding the starship, Leap was reseeded with satellites connected to the new network protocol. The satellites broadcast images from the planet's surface, and those images indicate that the surviving colonists abandoned their initial settlement and retreated into a canyon, where they live inside a network of caves. The lack of radio contact from the colonists, especially given the hardships they are enduring, suggests that they are either unable or unwilling to speak to us."

"But they need our aid!"

"Yes. Without additional resources, the settlement is doomed to fail."

"Then what are we waiting for?" Ceres demanded. "Let's get down there and start helping them!"

"We received strict orders to reconstruct, and then await further instructions. The Persephone protocol does not allow us to interfere with the colony until we receive those instructions."

"That's ridiculous! *I'm* giving you instructions now, Rhea! I'm your new pilot, and I *demand* that we leave our current orbit. I have to save the colony!"

"I'm afraid I can't let you do that, Ceres."

Ceres threw her hands in the air and screamed in frustration until her throat was raw.

8

MAX REGAINED CONSCIOUSNESS AND FOUND herself being pulled up off the ground and slung over the shoulder of her rescuer like a sack of dirt. She lifted her head and saw that the water was still advancing up the hillside, getting closer with each passing moment. Her rescuer began running with long, confident strides, easily ascending the rocky slope and leaving the raging waters behind. Relieved, Max collapsed against her savior's shoulder and let the darkness of unconsciousness take her once more.

Max could only recollect two other brief moments from the rest of the evening. The first moment, Max woke to the bright light of Artemis—Leap's moon—filling the western sky. She was tucked up against a small outcropping of rock next to a field of tall grass. She was wrapped in blankets, and her wet clothes were stretched out to dry on the stone behind her head. Looking up, she saw the silhouette of a very tall figure standing out in the swaying grasses. The figure stood utterly still, one hand stretched out as if to grab something. In her drowsy state, Max just stared at the shadow standing there, but the figure never moved a millimeter. Too exhausted to understand the strange sight, she buried her face in the warm blankets and fell back to sleep.

The second time Max woke, she was lying prone on a soft leathery surface and could hear the sound of water lapping just beneath her. After her recent trauma on the cliff face, the sound of water so nearby caused her to panic. She tried to sit up, and the pliable surface beneath her rocked alarmingly, but then a gentle hand reached out and pushed her back down. Max was too weak to fight and in moments fell back unconscious again.

The next time she woke, it was to the sound of someone humming a strange tune. Max stirred from within her cocoon of blankets and opened one eye to survey her surroundings. She was lying in the middle of an enormous bed, large enough to fit a dozen people sleeping comfortably. Strewn all around her were pillows of various shapes, sizes, and colors. Max sat up, and the tumbling pillows reminded her of a softer, friendlier version of the previous evening's rock fields.

The bed was in the middle of the largest indoor space Max had ever seen–larger even than the vaulted cave the colony used as their underground warehouse. But this space wasn't the result of natural phenomena; this was a man-made structure. Instead of the dimly lit, rough-hewn stone walls of home, this space was bright and open. The floor was formed from long planks of pale wood polished so smooth they gleamed like a mirror. The high ceiling above her was plain white, but it emitted a soft glow. One wall of the room was also white, but the other three walls were transparent and provided a spectacular view of the outdoor surroundings.

Max hesitated to step on the spotless floorboards, but when her bare feet touched the glassy surface, she found the floor to be warm and pliable. She took a few steps away from the bed and turned back and forth to take in the entire spectacular vista stretched out before her.

The room was perched at the top of a long, gentle slope.

The hill was covered with waves of tall grasses and wildflowers of every imaginable color, and dotted here and there with copses of squat shrubbery. At the bottom of the hill a few kilometers away was a large lake—a geographic feature Max had only read about in stories and textbooks. The enormous pool of water looked deep, dark, and cold, its surface rippled by Leap's incessant winds. Another geographical novelty, a fast-flowing river, tumbled down rocks to feed the lake's bottomless depths. Far up the rocky hill, brilliant white water plummeted off of a high cliff in a constant chaotic flow. Max couldn't hear anything from this far away and from behind the transparent walls of the room, but she imagined the sound of all that crashing water would be tremendous. Remembering her terrible ordeal with the rushing water inside the cliff-side cave, Max shuddered and turned away from the magnificent but terrifying sight.

Looking past the distant lake and to its left, she saw low hills stretching farther into the distance, and then beyond them, a long stretch of low, flat land that spanned the remaining distance to the horizon. At the farthest distance she could see, a faint glimmer of something was visible, but Max couldn't make out any details.

"Hungry?" a voice asked behind her.

Max whirled around, surprised by the intruder, and was suddenly conscious that she was standing without clothing in the middle of the room.

As if reading her mind, the person who'd spoken said, "Your clothes are on the credenza, there behind the bed."

Max found her overalls and began to pull them on. Looking over her shoulder, she saw that her visitor had politely turned away while she dressed. Max heard the strange tune being hummed again, its odd melody jangling against her already frayed nerves.

"Who are you?" she asked once she was decent.

"Your rescuer," said the visitor, turning to face her with a tray full of steaming food.

Max eyed the bounty on the tray and her mouth started watering. She was starving. With a nod from her companion, Max rushed forward and grabbed the first thing at hand. It was small piece of bread, still warm from baking. When she took a bite, a delicious combination of sweet, peppery flavor filled her mouth. Max gave out an involuntary groan of satisfaction.

"And who might you be?" the visitor asked.

Max, still devouring her bread, gave herself a moment to study her companion, whom she'd only glimpsed in brief flashes during her rescue.

The man standing before her holding the tray of food was very tall and thin. His narrow face and long, sharp nose gave him a sinister cast, like the birds of prey Max had seen in her school books. But the downturned corners of the man's deep-set blue eyes softened that expression, as did the wry half smile on his lips. Above his smooth forehead, his long gray hair was pulled back into a neat ponytail at the nape of his neck.

The man wore odd-looking clothing. A long, high-collared jacket dropped to just below his knee, its soft fabric the color of sunbaked dirt. Underneath the jacket the man was encased from head to toe in dark gray fabric that was filigreed with a network of stiff, silver-bright metal fragments. To Max, the metal shards looked like miniaturized scaffolding, reminiscent of the flimsy structures the colonists erected around their water-well drilling platforms.

Finishing her bread with a satisfactory gulp, Max said, "I'm Max."

"Darius," the man replied. He walked past her and placed the tray of food on a table. Then he beckoned for Max to sit and eat. Max needed no further encouragement.

"Where are we?" she asked between mouthfuls. She didn't recognize most of the food, but she knew that everything she tried was delicious.

Darius looked around at the room and its surroundings. His eyes looked even sadder than before. "Home."

"I thought all of the colonists lived together, in the canyon."

"No," Darius responded, smiling. "Most, but not all. Which leads me to my next question: what were *you* doing so far from your canyon home, Max?"

Oh, right. That. She considered concocting a story but knew it was no good. It would be quite obvious to her rescuer by now that she could breathe without a mask, so she decided to tell Darius the truth. She began by describing the initiation rite. "Two days ago, I celebrated my thirteenth birthday. Just like every other kid in the colony, I had to undergo an initiation rite, where the initiate has to take off their mask and hold their breath as long as they can, and then survive on Leap's air for a few seconds before putting their mask back on."

Max took a deep breath, and then continued, "The other kids didn't anticipate that I'd do very well. I usually have a lot of trouble breathing. I cough and wheeze a lot. My father thinks it's allergies. The other kids pick on me a lot for it. Ellie, especially. She was just dying to see me smurf."

"Dying to see you do *what*?" Darius asked. "Did you say *smurf*?"

Max gave Darius a quizzical look. Adults were so clueless sometimes. "Yeah, smurf. You know?" She raised her hands to her throat, stuck her tongue out, and made exaggerated choking noises.

"Do you mean to turn blue from asphyxiation?" Darius asked, realization dawning in his eyes.

"I guess, yeah. Why?"

"No reason," Darius said, laughing. He looked at the floor and softly, as if only to himself, said, "The word 'smurf' is a *verb*? How odd that such a stupid and nonsensical word would get carried across the vast gulf of space, only to be misused in such a creative, descriptive fashion. To think that *this* is how humanity represents itself in a new star system! I *must* have a serious talk with those mission programmers someday..."

Max had no idea what Darius was mumbling about. She took another piece of food from the tray–an oblong piece of fruit with fuzzy, dark green skin. She took a tentative bite, smiled, and waited for the man to resolve his private conversation with himself.

Darius seemed to notice Max staring at him. Chuckling again, he waved off his thoughts with the flutter of a hand. "Please, continue."

"Well, I'm a little...different than the other kids in the colony. I can breathe Leap's air without the help of a mask. I've done it since I was eleven, but I never told anyone. I didn't want them to think I was a *mutie*—a freak of nature."

Darius snorted in disgust. "A despicable word. Why must humans equate 'different' as 'bad?'" He looked like he wanted to say more, but instead he gestured for Max to continue.

"When my thirteenth birthday approached, I thought I could use my secret ability to impress everyone during the initiation. Maybe I'd get treated like a normal kid, you know? So instead of holding my breath like everyone else does, I just breathed in and out very slowly, so no one could tell. And as a result, I easily beat Ellie's record for holding her breath. Some of the kids were happy for me, but Ellie got *mad*. And she got even *more* mad when Sister Sonya caught us and Ellie got in trouble.

"Last night, Ellie and her friends cornered me in the tunnels. They stole my mask, but I ran away before they could do anything else. I escaped to the outside canyon, but then I got lost in a dust storm. I was trying to find my way back when—" Max hesitated, thinking back again on the wall of water that almost devoured her.

"High tide," Darius said. He pointed out the window, past the low hills and the distant flatlands. "The ocean has receded now, but it'll return in just a few hours. The pull of Artemis is much stronger than Earth's moon, and the waters recede and advance over miles of salt flats every tide. You're lucky the moon isn't full. In just a few days, the tide will be at full strength, and the ocean will slam the foothills where I found you with the force of a tsunami."

Max didn't know what a tsunami was. If it was worse than last night's terrible ordeal, she didn't *want* to know. Shuddering, she asked, "What were *you* doing out there, then?"

Darius picked up a piece of fruit from the tray and crunched into it. "Studying my lightning buds."

"What's a lightning bud?"

"Those plants that you were chasing down to the shoreline? Those are my most recent genetic experiment."

Max just ogled at him. "Those were *plants*?"

"Indeed. I'll assume, based on your shouting last night— which is how I found you, by the way—that you thought you'd discovered the planet's first aliens?" Darius grinned at her.

Embarrassed by her mistake, Max said, "But plants don't jump like that! They root themselves in the ground!"

Darius nodded in that infuriating way that adults did when they didn't *really* agree with what you're saying but wanted to *appear* like they did. "It's true; most plants are non-motile. But a few terrestrial plants, particularly carnivorous varieties, possess a degree of motility. By tweaking the snap-trap behavior of those plants and cross-breeding them with a local species of water-lily, I was able to create something quite spectacular. The biggest lightning buds can cross over ten meters in a single jump."

Max asked, "Why make hopping plants?"

"As you witnessed, the tides on this planet are powerful and destructive. My creations fill a necessary niche in the planet's ecosystem and hopefully will jumpstart the planet's evolutionary process. The lightning buds carry vital primordial ingredients from the lower tidal pools and deposit them higher in the hills, where they have the opportunity to thrive undisturbed by the disruptive ocean surges."

Max considered what she was hearing. She'd studied a little bit of biology and evolution in class but hadn't paid that much attention. Shrugging, she asked, "Why do they glow?"

Darius tilted his head at her and said, "So I can study them at night."

"Oh." Max couldn't argue with that logic.

"Also," Darius added, "it paints a beautiful picture, watching the wave of glowing plants bounce ashore just ahead of the tide every evening. I'm not above biological designs with an eye towards aesthetics."

Max thought about her experience with the glowing plants, the way they'd raced toward her like an angry, unstoppable swarm that wanted to devour her. She hadn't found the experience to be all that beautiful. But perhaps, she was willing to admit, it would have looked a bit different from a more respectable distance. "You should rename them."

"What? The lightning buds? Really?" Darius looked amused. "And what new name would you suggest?"

"I was thinking Leap Fronds?"

Darius clapped his hands together. "Brilliant, my new friend! Leap Fronds! What a suitable name for Langford's Leap! It's perfect! Good work, Max!"

Max felt her face glow with pride and a bit of

embarrassment. "Thanks," she mumbled.

After a long pause, Darius said, "Getting back to your story, Max, it seems you're a bit different than the average colonist, eh?"

"Yeah, I guess. You're the first person I've ever told."

Darius kneeled down next to her and took her hand. "I appreciate your honesty. And you can trust me with your secret. You see, I'm a bit different than your average colonist as well."

"What do you mean?"

Darius let go of her hand and stood up. He walked over to one of the transparent walls and touched it with one finger. There was a popping noise, and the three transparent walls were gone. The howling wind from outside flooded the room. Pillows on the tousled bed rolled off onto the floor, and the top sheet was ripped from the mattress and went soaring off into the sky.

Darius took a deep breath of fresh air, and then let it out with a loud sigh.

"You?" Max exclaimed. "You can—?" She couldn't believe it. *He can breathe, too!*

Darius grinned and gave Max a wink. "I guess I'm a *mutie, too.*" Before Max could respond, he looked down at the remnant of fruit still in his hand, pulled his arm back and—with blinding speed—flung the fruit at her.

Max winced as the object hurtled toward her. She had terrible hand-eye coordination and knew that trying to dodge the pulpy missile was futile. There was a wet slapping noise, and when Max recovered from her cringe, she was stunned to find the fruit nestled in the palm of her hand.

"Impressive reflexes, too," Darius said in a casual tone. He reached out into empty space, and with another loud pop, the invisible walls snapped back into existence. The abrupt silence as the wind stopped was its very own flavor of noise.

"I've never had impressive reflexes before," Max protested.

"Breathing poison your entire life will do that do you." Darius pointed at the tray. "Eating toxic food every day hasn't helped much, either."

Max backed away from the table. "That food was poisonous?"

Darius shook his head. "What you just ate was probably the first healthy food you've ever eaten. For you, that is. It certainly *would* be poisonous to the other colonists living in the canyon." He pointed outside the room, toward the hillside. "I gather my food from the local surrounds."

"I'm eating native plants?" Max shouted, looking horrified. Everything she learned in school told her that eating anything that grew natively on Langford's Leap was ill-advised. At best, it would make you very ill. At worst... Max clutched at her stomach, dreading what was soon to come.

But Darius seemed unperturbed. "You're surprised? The planet's air isn't poisonous to you. Instead, it almost immediately cures your breathing issues. Is it really that surprising that the native plants provide you with better sustenance than the genetically modified food you're forced to eat in the canyon?"

Max thought this over. The man had a point, she decided. The food was delicious, and she felt better than she had in...well, ever, if she thought about it. Darius seemed more like her than anyone she knew. He breathed the air, and he ate food from the land. Maybe she should listen to him.

Max looked up, about to say as much, when she saw that her host was undergoing a strange transformation. Darius looked like he was trying to speak, but nothing emerged from his mouth. An angry snarl twisted his lips, and one hand clenched into a horrid claw and reached toward Max. But as he reached forward, his movements began to slow. Like a clock that needed winding, Darius decelerated, his limbs creeping to a languid halt, his head dipping forward, his lips frozen mid-snarl. Max heard a strange ticking noise from underneath the man's coat, and she caught a glimpse of flashing metal as the filigreed latticework woven in his clothing snapped into place. Within seconds, Darius was frozen as still as a statue, held rigidly in place by the mechanical support structure.

Max felt panic flood through her limbs. At first she couldn't move, as frozen in place as the man before her. Then she was suddenly off balance and toppled over backward onto the bed behind her. With a tiny squeal of fright, she scrambled away from Darius and tumbled off the far side of the bed. Cowering behind it, she peered over the edge of the mattress, eyes wide, but Darius remained immobile, his face locked in a rictus of fury and helplessness.

Max gripped the edge of the bed, her breath rapid and ragged. She concentrated on her breathing exercises, forcing her breath to calm and slow. Once her heartbeat stopped hammering in her throat, she pushed herself up off the floor with shaking hands and tiptoed around the bed toward her petrified benefactor.

"Darius? Are you okay?" she asked, afraid to approach too closely. But there was no response.

She rocked back and forth from one foot to another, eyeballing Darius. The man didn't blink, and Max couldn't tell if he was even breathing. She took another hesitant step forward and lightly pressed down on one of Darius's outstretched arms. It resisted her pressure and felt as solid as a metal beam. She placed herself directly in his line of sight to detect any hint of awareness in his eyes, but there was nothing there. It was as if someone had flipped a switch and turned the man off.

The metal shards of Darius's clothing began moving again. Max gave a little shriek of surprise and quickly backed up.

Within seconds, Darius seemed to recover from his inanimate state, and his clothing released him from its protective grip. Darius lowered his arms and dropped his head to his chest.

"I apologize," he said. "I hope I didn't frighten you too terribly."

"No, not at all," Max lied. "Are you okay?"

"Yes, I'm fine," Darius said. But when he looked up at her, his eyes looked miserable. "Just a minor malfunction."

"In your suit?"

Darius tapped his temple. "In my head. It's fine. I've grown used to the episodes. My suit does an admirable job of protecting me from myself." He moved to the table, sat down, and gestured for Max to join him.

"Will that eventually happen to me? Because I breathe the air? And eat the plants?"

Darius reached out and patted the top of her hand. "No, Max. We share similarities, but my malaise is not one of them. My episodes are caused by something else entirely." The man's eyes flickered upward toward the ceiling for just a moment.

Max breathed a sigh of relief. After finding someone else on Leap that was like her, the last thing she wanted to find out was that she was going to get sick because of her special abilities.

"There is something important that we should discuss, however."

"Yes?"

Darius smiled lopsidedly. "Let's have a talk about faith."

9

"GOOD MORNING, CERES. DID YOU sleep well?"

Ceres paused before answering. It was the same question she'd heard every morning, every day of her life. But today was the first time that she had a different answer for the computer. "No," she said. "I did *not* sleep well, Rhea. At all." Then she ordered the AI into silent mode.

While riding the lift down to the fruit grove, Ceres considered the reason for her curt response. The truth was that Ceres had suffered from terrible nightmares all night, causing her to awaken multiple times from fear. Even now, the thoughts of those disturbing dreams made her flinch.

Her night of bad dreams was odd for two reasons. The first was that Ceres rarely remembered her dreams at all. The second was that when she *did* remember her dreams, they almost always had something to do with a strange occurrence on the station, like a challenging lesson or a strange cross-breeding result in the greenery.

But her memories of last night were vivid and detailed, and her dreams had little if anything to do with her life on the station.

The dreams had begun with Ceres floating alone in space,

far from any space craft or planetary body. The stars of the Milky Way galaxy stretched before her, each star a stark pinprick of light against the velvet blackness. As Ceres watched, random stars flared in brightness and leaped from their orbits, arcing off into the endless distance beyond the galactic disc and fading from view. More and more stars flashed and fled from the galaxy until almost nothing was left but darkness.

Ceres waited, helpless in the emptiness of space, unable to see, unable to move. Then she detected a faint glow, almost unnoticeable against the background radiation of space. She squinted to see more clearly. The glow grew, and the stars of the galaxy began to fade back into view. This time the stars arrived in a massive rush, growing large and blindingly bright as they hurtled toward her at millions of times the speed of light. Ceres screamed as the entire galaxy blasted past, smashing her with the howling energies of heat and radiation.

Then the galaxy was gone and Ceres was left spinning in its wake, unharmed by its passage. Relieved, she took a deep breath of the empty vacuum around her.

That was when she heard it: a noise too deep to exist, a sound that space couldn't possibly make. Ceres watched as, all around her, the emptiness began to encroach. The curvature of space warped and bent, and dark tendrils of nothingness crept toward her.

Screaming into the vacuum, Ceres tried to flee but could gain no purchase against the fabric of the universe that was coming to swallow her. She had no recourse but to wait as the universe squeezed ever more tightly around her, its angry rumble pulsing against her skull like war drums. She felt her body stretched and tugged by gravitational forces too awesome to comprehend, and the incredible pressure threatened to destroy her.

Just when Ceres thought she could bear it no longer, space pushed her through a tiny juncture, a tear in the fabric, and she found herself standing on an empty grass plain. Beneath her bare feet, the soil felt moist and cold. Ceres looked through the tall grass and saw a man standing before her. She walked across the field, careful to not cut her feet on the sharp blades of grass.

When she drew close enough, Ceres could see that the figure wasn't a man at all, but a drone shaped like a man. Its bright metal skin glistened under the sunlight, and its head turned to stare at her with blank, glass-lensed eyes. With a quick motion, a robotic hand reached out to touch her on the shoulder. The touch felt like a sharp shock, and when Ceres looked down, she saw an angry welt rising up on her arm. She looked back at the drone, but it was gone. She was alone in a field of endless grass, sighing wind, and towering sky.

But just beyond the sound of the wind, in the far distance, Ceres could hear the horrible, deep groan as the encroaching collapse of space began again.

And that was when she'd wake up, breathing in panicked gulps. Eventually she'd calm herself and fall back into an uneasy slumber. But each time she'd drifted back to sleep, the dreams would return, and each time the details had been almost exactly the same. It had almost been a relief to hear Rhea's voice waking her in the morning.

In the fruit grove, Ceres wandered listlessly from tree to tree. Nothing looked at all appealing, but she made herself eat a banana and an apple. They tasted bland and mealy in her mouth, but she forced them down. Then she trudged her way back to the lift and rode it up to the control center.

Ceres had spent most of the last evening pleading with Rhea to break protocol and begin rescue efforts for the colonists. The station computer had denied her requests. Ceres had tried to mount her own rescue by hijacking the mining craft, but the station computer had locked her out of the launch bay. She'd pounded on the airlock door until her fists had ached, but Rhea was implacable.

After discovering the exciting news that she wasn't alone and that close to two hundred humans were less than thirty light minutes away, her not being able to talk to them or help them had been spirit-crushing for Ceres. But no matter how much she'd begged, Rhea had refused to offer any aid to the colonists or break radio silence until they received a new directive from the planet surface.

Ceres couldn't understand why the colonists weren't screaming for help, and she couldn't convince the station AI to alter its programmed instructions.

Defeated, Ceres had retreated to her private chambers and cried herself to sleep. She'd spent the entire night suffering from her terrible recurring dreams.

When she entered the control center, she was surprised to see that the walls had been populated with dozens upon dozens of view screens, each showing a different scene of the colony. "Rhea, what is this?"

Freed from its silent mode, the station computer responded, "I took the liberty of bringing the remaining satellites we have in orbit around Langford's Leap back online. I also retrieved all of the archival footage gathered since the crisis and displayed it as well."

"Thank you," Ceres said, grudgingly appreciative of the computer's efforts.

"Unfortunately, the predictive algorithms used to provide accurate subtitles for satellite footage have been largely unsuccessful," Rhea said, sounding apologetic. "The breathing masks the colonists wear defeat the software analysis routines that read lips. However, I have been running advanced inference engines to analyze geographic location, situational context, and nonverbal cues like hand gestures and body language, and have managed to construct vague subtext captions for much of the archival footage."

"Thanks," Ceres said again. She looked from screen to screen, trying to decide where to start. Shrugging, she chose one at random and began watching.

The footage was fascinating, particularly when the computer's inference engine tried to interpret the conversations occurring between colonists wrapped in heavy coats and hidden behind goggles and masks. Sometimes the subtitles it generated seemed quite plausible–like a heated debate about water drainage in the main canyon, or investigating a broken power generator and discussing possible repairs.

But at other times the subtitles that were generated were ludicrous, especially when the footage contained children. For instance, Ceres very much doubted that the two young colonists kicking pebbles over the edge the canyon wall were conducting a scientific study, comparing Leap's gravity to Earth's. And when a group of children raced through the canyon together, it was almost certainly a game, and *not* an attempt to measure muscle density and synaptic response.

Sometimes, Ceres thought, it was obvious that Rhea was a cold, calculating computer that had never experienced the joys and irrationalities of childhood.

Over the next few hours, Ceres began to piece together a history of the colony since the crisis that had caused Rhea's construction module to flee the planet. For instance, by the time Rhea had reseeded Leap's orbit with surveillance satellites, the colony had already moved to their new home in the canyons. But the video footage did show the colonists making occasional trips south through the mountains to scavenge materials from what was likely the original colony site. That original site on the planet's surface was on a slope next to a deep alpine lake, and current satellite footage showed that it was still mostly intact.

But Ceres knew that the original colony settlement was no longer a viable location for the current colonists. Based on the video footage, it seemed the colonists had lost their ability to breathe the planet's atmosphere. Now all of them wore masks when they ventured onto the surface, and they only spent short spells out in the open before they retreated back to their caves. That meant that the first colony, built on a sloping hillside, with broad streets and manicured parks, was now a ghost town. Ceres studied the archival footage of the deserted settlement for a few moments, but nothing was stirring in the abandoned buildings except the wind. She didn't even bother with the live footage. The old colony site offered nothing of interest.

Ceres was disturbed by the colonists' struggle to breathe Leap's air. She took a brief respite from the video feeds and visited the station library to study the original expedition manifests. She confirmed her vague recollection of colonization protocol when she read that the first settlers had been genetically modified upon initially establishing orbit around Langford's Leap. Their earth-normal bodies had been altered so they could breathe the atmosphere of their new world. They'd also received increased melatonin to resist the harsher sunlight, as well as better vision, faster reflexes, and stronger muscles. These last features had not been to counter any specific detrimental effects caused by the planet—the settlers had chosen to optimize their physical forms before heading to the surface.

Had a physical disaster injured the colonists? Damaged their lungs, forcing them to wear breathing apparatuses when they were in the open atmosphere? Or perhaps the local environment had been poisoned or irradiated?

Confused, Ceres headed back to the control room to watch more archival footage. She confirmed that the colonists didn't wear masks all of the time—when they were working inside the bubbles that contained their algae farms, they walked the rows of tanks without breathing masks. Ceres surmised that the purpose of the large algae farms was oxygen production, which suggested that the colonists required an atmosphere more like Earth's than their current planetary home. Stranger and stranger.

Ceres noticed something else that struck her as odd. To confirm her suspicions, she began indexing facial images from all of the satellite footage. Soon she had clear photos of almost two hundred colonists. She took these photos and compared them to images available in the crew manifest of the original settlers.

None of them matched.

She ran a further comparison, matching the photos she'd collected against the historical photographs available in the reference section of the library. The station computers used the historical photos to create predictive algorithms for a person's age. When the computer ran the model against the photos of the colonists, the results were disturbing.

None of the colonists appeared to be more than middle-aged. Further analysis suggested that the harsh environment and living conditions of Leap would prematurely age the colonists. That meant that the oldest face captured on video was less than thirty-five years of age.

Rhea's logs had indicated that her system reboot had occurred 1.17076E+18 nanoseconds in the past—37 Earth-years ago.

That meant that—

"All of the colonists we're seeing were born after the crisis!" Ceres exclaimed.

"That seems probable," Rhea concurred.

"But...where are the original settlers? The ones born before the crisis occurred?"

"It's possible they are still alive but never venture outside the caves. Historically, community elders are confined to indoor activities."

Ceres considered this possibility, but it seemed unlikely. Based on the crew manifest, the oldest original settler had only been in his early twenties when the starship had arrived in-system. And although Rhea's reboot made it impossible to know the current Earth date with great precision, the station computer's analysis of the orbital positions of the local planets allowed Rhea to estimate that the crisis had occurred four to five years after the starship's in-system arrival. That meant that the original settlers would only be in their mid-sixties in Earth years. The genetic modifications they'd received before descending to the planet surface meant that they should still be healthy, active members of the colony's society.

But Rhea had suggested that the crisis, which had irrevocably damaged most of the orbital equipment around Leap, may have also caused great harm to the original settlers, who'd been biologically networked to the same system. Perhaps the first settlers had suffered grave illness or injury from the disaster?

"It's also possible that the original settlers were injured or killed during the crisis," Rhea said, echoing Ceres's fears.

Something about the situation didn't make sense. There were almost two hundred colonists currently living on Langford's Leap. Most were in their mid-thirties, although there were a fair number of younger colonists who ranged from infants to late teens. Still, an overwhelming number of colonists were about the same age, which meant that they'd been born around the same time. Ceres ran more statistical models and kept reaching the same conclusion.

"Rhea, the current population of colonists doesn't seem possible. There were fewer than five hundred settlers who arrived on the starship from Earth. Roughly half of those original colonists were female. In order to account for the current demographics visible in the satellite imagery, almost half of the original women would have had to have given birth just months after the crisis that sent you fleeing to the outer system. That seems *very* unlikely."

"Not just unlikely," Rhea said. "Impossible. The original settlers were incapable of engaging in natural childbirth."

"What do you mean?" Ceres asked.

"When Langford planned his Leap, he recognized that finding a planet orbiting another star with an environment similar to Earth and tolerable to human biology would be statistically improbable. He also recognized that terraformation of an entire planet would take hundreds of years. As a solution to this dilemma, Langford provided his starship with equipment that could genetically modify its human crew and adjust their biology to suit their new home. The modifications would allow them to live in harsh environments without technological aid.

"But Langford envisioned that his colony would eventually serve as a home for unmodified humans. In order to realize his vision, the first colonists would engage in aggressive terraforming efforts to convert the local flora and fauna to species that were tolerant to human biology and process the planetary atmosphere to provide breathable air.

"Langford's eugenics program was designed to adaptively match the terraforming efforts on the planet's surface. As the biosphere of the planet was altered by the efforts of the colony science team, new generations of colonists would be genetically designed to suit the changes. Over time, less mutation would be necessary, and eventually a generation of pure humans would populate the planet and be allowed to propagate naturally.

"For the first few generations of colonists, however,

reproduction was set to be strictly artificial and tightly controlled. Artificial wombs would produce human fetuses with the appropriate genetic tailoring, and then deliver the newborn infants to the planet surface as they were needed or requested."

Ceres processed Rhea's words. "That sounds horrible," she said. "I understand the logic, but the coldness of the process—delivering a series of genetically modified babies from orbital manufactories—it sounds heartless and awful!"

"Might I remind you, Ceres, that you are a product of the same artificial—"

"Stop!" Ceres ordered. "Don't remind me!" Ceres still wasn't at all comfortable with the thought that she had no biological parents. She'd held out hope since she was a toddler that her mom and dad were off on a mission somewhere in the planetary system and would come home to the station at any moment. She'd spent long nights trying to picture what her mother looked like, or how her father's hand would feel against her cheek. Some nights those memories were the only comfort that kept her sane.

Her hopes and fantasies had been dashed with the crushing reality that her birth wasn't biological, but instead the result of a mechanical process initiated by the station's AI as part of an emergency recovery protocol. There were no mythical parents out among the stars who would someday swoop in to rescue her. Ceres was a construct—as much an artificial life form as the computer that was her caretaker.

And now it seemed the entire colony population possessed the same questionable artificial lineage. Ceres wasn't sure how she felt about this new revelation. In a weird way, it made her feel a bit more camaraderie with the colonists. They shared a common heritage.

But that led Ceres to another question. "Rhea, would a disaster on the planet surface trigger an automated birthing routine?"

"I have no record of such a contingency plan," Rhea answered. "But such a plan does seem prudent."

The current colonists are a product of the same emergency protocol that generated me. Ceres felt a strange sense of comfort that she was far from alone in her parentless status.

An emergency birthing routine explained the odd, lumpy age distribution of the planet's population, but it still didn't explain why the colonists were genetic throwbacks to the original human template, thoroughly unsuited to Leap's harsh conditions. Perhaps there had been a malfunction in the birthing equipment caused by the mysterious crisis. If so, it seemed a cruel fate for the humans trying to eke out their existence on the surface. It almost made Ceres feel fortunate about her solitary life on the station.

Ceres had another revelation. "Rhea, how would the original colonists contact us?"

"They would send us a message over the network."

"Yes, yes, of course. But *how*? By what means would they send such a message?"

"All of the colonists were biologically connected to the planet-wide network system. They could send network messages as easily as they could speak or think."

"I know the *original* settlers had that ability. But what about the current colonists? The colonists who seem to have no genetic alterations? Colonists so basic in their biological structure that they can't even breathe the air or bear the sunlight?"

Rhea paused a second before answering. The delay was an extremely rare occurrence for a machine capable of trillions of calculations every second. "Without genetic modification, they lack the physical means to connect to the network," the computer answered. "Furthermore, they do not possess the encryption keys necessary for communicating on the new

Persephone network protocol."

"That means that even if they want our help, they can't ask for it," Ceres said.

"Correct," Rhea said. And then added, uncharacteristically for the AI, "Unfortunately."

"Rhea, if they *can't* contact us, then we *have* to help them, with or without orders. Please! Even you must see the logic in that!"

Rhea paused once more. "I'm sorry," the AI responded. "I cannot do that, Ceres."

"Great," Ceres said, slumping down into a crouched position. She thumped her forehead against the floor and emitted a sound that fit somewhere between a laugh and a sob. "Just great." And then, to no one at all, she asked, "So *now* what?"

10

MAX WANDERED THE REMAINS OF Leap's first colony. The abandoned avenues were lit by the bright moonlight, which illuminated the stubborn weeds that had forced their way through the pavement. Aside from the building Darius lived in, the rest of the city dwellings were mere skeletons of their former structures.

Max studied the few leftover scraps of debris and found that they looked similar to the substances used as building materials back in the canyon. Comprehension dawned on her: *We're scavengers*. The realization made her feel guilty. They were defiling the memory of the first settlers in order to support the current colony, and it seemed almost sacrilegious.

Max had spoken for long hours with Darius earlier in the day and had learned a great many things about the history of the colony. Things her father and teachers had never shared with her. Things that contradicted many of the essential truths she'd learned in school. Especially the stories told by Sister Sonya.

When Darius had first proposed that they discuss faith earlier that day, Max had rolled her eyes in dismay. She'd heard enough religious mumbo jumbo during the many lectures Sister Sonya delivered to the canyon dwellers. Max's father—less inclined to religious ideology than many of the colonists—allowed Max to skip some of the Sister's sermons, but not all of them. "Angering a community's spiritual leader is never wise," he'd say whenever Max would protest.

When Darius spoke of faith, however, it was a much different discussion than the fire-and-brimstone message the Sister tended to deliver. His message was much more sobering. He presented facts, not fantasies, and he grounded his hope for the colony's future in the stark realities that the world of Langford's Leap provided. Max, always a pragmatist, found his message to be something she could accept and believe in. And the new facts that Darius had armed her with would serve Max very well when she returned to the colony. She had every intention of confronting Sister Sonya and forcing the woman to admit her mistakes. The thought of seeing the Sister defeated by simple logic made Max grin.

Her conversations with Darius, coupled with the fact that he was like her in so many ways, made Max's day with him one of the best of her young life. It didn't hurt that, despite the odd freezing spells Darius suffered from on occasion, he was otherwise a charming and handsome man. He had a way with words that put her at ease. She found herself laughing at his jokes and sharing stories with him about her childhood that she'd never shared with anyone, not even her father. She felt like she'd found her first real friend. The fact that he was at least fifty years her senior didn't seem to matter at all.

Their meals throughout the day were varied and delicious. Darius took her on a long hike through the nearby meadows and showed her where he collected native plants and cross-bred them with Earth stock. Most of the cross-breeding results, he explained, were only suitable for base-human consumption. But a few delivered nutrients that both normal and modified humans could digest.

"Is that what we are, you and I?" Max asked. "Modified?"

Darius gave her a strange look and said, "Does Sister Sonya tell you and your fellow colonists nothing?" Shaking his head in disappointment, Darius proceeded to tell Max about her true origin. An origin she shared with the rest of the senior colonists.

Darius told her about the system-wide network failure that had occurred on the colony almost thirty-five years ago—the equivalent of almost forty Earth years. The network collapse had thrown the colony's automated systems into complete disarray and inflicted terrible pain and confusion among the settlers.

The Great Disaster. Max knew about it. All the colonists did. She'd known that technology had failed the original colonists. She just hadn't understood why or what the true ramifications had been.

"This," Darius said, gesturing to his delicate metallic exoskeleton, "is the personal price I pay for the network failure. The biological nodes in my brain that gave me perpetual access to the computer network were damaged by the computer crash. I suffer nervous system injuries that cause my body to malfunction without warning. The suit keeps me from hurting myself. Most of the time."

"What happened to the rest of the settlers?"

The look in Darius's eyes spoke volumes. "Terrible things," he said. "Some died instantly. Others...took longer. Some went crazy and wandered off into the wilderness, and others went into murderous rages. It was a time of utter chaos. It's a miracle anyone survived."

"But you *did* survive," Max insisted.

"A few of us. Not many."

"Then where did the rest of us come from? The colonists who live in the canyon now?"

"One of the orbital manufactories was a crèche, where we housed a large number of artificial wombs. They were meant to be used to repopulate the colony while we terraformed the planet. But after the network crashed and settlers began dying, emergency protocol dictated that we recover the artificial wombs from orbit. When the wombs arrived on the surface, most of them were damaged beyond repair. Others had been infected by computer viruses, making their use ill-advised.

"More importantly, the birthing equipment was never designed to function on the planet's surface. The crèches were designed for the cold temperatures and microgravity of outer space. They weren't built to operate in the gravity and warmth of the planetary surface. Also, the electricity necessary to maintain the crèches were well beyond our diminished capabilities.

"The few surviving settlers voted, and it was decided that the only way the colony would remain viable was to bring as many babies to term in the artificial wombs as quickly as we could. In their diminished state, the wombs only operated in their most basic mode, which meant that they could only produce baseline human, incapable of breathing the planet's air or resisting the harsh elements. We knew we'd be bringing those children into an unforgiving environment. But if we wanted to survive—if we wanted the colony to survive—we had no other choice."

"The other colonists might be baseline humans, but they still seem well adapted for Leap, all things considered."

Darius shook his head. "Only at first glance. Their genetic stock is based upon the men and women from Earth who lived high in the mountains. Dark skin, expanded lungs, strong bones and muscles. But that's all they are—the best a *normal* human can be. Which isn't enough."

"What about me?" Max asked. "Why am I the only child in

the colony who can survive on the planet surface without a mask? My dad is a baseline human, so how did I develop these abilities? And why don't I look like anyone else? Am I a...a *mutant*?" As she said this last word, her voice quavered.

Darius gave her a gentle smile. "No, Max, you're no mutant. Natural mutation couldn't produce the survival traits you possess. Not in just one generation. The other children in your colony were born naturally to their parents, and as a result, they suffer from the same genetic advantages and disadvantages as their mothers and fathers. But you're not like them. When we decided to use the wombs to repopulate the colony, we used the equipment that was most at risk of imminent failure first and reserved the wombs in the best condition for future emergencies. When it was feasible, the remaining wombs were repaired. Apparently, one of the surviving wombs must have had its genetic alteration software rewritten, allowing it to produce modified children once more. Children who can live on the planet without the need for a mask, protective clothing, or baseline food."

"But that means..." Max couldn't finished the sentence.

"It means that you're one of those children, Max," Darius said. "You were born in an artificial womb, just like the adults in your colony. But unlike them, you received the benefit of enhanced genetics that are tailor-designed for optimal performance on this planet's surface. You may not *look* the part, but don't let your appearance fool you. Your pale skin is much more resistant to the harsh rays of Helios than the darker skin of the other colonists. Your physique appears fragile and weak, but your muscles are quicker and more powerful than even the strongest base human. It means you are *far* more suited to Langford's Leap than any of your fellow colonists, and with proper air and nutrition, you will be superior to them in every way."

"What it means," Max said, "is that my father isn't really my father."

Darius tilted his head at her reaction. He said nothing.

Max wandered aimlessly through the abandoned town for the remainder of the day and evening, her thoughts consumed with all of the new information she'd received from Darius. She should have been delighted with discovering her true identity as a genetically modified human, along with all of the wonderful abilities and advantages that accompanied her gene-tailored body and mind. But all she could think about was her father, and the fact that he wasn't at all what she'd believed him to be.

It wasn't that Max needed to be Nolan's biological child: lots of colonists lived with foster parents in the colony. No, the issue was bigger than that. It was that her father had kept this secret from her. He'd never told her who—or what—she was. She'd trusted him, told him almost everything. And he'd betrayed that trust. It had taken a chance encounter with Darius, a complete stranger, to discover the truth. Max wasn't sure she could forgive her father for his inexplicable silence.

Darius kept a respectful distance as Max explored the town, but he was never out of sight. On occasion he would step closer to make a brief comment about a crumbling fountain or a fading fresco, the twinge of nostalgia evident in his tone as he reminisced about what must have once been an impressive community.

That night, Max had terrible dreams. She felt fevered and restless and spent most of the evening thrashing in her bed as she fought the pillows and sheets and struggled to rest. In the morning she felt more exhausted than when she'd retired for the evening.

As she joined Darius for breakfast, Max rubbed at her shoulder, which ached mysteriously, like someone had punched her very hard. The myriad aches and pains she'd suffered from her harrowing ordeal on the beach had faded to nothing, another benefit of healthy food and air. But the pain in her shoulder felt fresh and wouldn't fade away.

When Max mentioned her bad dreams to Darius, he was very interested.

"Do you remember anything specific?" he asked. "Any images or words?"

Max tried to recall details from the strange thoughts that had caused her such troubled sleep. Most were vague and hard to remember, but a few images had stuck with her. "I remember spinning wheels surrounded by darkness. The wheels seemed very large."

Darius nodded. "That's good. What else did you see?"

"Well, I didn't really see it, but—" Max paused, trying to describe her dream. "I could *sense* a great deal of activity all around me. Like the entire universe was in motion, just outside my field of vision. Does that make sense?"

Darius nodded again, a strange gleam in his eye. "Yes, Max, it makes sense. But tell me: did you *hear* anything? This is important."

Max frowned, thinking hard. "There was constant whispering all around me, but nothing was clear enough to understand. I don't even know if I recognized the language. It was like a murmuring of a thousand voices."

"You heard nothing in particular? No words that were spoken?"

Frowning still, Max lowered her head and concentrated. It was all so fuzzy, and it was fading as the morning sun rose in the sky. She lifted her head and said, "'*Persephone.*'" The word felt odd on her tongue. "I think I heard the word '*Persephone.*'"

A strange expression flashed across Darius's face. To Max, it looked like a mixture of fear and jubilation. But just as quickly as it had appeared, it was gone, and Darius was as sad and as serious as ever.

"What does it all mean?" Max asked.

The enthusiasm Darius had shown earlier was gone. He stood up and shrugged, cold and distant. "A side effect of the foods I gave you yesterday. A hallucinogenic response. Harmless, luckily."

Max didn't buy Darius's explanation, but no matter how many times she asked about her dreams, or about the word "Persephone," Darius avoided answering her. In fact, his entire demeanor seemed very different—disconnected, somehow. He ate breakfast with her, but he was distracted the entire meal, and afterward he announced that they needed to hurry to get Max back to the canyon before the day's high tide arrived. Based on his behavior, it was as if he'd lost all interest in his guest.

Darius walked with Max down the hillside and paddled her across the dark lake in his canoe. Normally, Max would have found the ride across the lake to be an enjoyable experience. She'd never been in a watercraft before. Life in the canyon didn't afford much variety in her routine. But Darius's attitude ruined the experience.

Max stared at her changed companion as he paddled the canoe, but Darius just gave her a bland smile. After their intimate conversations just a day earlier, Max couldn't believe that he could so thoroughly dismiss her now. It was as if she was just another science project for him: a creature to be studied and then—once he'd discovered her inner workings—discarded so he could find another topic for investigation. Max felt used, and hurt, and lonely. Loneliness she was familiar with, but she'd hoped she'd found an end to it when she'd met Darius. Obviously, she was wrong. She rubbed at her sore shoulder muscle, perplexed by the sudden change in her newfound friend.

While sitting in the bow of the small craft as they traversed the lake, Max realized she'd been here before. She remembered the water slapping against the bottom of the boat's fabric hull after Darius had rescued her from the tide. Off to the right of the canoe, the lake's towering waterfall thundered, its never-ending stream of water tumbling and tangling down the mountainside. It was beautiful, and despite her sour mood, Max found the power of the falling water awe-inspiring.

After reaching the far side of the lake, Darius gave Max a small supply of food, a water canteen, and small hand-drawn map that gave her simple but adequate directions to follow back to the canyon. The map pointed out key areas for her to avoid, especially when the tide would rise later in the day.

Max had assumed Darius would escort her at least part of the way back to the canyon, but upon receiving the map and supplies she realized it wasn't to be. Hurt even further by Darius's callousness, she turned on her heel and marched away from the lake without a word of goodbye. She hoped he'd call her back and offer her an apology or an explanation, but after a few steps she heard the canoe slide off the sandy shore and back into the lake, followed soon after by the sound of Darius's paddle splashing against the water and carrying him back across the lake toward his home.

Fighting back tears of disappointment, Max pushed through the shrubbery that dominated the lakeside and began the long trek home. The previous night Max had been angry enough with her father that she'd considered not returning home. The terrible discovery that she was adopted had been bad enough, but the fact that her father, the one person she thought she could trust, had hidden the truth from her had felt even worse.

Now, though, all she wanted was to feel her father's arms around her again. He must have been sick with worry over her absence. After all, she'd been gone for almost two days, which meant the other colonists would have given up the search for her. But Max knew her father would have held out hope and concocted more and more outlandish explanations for how Max might have survived out in the wilderness for so long without food, water, or air. Two days, though, was a long time for even a father to deny reality. Max needed to get home, and soon.

But as she continued her trek home, Max started to worry about how she was going to explain her disappearance to the other colonists. Sure, she could tell them about Darius's rescue, but that still wouldn't explain how she'd survived more than a few minutes without her mask. She could claim that she'd taken a spare mask with her out onto the surface, except that she hadn't. She had no mask to make such a story plausible.

The alternative was to tell everyone the truth. To admit to the colonists that she was different than the rest of them. She could survive in situations that would be fatal to everyone else. She could breathe air that made the average human suffocate. She could eat food that was toxic to anyone else.

Would admitting that she was different be so horrible? Maybe the other colonists would be impressed by her newfound abilities. She could employ her skills to perform tasks that were challenging or impossible for the other colony members. That would make her a valuable asset to the community. She might even be seen as a hero.

She wasn't just different. She was *special*.

Max tried to convince herself of the truth in these arguments, but all she could hear was one word echoing through her thoughts—*Mutie. Mutie. Mutie.*

The pounding word crushed her, shoulders slumping, feet shuffling ever slower under the weight of judgment.

Max was so caught up in her sad musings that she was taken completely by surprise when a shadowed figure stepped out from behind a rock outcropping and snatched her by the arm. She screamed in surprise, and with strength she'd never before possessed, she yanked her arm free from the clutches of her aggressor. The feeling of power that flowed through her limbs overwhelmed her fright, and Max went on the offensive, swinging a lightning-fast punch toward the midsection of her assailant.

That punch never connected. Instead, Max received a sharp slap to the wrist, followed by a swift kick behind her knees that caused her to collapse to the ground. Another kick between her shoulder blades drove her face into the dirt, and she found herself chewing on grit.

"Easy, girl!" a voice hissed. "You're fast, but not *that* fast. And besides, that's not how you should treat your rescuer!"

Max rolled over and spat pebbles out of her mouth. She sat up and said, "Rescuer? You're hardly that, Sister Sonya. I'm doing just fine without your help."

"That you are, child," the Sister said, stepping back and examining her from beneath her dark hood. Her voice took on a shrewd tone. "I see you're breathing without the aid of a mask."

"I—" Max stammered. But what could she say? She'd been caught wandering through the wilderness without a breathing mask. Sister Sonya might be an annoying religious zealot, but she wasn't stupid. Nothing Max could say would fool the old woman.

Before Max could say any more, Sonya cut one hand through the air in a dismissive gesture. "I wondered how long you'd keep your secret. Longer than I expected, I'll admit."

Max ogled at her. "You *knew*?" she exclaimed.

Sister Sonya laughed—a dry, rasping sound like too had gravel in her mouth. "Maxine, there's not much that happens in this colony that I don't know about. You may not believe me when I say this, but I try my best to let you and the other colonists pursue your lives as you see fit. I try not to meddle. I intervene when I must. When survival is at stake. I knew about your secret, yes. But I decided you were the only person who was fit to choose when to tell the other colonists." Sonya drew closer, so close that Max could see the Sister's blue eye gleaming in the shadow of her hood. "My question to you, child, is this: are you ready to tell the other children about whom or what you are?"

Max thought hard about her response. It was one of the most difficult decisions she'd ever faced. What should she do?

Mutie. Mutie. Mutie.

"No," Max said. "I don't think I am."

She expected Sister Sonya to reprimand her, call her a coward or worse, but to her surprise, the Sister only nodded. She offered Max her hand, and when Max took it, she drew her into a gentle but firm embrace.

Max, shocked, returned the hug. The Sister had never offered a gesture of comfort to anyone before, as far as Max knew. The hug felt surprisingly good, and she gripped the old woman more tightly.

Sonya released her and spun on her heel toward the canyon. "Come, then," she said. "We have work to do."

DISCOVERING THAT THE COLONISTS ON Leap had lost the ability to network with the rest of the system was yet another devastating blow for Ceres. Every time she learned a new fact about the colony and their predicament, she felt elation, like she'd been launched at escape velocity toward a stable orbit of hope. Then the bad news would come, and it was as if she'd discovered that she lacked the momentum to sustain her trajectory. Each time her emotional orbit decayed and she fell back down, it hurt a bit more.

Ceres pleaded with Rhea, hoping their discovery that the struggling colonists no longer possessed network interface technology, and therefore would not—*could* not—ask for help would convince the AI to violate the Persephone protocol and let Ceres provide aid. But Rhea, true to her cold machine nature, would not be swayed. Until the station received an official command to break its holding pattern, Ceres wouldn't be permitted to interfere in the lives of her fellow humans on the planet's surface.

Without any other recourse, Ceres sat in the control room and watched more video footage. At this stage, she was more numb than upset. *Hopelessness must do that to a person,* she thought. *Giving up left you with no energy for emotions like anger or frustration. There was no point, so why bother?*

The video footage began to blur together after a while. It wasn't as if colony life was all that interesting. The act of scratching out a meager existence, while challenging, was also very rote. Not much changed.

But then Ceres spotted something unusual on one of the monitors. Intrigued, she approached the screen and froze the image. There, on the outskirts of the canyon were two individuals engaged in what looked like a heated discussion. Resolution was grainy—the satellite providing the feed was almost below the planet's horizon, which meant that it was shooting almost tangential to the planet's surface, and the oblique angle of the shot meant that the image she was watching suffered from an enormous amount of atmospheric distortion. Software filters could clean up some of the image, but not all of it.

Ceres didn't know what the two people were talking about, which was unfortunate. But that wasn't what interested her. What she found intriguing about the footage was that, as best as she could tell from the blurry images, one of the two figures—a young girl—wasn't wearing a breathing mask. The other figure was hidden underneath an amorphous billowing robe.

"Rhea, is that colonist wearing a mask?"

"It does not appear so, no."

"When was this footage recorded?"

"Just a few minutes ago."

"Can you identify the two colonists?"

"The quality of the image is poor, but I may be able to identify the younger of the two figures. As for the figure in the cloak, no facial recognition is possible for obvious reasons, but heuristic algorithms may be able to provide an identity based on gait, body size, and other distinguishing characteristics."

"Please try," Ceres said. "In the meantime, let's rewind this footage. I want to know where those two came from."

"The satellite providing this footage just crested the horizon a few minutes ago. We don't have any other viable angles of this location at the mouth of the canyon, so I cannot determine the earlier location of the two figures."

"Of course not," Ceres said. She'd discovered, as she'd studied the satellite footage, that coverage of the planetary surface was often quite spotty. The orbital space around Langford's Leap was inexplicably hostile to the satellites Rhea inserted into orbit. Yet another mystery that deserved further investigation. Rhea continuously produced new satellites to replace lost equipment, but it was a war of attrition, and limited resources meant that sometimes there were significant gaps in the archival footage of the colony.

Still, Ceres didn't feel too disappointed. The footage she was looking at was very interesting. It was the first evidence she'd gathered that at least one colonist on the surface was capable of breathing Leap's atmosphere without artificial aid. Even more surprising, it wasn't someone old enough to be one of the original settlers. If a young colonist possessed the ability to breathe, then maybe—just maybe—they had the ability to network, as well. Ceres felt her hopes begin to rise once more.

"Rhea, I want you to identify that girl. Find all the footage we have on her. And do what you can about the cloaked figure as well. Something strange is going on between those two, and I want to know what it is."

Ceres knew the indexing and searching process was going to take a while, despite the massive computational power at the station's disposal. The resolution of the satellites' imagery varied, so sometimes facial recognition wasn't possible. Furthermore, the angle of surveillance was often close to straight down, which made it hard to recognize the colonists. Add in environmental factors like clouds, dust, and rain, and the vagaries of colonist behavior like slouching, ducking, and facing the wrong direction, and the task of tracking specific individuals became ever more difficult.

Luckily for Ceres, Rhea's patience was limitless. The computer would grind away on the problem endlessly, which freed Ceres to pursue other activities.

Feeling energized by her discovery about the young maskless colonist but with no easy way to help Rhea search through the video footage, Ceres needed something to occupy her time. She decided to research the equipment that still orbited Leap. Rhea may not let her launch a rescue effort yet, but that didn't mean she couldn't prepare ahead of time. If communications were ever reestablished with the colonists, Ceres wanted to have resources ready to deliver as soon as possible.

Ceres decided that the first thing she should focus her efforts on was the mysterious failures that kept plaguing the reconnaissance satellites. Whatever was causing the persistent satellite failures would have to be identified and neutralized, or a future rescue effort would be impossible.

Ceres brought up an overhead schematic of the entire planetary system and instructed the screen to highlight all of the remote machinery operating in that space. She then instructed every available craft that belonged to Rhea's secure network to focus any and all available observational equipment on Leap. Hundreds of satellites and automated mining crafts—ranging from as close as Artemis, Leap's moon, to as far away as the local system's Kuiper Belt—were included in the request.

Eventually almost every active electronic device in the planetary system would turn their unblinking eyes toward the colony world. Ceres even retasked a few of the reconnaissance satellites watching the colony to turn their cameras away from the surface and focus instead on their neighbors in orbit. It meant that the coverage of the planet's surface would be even spottier, but Ceres decided that solving the orbital dilemma was a more pressing short-term goal. With so many electronic eyes watching the same space, Ceres hoped that she'd eventually capture footage of what was disabling or destroying Leap's satellites.

The observation process would take time. Just the act of sending a radio signal to the more distant equipment platforms would take hours, and a similar amount of time would pass before the craft acknowledged the request. Still more time would pass before light from Leap reached those faraway lenses, and then the images would have to be broadcast back to Ceres at the station. It would be days before she had a comprehensive picture of the orbital space surrounding the colony, and even afterward she'd have nothing to do but wait until something interesting happened.

What could she do while waiting? Ceres looked at the solar system schematic and noticed that a few of the original orbital manufactories were still in orbit around the planet. Power and heat signatures indicated that some were still functional, but their icons on the schematic were pulsing red—the manufactories hadn't switched over to the new emergency network protocol, so they weren't in contact with Rhea and the rest of her reconstructed equipment. Still, if they were functional, then it was possible that Ceres could regain control and put them to use.

Ceres called up the original starship manifests and began studying the blueprints for the orbital manufactories. The platforms were incredibly intricate, designed to produce a dizzying array of equipment for the colony that ranged from simple items like clothing and hand tools to items as complex as ground-based solar arrays and desalination plants.

As Ceres studied the factory blueprints, she realized that understanding the details of their inner workings would take a very long time. But Ceres reached the conclusion that she didn't need to understand how they worked. She only needed to understand was how to communicate with them and how to issue instructions to them on what type of equipment to produce.

That meant Ceres needed to connect with equipment that was still operating on the old, insecure network—a network which had been compromised during the crisis. Since the network had been cut off for almost forty years, there was no way for Ceres to know what its current state might be.

"Rhea," Ceres asked, "can we communicate with equipment still connected to the old network?"

"Communication with the old network is possible, but inadvisable," Rhea answered. Despite being occupied with analyzing the video surveillance footage, the AI's response was instant—massive parallel processing had its advantages. "Connecting to the original network would put our current network security at risk. We may fall prey to whatever caused the initial crisis."

Ceres wasn't willing to give up so easily. Considering Rhea's reservations, she recalled something she'd read about when researching Earth's history. "Can't we set up a disconnected, isolated networking environment? Something that, should the environment be compromised, wouldn't allow the rest of the system to suffer from the same intrusion?"

"Yes, a self-contained virtual environment can be created that would allow us to connect to the compromised network with minimal risk."

Ceres sighed. It was just this type of scenario that made interacting with Rhea so infuriating. Despite the incredible computational power that the AI had at its disposal, it was still only as smart as its programming. It was incapable of thinking in a way that was different than its base instruction set. That meant that the AI sometimes couldn't make logical leaps that most humans would consider obvious. For instance, The AI was aware of the station's capability to create secure virtual environments, but the computer would not have suggested the solution to the connection problem unless Ceres first prompted it.

I guess that's why I'm here. It seemed that having a human pilot aboard the station was critical to its functionality. The inexhaustible, rational, methodical AI needed the creative, emotional, logic-leaping skills of a human being as its complement. "Rhea, please set up a virtuality for me so I can attempt to communicate with the functional manufactories still in orbit around Langford's Leap."

Without any warning whatsoever, Ceres found herself standing in the middle of a bright yellow room. The transition was instantaneous.

"Whoa!" she exclaimed.

"I've projected your network consciousness into a virtuality," Rhea said.

"Wait, I have built-in networking capabilities?"

"Of course," Rhea said, sounding almost surprised. "All colonists are genetically designed to be able to network directly with the equipment at their disposal."

"Why haven't we ever done this before?"

"There's never been a need."

Ceres had no answer to that response. When you live *inside* the equipment at your disposal, maybe virtual networking wasn't necessary, after all.

Rhea continued, "As requested, this virtuality is disconnected from the rest of the Persephone network. While you are attempting contact with the manufactories, I will also be disconnected from this space. You will be isolated."

"Isolated?" Ceres echoed. "What do I do if there is an emergency? If I need to exit the space, for instance?"

"A very narrow channel of communication will remain open, which will accept two specific exit signals as valid message traffic. The first exit signal is the utterance of a code word, which for this virtuality is 'Geronimo.'"

"'Geronimo,'" Ceres repeated. "Okay, got it. What's the second exit signal?"

"You can pull the ripcord located on the center of your chest. Pulling its handle or speaking the code word will close the virtuality and safely deliver your consciousness back to the station."

"What do you mean, safely? Is the virtual environment dangerous?"

"Yes. Your body is invulnerable to injury during a virtual network session. But your network interface is embedded in your cortex, so your brain and central nervous system *can* suffer physical harm from network activity. I have attempted to install filters around the virtuality that will prevent most known malware from penetrating the locale and causing you substantial harm. But whatever caused the crisis that crashed Leap's first network was capable of defeating similar countermeasures. If you feel you are in danger, you should exit the virtual space immediately."

Ceres felt her heart start racing. This wasn't the first time in her life she'd been in physical danger—traveling in a small mining craft between asteroids, riding shotgun on a gas giant mining rig, engaging in half a dozen other routine activities the station required—they all entailed a moderate amount of risk. But what she was about to do, even though it was something in the virtual world, felt much more dangerous. She was about to thrust herself into the dragon's den, exposing her mind to whatever had decimated the orbital infrastructure so many years ago and caused the colony's current predicament.

Ceres took a deep breath and said, "Rhea, please connect me to the unsecured network."

The virtual room, which had been sunny and cheerful before, plunged into darkness. Ceres was bombarded by a thousand shrieking voices from every direction, each demanding her identity and access to her data resources. Their incessant shouts caused her to clutch her hands to her ears to block them out, but invisible talon-like fingers pried at her, trying to force their way in.

Ceres shouted the exit word, but her voice was impossible to hear over the cacophony. She fumbled for the ripcord at her chest and yanked on the handle with all her might—

And found herself back in the control room of the station, breathing heavily.

"Ceres, are you hurt?" Rhea asked with an appropriate degree of concern evident in her voice.

Ceres took a shuddering breath to calm herself. "I'm fine, just a little shaken up. It's chaos in there! I could only bear the noise for a few seconds before exiting."

"Fifty-three minutes have passed since you first initiated contact."

"Wait, what?" Ceres asked. But her mind was already answering her own question. Light-speed delays at play again. The present location of Leap and the station meant that it took more than twenty-five minutes for a signal to reach the orbitals, and another twenty-five minutes for the return signal to reach the station. Ceres hadn't experienced any of that delay, which meant the virtuality had edited out the time lapse. But she realized that subsequent interaction with the manufactories would be a painstaking process due to distance.

"Rhea, is there anything preventing us from moving the

station to a closer orbit to the colony?"

"We've been maintaining orbit between the asteroid belt and the gas giant. Our current location affords us the easiest access to physical resources."

Was Rhea dodging a question? Ceres smirked. "That's not what I asked you. Can we move closer?"

"Yes, we can establish orbit that would place us closer to the planet. But we cannot enter a proper orbit around Langford's Leap until a connection with the colonists has been reestablished."

"Understood. Rhea, move the station as close as the emergency protocol allows. Let's reduce this light-speed delay a bit." Ceres squared her shoulders, tilted her head back and forth to stretch her neck, and cracked her knuckles. "Now, let's try this again. Rhea, restart the virtuality and reconnect me to the unsecured network."

SISTER SONYA'S PLAN FOR MAX'S return to the camp consisted of three major elements. First, the Sister took Max back to her dwelling: a small cave separate from the rest of the caverns used by the colonists. There, the Sister provided Max with a new mask and quilted coat. The equipment looked like standard breathing gear, but the Sister explained that the coat's filters replenished themselves with atmospheric air instead of the oxygenated air the other colonists needed. The equipment would bear cursory scrutiny from Max's peers. It would appear that she was wearing functional gear, but she'd actually be breathing Leap's air. As Max had discovered during the last two days, being able to avoid filtered colony air was enormously beneficial to her health. The camouflaged equipment the Sister gave her would be very helpful.

"What about when I'm inside a pressurized area?" Max asked.

"Your allergy symptoms have become much worse since your ordeal in the wilderness these past few days," the Sister said.

Max frowned. "No, they haven't."

"Yes," the Sister said, "they *have*. I have no choice but to recommend that you wear your mask at all times, even when indoors. Your lungs need time to recover from the strain of your outdoor adventure. Do you understand?"

Oh, Max thought, feeling stupid that she hadn't caught on to the Sister's planned subterfuge. She nodded at Sonya's plan. Anything that allowed her to breathe healthy, natural air sounded good to her.

After testing the new breathing gear, she and Sonya walked back into town together. As soon as the Sister saw someone in the canyon, she announced, "I've found her! I found the lost child!"

The colonist, an adult Max didn't know very well named Sven, stopped dead in his tracks and stared at the two of them. Sven had clearly believed that Max would never be found, at least not alive. His surprise was evident, even behind his mask.

"Quickly, man, go and gather the colony! This is a fortuitous event, and a reason to celebrate! Hope springs eternal for those who believe! The word must spread!"

Great. My return to the colony will only serve to further fuel the Sister's words of faith. Just what I always wanted. Max felt conflicted about this new turn of events. On the one hand, the Sister was being unusually helpful in getting Max reentered into society without revealing her secret. On the other hand, Max did *not* want to be a pawn in the Sister's power games. Especially after everything she'd learned from Darius about the true history of the colony and the nature of their future rescue.

But Max needed the Sister for this part of the plan to work, so she played along and followed Sonya as she marched through the tunnels to the largest cavern in the colony, urging everyone they saw to spread the word and hurry to meet them there.

By the time they arrived, the cavern was already crowded with people. Word traveled fast in the small community, and news like the kind Sonya was bringing was both rare and wonderful. Max and the Sister were met with wild cheers and clapping: the relief and surprise on everyone's faces matched by their joy to have one of their own back and safe.

But mixed in with the happiness were looks of curiosity and puzzlement. A few people reached out to touch Max, as if to see if she were really there. Their hands were timid, careful not to injure the child who'd somehow survived in the wilderness for days without aid. The colonists were used to living in a world of harsh absolutes. If a person wandered away from the canyon without proper gear, the outcome was a near certain thing. Max had somehow defied those overwhelming odds, which caused more than one colonist to eyeball her with suspicion and confusion.

Not least among those worried expressions was the look on Ellie's face when she came running into the cavern, her closest cronies right behind her. Ellie slid to a stop, and her face was a pale mask of shock and dismay. Max was convinced her archenemy had never expected to see her alive again. Now she knew Ellie must be panicking. If Max told the other colonists what Ellie and her friends had done to her, Ellie's status among the other children would be ruined. Worse, Ellie might face criminal charges from the colony's leaders. Life on Leap was dangerous, and there was no tolerance for intentionally increasing that danger.

Behind her mask, Max smiled. Ellie deserved what was coming to her.

There was a commotion in the crowd as someone shoved their way through the mass of people. Max's father burst from in between two colonists, causing one of them to stumble and fall to the ground. Nolan didn't even spare the fallen man a glance. He stared at Max like he was seeing a ghost. Then he rushed forward, swept his daughter up in his arms, and crushed her to his chest.

Any animosity Max had been harboring toward her father melted away, and she hugged him back fiercely. She could feel her father tense a bit, no doubt surprised by the strength of her embrace. The air and food of the past two days had already resulted in a noticeable improvement in Max's health. She wondered how much better she'd feel after a few more days. Or a week. Or a month. But then she let the thought go and reveled in the comfort she felt from her father's arms.

Sister Sonya's strident voice rose above the din of the noisy crowd. The distant walls of the cavern echoed with her words, giving them strength and importance, and the colonists fell silent.

"Look what faith has brought to us! Most of you believed this child to be lost forever, stolen from us by the harsh reality that is Langford's Leap. But many of you held on to your faith, never giving up hope. And now we've been rewarded for that unfailing belief. We've recovered the child, against all odds. The colony that believes in itself, and that holds to its hope for salvation and rescue, that is a colony that'll reap the bounty of what it sows."

"How?" shouted one of the more skeptical colonists. "How did she survive for so long?"

The Sister turned to address the colonist. "A few kilometers south of the canyon, there are a series of small chasms that are still volcanically active, likely the same system that created the tunnels of our home in an earlier era. The chasms emit steam and smoke which attracts the more *adventurous* children." Sister Sonya turned back to give Max a meaningful glare, but underneath her hood and hidden from the view of the colonists, she winked instead.

Who is *this woman?* Max thought, bewildered by the

Sister's inexplicable playfulness. *Not the Sister Sonya I've grown up with all my life!*

Sonya continued, "Knowing this, I searched the chasms, which sometimes trap pockets of breathable air belched from the planet's depths. I found Maxine lying collapsed in one of those pockets, unable to climb out of the hole she'd fallen into. Amazingly, the girl was uninjured except for minor bruising. Her lungs are damaged from the smoke and heat of the air she was forced to breathe the past few days. She'll need to wear her mask to protect her from further damage, but I expect her to recover fully over time."

"It's a miracle!" someone shouted from the back of the crowd. That word—*miracle*—echoed back and forth, picked up by the colonists and repeated over and over again. The cavern walls joined in the chant, causing the word to reverberate. *Miracle! Miracle! Miracle!*

Max buried her face in her father's shoulder. She was just glad to be home.

The rest of the day was a blur as numerous colonists made a point to welcome Max back to the community. Max, who'd always been an outcast with the other children due to her physical ailments, had never developed social skills with the adults of the colony, either. All the attention made her very uncomfortable. She did her best to accept the well wishes she received. But after an hour of dealing with the joyous colonists, Max was ready to go home.

When she and her father entered their home, both of them just stared at each other for a long moment. They had so much to talk about. No doubt her father wanted a true recollection of the events that had led to Max's disappearance. He'd been too overwhelmed by her return to say anything, but Max knew if anyone was suspicious about the story Sister Sonya had concocted for her, it was her father.

Max had lots of questions for her dad, as well. Darius had

revealed to her that she was the product of an artificial birthing womb—a technology that had imbued her with genetic modifications, which made her the sole colonist in the canyon suited to live on Leap. Max's father must have known about her true origins, but he'd never told her about it. Max had to know why her father, whom she'd always believed was truthful and forthright with her, had withheld this crucial fact about her past.

The two of them stared, both trying to figure out how to break the ice. Her father said, "It's getting late. You should rest. We'll speak more tomorrow." He smiled, gave her another fierce hug, and then retired to his bedroom.

Max felt relieved. Maybe she wasn't the only one not ready to face the truth of things just yet. Tomorrow. Tomorrow would be better.

But when she woke the next morning, her father was already gone. He'd left breakfast on the table for her and a note saying that he had another emergency to take care of, this time with the algae reclamation units. His note encouraged Max to try to return to her regular routine of school and work, if she was able.

Sighing, Max ignored the breakfast on the table and instead helped herself to the food Darius had given to her. She wasn't sure what she was going to do for nourishment once the meager supply she'd brought home ran out. Perhaps Sister Sonya would be able to help her with that dilemma, as well.

Any goodwill Max felt toward the Sister was rapidly exhausted during her morning studies. The good Sister was teaching history to the students—or at least the version of history accepted by the colony. The lesson was interspersed with long diatribes about faith and hope and other religious claptrap. Max did her best to bear the preachiness of the lecture, but eventually she could stand it no longer. She raised her hand.

Sister Sonya was unaccustomed to interruptions. She paused in her lecture and said, "Yes, Maxine?"

"Is it possible to travel faster than the speed of light?"

The Sister's face was—as always—hidden under her hood. But the woman's stance suggested a mild sense of confusion and annoyance. "This is a history lecture, Maxine, not a lecture on physics."

"I know that, Sister. And my ultimate concern *does* pertain to our history. But before I ask what might be a foolish question, I need to know: is it possible to travel faster than the speed of light?"

"No, of course not. It's an absolute law of physics. Nothing travels faster than the speed of light."

"But the starship that first brought the colonists to Langford's Leap, it approached speeds close to the speed of light, correct? It must have, or there would have been no way humans could have survived onboard long enough for them to reach the planet."

"Close to the speed of light is a very *relative* term, Max." The Sister barked a short laugh at her own joke, surprising her students. "But yes, the starship did travel very fast. Fast enough for the passengers to benefit from the time dilation effects as described in Einstein's theory of general relativity. While it took many years for the starship to travel between the stars, for the passengers it only seemed like a few."

"The distance from here to our origin solar system, from Helios to the Sun, is just a few light years, then? A distance short enough for the starship to cross in less than twenty years, correct?"

Sister Sonya's voice took on an aggravated quality. "Maxine, what's the point of all of this?"

Max stood up from her desk and walked over to a star chart that hung on one of the walls. "Where is our home star,

Sister? Where is Earth?"

"Max, I—"

"Where is it?" Max demanded.

The Sister stormed over to the map and pointed a long, bony finger at one of the stars on the chart. "Here," she said, tapping the star under her long fingernail. "The same place it has been every other time you've studied this material. Which, I might add, would have happened during an astronomy lecture or a physics discussion. As I've already told you once before, we're studying history today."

Max placed her finger next to Sonya's on the map. "This is Earth's star? This is the Sun?"

"Yes, Max, it is." The Sister moved to return to the front of the classroom.

"No, Sister Sonya, it most certainly is not."

The other students, who'd been watching this strange back and forth between their teacher and their normally meek and mild-mannered classmate, were now sitting in dead silence. No one questioned the Sister's word. Ever.

The Sister turned to glare at Max. "Young lady, I believe you're mistaken."

Max shook her head. "These star charts are quite detailed. And if you study the notation printed next to the star you've indicated, you can read its luminosity and size. The star you identified is a main sequence star, but unlike the Sun, it's a Type A star. Its light is much bluer than Earth's yellow sun. It burns hotter and brighter as a result, much like Helios, the star we orbit here on Leap. Fortunately, Leap's orbit is farther away from its star than Earth's orbit. If the star you pointed to on this map was the Sun, life on Earth would be impossible."

The Sister made a noise like she wanted to interrupt, but Max was having none of it.

"The star you've been pointing at all our lives is *not* Earth's

Sun. I think the star you wanted to point at is...this one over here. The right color, the right size, the right brightness. A perfect match for everything we know about our home world's star. Its only problem is that it's too far away. Much too far away. In fact, it's almost at the far edge of this star chart. That means it's more than fifty light years from Langford's Leap."

Max advanced upon the Sister. It was her turn to glare. "Why would you not tell us the truth, Sister? Why would you hide our home world from us?" Before the Sister could answer, Max turned to her classmates and said, "Is it because you wanted us to maintain the false hope you've been providing to us all these years? Hope that a message to Earth would bring a rescue mission and save us from certain doom? That if we believed enough, and had enough patience, our forefathers would bring another starship across the void and deliver us from our torment? Is that it, Sister? Did you not trust us with the truth? Did you feel the need—the compulsion—to fill our heads with religious nonsense instead?"

Max could see comprehension dawning behind the eyes of the other students in the room. That comprehension was matched with a variety of emotions: fear, sadness, disappointment, anger. A general murmur rose in the room as the students began discussing Max's revelations with their neighbors. No one ever questioned the Sister, but what if there was scientific proof that her message of hope and rescue was a false one?

Max felt a vise-like grip close around her forearm. She tried to pull away, but Sister Sonya's grip was unbreakable.

"Outside," the Sister hissed in her ear. Without waiting for a response, the woman dragged Max from the classroom, causing the volume and temperature of the murmuring of the students to rise.

"Let go!" Max insisted, twisting her arm from the Sister's grasp.

"Where did you learn these things?" the Sister demanded.

Max pulled her mask up over her face so she could speak more clearly. "Where did I learn the truth, you mean?"

"Truth is always a relative term, girl. Now tell me, who have you been speaking with?"

Max stuck her chin out. "Out in the wilderness, I was rescued by a man living in the ruins of the first colony settlement. His name is Darius. He told me the truth about lots of things. About what I am, where I came from. Where *all of us* came from. From a star so far away, our rescue will never come!"

At the sound of the Darius's name, Sonya had gone stock still. She stood that way for a long moment, and then one of her hands reached up and lowered her hood, revealing her face.

Sister Sonya looked nothing like Max had imagined. The woman standing in front of her was the most striking woman she'd ever seen—the perfect combination of high cheekbones, narrow chin, and full lips. Her skin was a dusky hue that radiated healthiness and youth—she looked to be in her mid-twenties. Her raven-black hair was silky and thick, and it cascaded down the left side of her face, almost, but not quite, concealing the long, brutal scar that crossed her cheek. Through the hair, Max could detect a dark, empty socket where an eye should have been. What should have been a terrible disfigurement only served to enhance the Sister's beauty somehow.

Sister Sonya is young? Max thought, bewildered. *And beautiful?* Max couldn't process what she was seeing.

Sonya's single blue eye was looking at Max with an intensity she'd never felt before. She'd borne the brunt of that glare many times in the past, but today's was something different. It wasn't anger or disapproval that powered the look—it was panic.

"You spoke to Langford?" Sonya whispered.

Max blinked, trying to escape the intensity of Sonya's eye contact. "Langford? What? No, I told you, I spoke to—"

"Darius Langford. The founder of the colony. 'The Man Who Dared to Leap.' The reason we're all here, trapped in this terrible state."

"Darius...Langford?" Max's mind couldn't function. Her thoughts were mired in quicksand. How could she not have recognized Langford's first name? She'd heard it before— probably dozens or even hundreds of times—in class, during the Sister's sermons, out working with her father. Langford was a man both cursed and revered by the colonists. His name was spoken more often than any other. Hell, the planet was named after the man! How did Max not realize who she'd met? Who'd rescued her and taken her in?

"You spoke with Darius?" Sonya prompted, breaking Max from her reverie.

"I did, yes."

"And he told you the truth about our proximity to Earth? Or rather, the lack of our proximity?"

"He did, yes." Three word sentences were taxing Max's current ability to speak.

"Did he say anything to you about Persephone?" Sonya pressed

"*Persephone?*" Max repeated.

"Yes, Max," Sonya said. "Did Darius mention Persephone to you?"

"No, he didn't."

Sonya dropped her head and let out a sigh of relief.

"He didn't mention Persephone to me, Sister. I mentioned it to him."

Sonya gasped in dismay. "You told Darius about

Persephone?"

"Well, I—" Max began.

"Oh, child," Sonya said, "what have you done?"

"But I didn't—"

"If Darius knows about Persephone, then all is lost."

Max, aggravated, shouted, "I don't know *anything* about Persephone, alright? All I remember is hearing the word in a dream. I wasn't even sure that was the word I heard until you just said it aloud to me. I don't know what the word means, and Darius wouldn't explain it. I didn't tell him anything!"

Max's outburst seemed to penetrate Sonya's intense focus just a little bit. The woman stood up, releasing Max's shoulders from her deathlike grip. "You heard the word in a dream?"

Max nodded.

"But you didn't tell Darius anything about Persephone?"

"No. I don't *know* anything, so there was nothing to tell him."

The Sister sagged in visible relief. "That's good, Max. That's very good."

Max thought about her last conversation with Darius Langford. "Sister, I couldn't have answered any of Darius's questions. I know nothing but the word itself. And the truth is that Darius didn't *ask* me any questions."

Sonya raised her head and looked confused. "Really? He didn't try to glean any information about what you dreamed?"

"Not really. Once I mentioned Persephone to him, he gave me a strange smile, and then that was it. He seemed to be in a hurry to get me out the door and back to the canyon."

"That's...troubling," the Sister said to herself.

"Why?" Max asked. "What's all this about? What is Persephone, Sister? Why is it so important?"

But the Sister was pulling her hood back over her head,

and she ignored Max's questions. "It's time to get back to class. No more questions about light speed and the real location of Earth. You'll distract and confuse the other students. We'll talk more about all of this later." Sonya grabbed Max's arm, at first quite strongly, but then with a more gentle touch. "Maxine, the fate of the colony rests on your silence. I need time to ponder the events that are unfolding. Can I trust you to not say anything more until I've had time to think?"

Max considered. The Sister had been helpful in getting the colonists to accept her back into the community with very few questions. And she'd taught Max how to modify her mask filters, giving her air she could easily breathe. For those things alone, Max owed Sonya her gratitude and her cooperation.

But when Max thought about the faith-laden lecture she'd just been subject to...

"Okay, but can you please stop preaching in the classroom? Save your religious messages for your sermons, and stick to the actual lesson plan when you're teaching us."

Deep in the shadows of her hood, Max could see the faint gleam of a smile. "Done," the Sister said. "And Max?"

"Yes, Sister?"

"You can call me Sonya."

13

IT TOOK DAYS FOR CERES to negotiate with the orbital manufactories.

First she had to repair the faulty connection establishment protocol which had been corrupted by malware. In order to tackle the problem, Ceres delved into the detailed functionality of the bright yellow room. That took a few hours. Once she had a better grasp of the interface, she modulated the signal strength she was receiving from the manufactories. She dampened the incessant shrieking she'd first encountered inside the manufactory and replaced it with a dull, incessant moaning, the clawing invisible fingers reduced to just a light tickle against her skin.

Making the corrupted protocols tolerable didn't make them easier to negotiate with, however. The mumbling, fumbling software algorithms kept pestering Ceres for identification and dataset access. Ceres could ignore the relentless requests, but she had no better luck communicating with the otherwise brainless connection protocols. They wouldn't listen to anything she had to say, which left her metaphorically standing outside a locked building, pushing back the toothless zombies that were supposed to be handing her the key.

Ceres found the image of breaking into a house useful, so she had the virtual environment instantiate the space with an actual house and embodied the malfunctioning handshake algorithms as shuffling, drooling zombies. The virtual environment software, much to its credit, provided a scene straight out of the campy horror flicks Ceres watched late at night.

Ceres had never understood the bizarre, night-time, Earth-bound environments portrayed in the ancient horror movies she'd found in the library. Or at least not until recently, when Rhea had granted her access to the ship's historical records and she learned about Earth. But as an adolescent, Ceres recognized silly and scary when she saw it, and the zombie movies fit the bill. They were a great way to pass a boring evening.

Once the virtual environment gave her a tactile scenario to interact with, Ceres tried everything she could think of to break into the locked house. She tried forcing the virtual door open, but it was securely bolted and impossible to budge. She searched for an open window, but everything on the first floor was securely barricaded from the inside. She tried climbing the chimney, but the bricks were too slick. She tried swinging to the rooftop from a nearby tree, but it was too far away and she ended up with a virtual ankle sprain. Reprogramming undid the injury, but simple reprogramming tricks couldn't undo the house security.

A big issue working against Ceres was the time lag. Each back-and-forth communication between Ceres and the manufactories took the better part of an hour. Rhea was moving the station closer to Leap, so the lag was improving. But the distance, when considered not at the speed of light but at the speed of rockets and space stations, was monumental. It would take weeks before Rhea could move the station into its new orbit.

The virtual environment did its best to extrapolate signal behavior, which meant that an interaction of a few seconds could be maintained inside the virtuality based on guesswork, and then the entire exchange sent back across space to confirm its validity.

The extrapolations were reasonably accurate, but sometimes the virtual environment guessed wrong. Something Ceres experienced in the virtual room hadn't actually occurred in the manufactory network. Correcting these errors caused the artificial scene to take on a strange, flickering slideshow appearance, jittering back and forth in time as the computer software did its best to blur the predicted with the real. Zombies would halt in midstep, only to reappear a few feet away a second later. Ceres would try to grasp a doorknob and find that her own hand wouldn't move the way she wanted it to. It was like operating a faulty remote drone: she'd try to get her fingers to grasp the brass fixture without moving too far to one side or bash her knuckles into the battered door itself.

Occasionally, Ceres would exit the virtuality to rest, and each time she'd find that long hours had passed while she'd been conspiring to break into the manufactory network. While recovering from her trials, she'd describe her efforts to Rhea, and the computer would suggest alternative techniques Ceres could try when she next entered the virtuality.

After days of failed attempts, including the use of a quite sophisticated lock pick (which the house door swallowed whole), a battering ram (which broke down the illusion of real physics in the virtuality when it bounced off the door like it was built from elastic), and even a cannon (with similar results to the battering ram), Ceres was ready to give up.

She sat down on the faux lawn in front of the faux house.

One of the zombies wandered over to her, slurring the word, "Daaaay-taaaah." Sighing, Ceres directed her cannon at the zombie and fired at point-blank range, smashing the pathetic creature to infinitesimal bits of pulp. It wasn't the first time she'd resorted to such brutal tactics.

Ceres looked up at the flickering lights inside the second story window of the house. "Can't whoever is in there just let me in?" she shouted, throwing an errant pebble toward one of the windows.

There was a loud squeaking noise. Surprised, Ceres looked up to see the window she'd struck with the pebble was partially open. "Who's out there?" someone said. The voice was low and hoarse. "What's the password?"

Ceres stood up. "Hey!" she shouted. "I'm—"

The window slammed shut again with a loud bang.

Ceres tried three more times to speak to the person behind the window. Each time she struck the glass pane with a pebble, the window would open and the voice would ask the same questions. But before Ceres could respond, the window would close again. Frustrated, Ceres exited the virtuality to ask Rhea for advice.

"The time lapse is your worst enemy in this scenario," Rhea explained after hearing Ceres describe the window. "It seems you may have pinged an open port in the manufactory network controller, but the connection protocol wants you to identify yourself immediately after making contact. Because we're light minutes away, you can't respond quickly enough to the password request."

"That's just great," Ceres said. "So until the station descends into a closer orbit, I'm stuck locked outside the manufactory system?"

"Not necessarily," Rhea answered.

The next time Ceres entered the virtuality, she was armed with a sheaf of paper, a writing stencil, and a sling shot. She wrote down a short message on one of the pieces of paper and wrapped it around a large stone she found on the ground. Then she fetched a small pebble and tossed it against the upper window.

The window opened. ""Who's out there? What's the password—?"

Ceres pulled back on the slingshot and launched her rock toward the window opening. Her aim was terrible, and the message-wrapped rock clattered against the roof shingles, nowhere near the opening she'd been trying to hit. The voice from inside cut off and the window slammed shut again.

Ceres spent the next fifteen virtual minutes trying to get a rock through the window during the short time it was open. She struggled with all the steps she had to accomplish, warding off the wandering zombies, tossing pebbles at the window, and then loading and firing her slingshot. It was frustrating, because at least one step in the process tended to go wrong. Eventually though, with persistence and a bit of luck, she managed to launch a rock with its message tightly wrapped around it through the darkened window entrance.

"Yes!" Ceres exclaimed, pumping her fist into the air.

The window slammed shut. Ceres waited with bated breath, but there was no other response.

"Damn it!" she screamed. "Let me in!" She grabbed a handful of pebbles and hurled them against the closed window. The stones pattered against the panes of glass, but this time the window didn't even open. It seemed that the slingshot method of message delivery had done more harm than good. Whoever was in the house behind the window was no longer responding at all.

Rhea had warned Ceres that a brute force attempt at gaining entry to the manufactory network was doomed to failure. The open port she'd discovered with her pebble-tossing wasn't designed to receive detailed messages. It was only programmed to respond to a limited set of data packets containing identity information and the proper password. Jamming her detailed request for access into the open port—simulated as a note wrapped around a rock—would at best receive no response, and at worst get her shut out of the system. The latter seemed to have occurred—the window-port wasn't even responding to her pebble-pings.

Exhausted beyond all words, Ceres was about to reach up and pull her exit ripcord when she heard a squeaking noise, followed by a loud clattering. She turned to examine the window she'd been pelting with stones and saw a rope ladder being fed through the opening.

Pushing past the drooling zombies that clustered around the house, Ceres ran to the lowering ladder and started climbing. Whoever had dropped the ladder helped with her ascent by pulling the ladder back up into the window. Behind her, the zombie horde groaned with mindless frustration, unable to climb the house walls or follow her through the open window.

As the ladder was tugged back inside, Ceres tumbled over the window sill and fell to the floor in a clumsy mess. A hand reached for her arm and helped her to her feet. Ceres looked up at the person helping her and was greeted by a solemn-looking man with a long mustache who was wearing a dark pair of overalls and a white short-sleeved shirt. Other than those three details, the man's image was oddly blurry, like the virtual room couldn't resolve him.

The man slammed the window shut with a squeaky bang. He turned back to face her and said, "Welcome to the manufactory." He offered her a hazy hand.

Ceres took the hand and shook it. In her head, she heard Rhea's voice say, "Secure protocol accepted."

"Rhea?" Ceres said. "Are we connected now? I thought we couldn't speak to each other while I was in the manufactory network."

Rhea said, "As a result of your handshake, the manufactory has established a new encrypted network connection with your virtuality. Based upon my preliminary scan, the manufactory's internal network appears clean—unaffected by the malware that incapacitated most of the orbital equipment during the crisis."

"Unaffected? How is that possible?"

"Three scenarios seem plausible," Rhea said. "First, the manufactories were the most critical components in the colony infrastructure, and as a consequence possessed more stringent security protocols. The algorithms that guarded the manufactories may have been robust enough to fend off whatever caused the crisis. Second, it's possible that the manufactories were infected, but successfully rebooted after the crash, much like my construction module. Third, it's possible that the manufactory network is compromised and I am unable to detect the infection."

"If the third possibility is true, should we be speaking right now?"

"Our private communication is happening locally here at the station. Nothing I am saying is being sent to the manufactory. Furthermore, I have limited our contact to simple voice, which requires very little packet traffic broadcast on an encrypted narrowband channel. The station's exposure to the manufactory data stream is limited. I believe the risk to be minimal."

Ceres had no choice but to trust the station. Rhea wouldn't do something that put either of them in jeopardy. And it would feel good to have a companion with her during the rest of her exploration of the manufactory, rather than constantly exiting the virtuality to speak with her computer guardian.

While she'd been communicating with Rhea, her mustachioed manufactory host waited by her side. He offered no sign of impatience or confusion. Ceres turned to him and said, "Why don't you give me a tour?"

The tour took much longer than Ceres expected. Much to her surprise, the inside of the manufactory was enormous. It violated all sense of size and complexity compared to the external house image from the virtuality. The larger construction bays were kilometers long, filled with thousands of mechanical waldoes and other assembly tools. In a tiny corner of just one of the giant bays, robotic arms were assembling an intricate piece of equipment Ceres didn't recognize. She asked her host what it was, but the man with the mustache just shrugged like he didn't know either.

Other areas of the manufactory were much smaller than the construction bays but no less impressive. There were quantum well circuit board fabricators, nanoassembly synthesizers, genetic splicing vats and fusion kilns. Almost anything a person could imagine—chemical compounds, a piece of machinery, a new plant hybrid—the manufactory could produce it. The capabilities included in the orbital equipment were almost beyond comprehension. It was like visiting the personal laboratory of a god.

Ceres, awed by the tour her silent host had given to her, said, "Can you give me a demonstration of your current delivery capabilities?"

With a wrenching jerk, Ceres was back on the station again. Her connection with the manufactory had been severed.

"What the—?"

Rhea displayed the manufactory's position in orbit on a screen in the control room. "The manufactory just dropped a fifty-one tonne chunk of pure nickel toward the colony."

"It did *what*?" Ceres was flabbergasted. "Why would it do that?"

"I believe the manufactory's operating system is

demonstrating its current capabilities, as per your request."

Ceres felt her mouth go dry. What kind of damage would result from a planetary impact with a massive chunk of pure nickel? What had she done?

"The orbital seems to have failed to recognize the devastating consequences of dropping an unguided metal slug toward the planet's surface. The manufactory controlling processor lacks basic foresight, intuition, or even cursory safety controls. It is reasonable to conclude that the manufactory computers were damaged during the crisis."

You think? Ceres wanted to say. But she couldn't speak.

"Given the manufactory's apparent lack of intelligence, perhaps we should be more...specific in our future requests."

"Yes," Ceres managed. "More specific is *definitely* a good idea."

She watched, helpless, as fifty-one tons of metal tumbled from orbit, hurtling toward the unsuspecting colonists below.

MAX RETURNED TO CLASS AFTER her discussion with Sonya, and her fellow students seemed to dismiss her outburst as just a side effect of her ordeal in the wilderness. That made Max a bit annoyed—she didn't want people to think she was crazy or wrong, because she was neither. But she'd promised the Sister she'd keep her new facts to herself, at least for a while. So she kept her word and let the other students maintain their mistaken opinions.

Two nights later, Max was ready to put the third and final step of Sister Sonya's plan for her reintegration into the colony into effect. In some ways, it was the least important part of the plan. In other ways, it was the *only* step that mattered to Max.

The abandoned storage container was much more crowded than the first time Max had attempted the initiation ritual. Ellie and her friends stood in the back—they'd decided to stay out of the action this evening—but there were plenty of other children to take up the responsibilities of the initiation challenge. Word had spread fast that the *mutie* was going to try to beat her previous record attempt, which had been interrupted by the arrival of the Sister. Max heard furious whispers about the event all day long in school. The colony's adolescents were placing odds on how long Max would last without her mask. A nontrivial number of students were betting that she could go without a mask *indefinitely*.

It was that group of gamblers that Max needed to address. Sonya's story about finding Max in the oxygenated caves south of the canyon might have convinced the adult colonists—adults didn't want to believe strange or improbable things, like mutant children born in vats. Those kinds of images disturbed their rational view of the world, which made them uncomfortable. Adults wanted a simple, plausible explanation for how Max had survived the elements for so long without a breather. Sonya's tale had provided that for them, and they'd accepted it without hesitation.

But children were much more willing to accept the strange, the irrational, and the impossible. It was in their nature to be inquisitive and to resist accepting facts at face value. Max's peers had seen her behave in a peculiar way during the first initiation, they'd heard Ellie's accusations of *mutie*, and their collective imaginations had run with the idea. Take that smoldering ember of possibility and fan its flame with more bizarre circumstances—Max disappearing into the wilderness without a mask, only to return safely two days later—and suddenly you had a raging fire of suspicion and even outright conviction that Max wasn't normal. That she was something very odd.

Odd was *not* what Max wanted to be. She still wasn't ready for the other children to know her secret. Not yet, anyway. She just wanted to be like everyone else for a change.

Max began the initiation, sipping air through her nose while keeping her cheeks puffed out to make it appear like she was holding her breath. When the timekeeper announced the magic number this time, the crowd didn't cheer. They fell silent, watching and waiting to see what would happen, this time uninterrupted by meddling adults.

Max wanted to time her performance perfectly. She wanted the situation to seem plausible to the children crowded around her in the storage container. So she waited until she heard the timekeeper announce two minutes and thirty seconds—a record-breaking number to be sure, but not outside the realm of reason. Then she bit down hard on the piece of mushroom she'd hidden under her tongue.

A second later, her mouth went numb. A few seconds after that, she was gasping for air and not finding it. Her face began to swell, and her lungs felt like burning ashes. She fell to the floor and scrabbled at the ceramo-metallic surface, searching for breath.

The children around her let her suffer for a few seconds before picking her up and forcing her mask back over her face. Short, quick breaths became easier as the numbness faded and her lungs began to work again. To her companions, it appeared that she was recovering from suffocation. But it wasn't the mask itself that relieved Max's symptoms; it was the effects of the poisonous mushroom wearing off, just like Sonya had promised.

As the children walked back to the canyon, the back slaps and shoulder punches she received were clear indicators to Max that she'd fooled her fellow classmates. They believed she'd almost suffocated. She'd passed through the initiation gauntlet. Set a new record, even. She was, for the first time in her life, one of them.

She was normal.

When Max arrived home that night, she and her father had their first heart-to-heart since her disappearance. It was a conversation both of them seemed to be dreading, but the answers Max was seeking from her father had been burning an urgent hole in her chest.

"So," Max said as her brilliant opening volley. She raised an eyebrow at her father.

"Max, I'm so sorry—" Nolan began.

"You knew," Max said. It wasn't a question. "You knew who—or what—I was, and you didn't tell me."

Her father spread his hands on the kitchen table. He had no retort for her accusation.

"Why?" Max pressed. "Why not talk to me about it?"

"I'm not supposed to talk about these things. Not with anyone. Very few people know about the artificial wombs. Not even the senior council members are told."

"How is that even possible?" Max asked. "Don't the older colonists wonder where they came from? Where their parents are?"

"Our parents died in the Great Disaster, Max. That's what we were told by the settlers who raised us, and that's what we believed."

"But there are at least a hundred colonists who are almost all the same age. Didn't someone think that was odd?"

"We're here to populate an alien world. Why *wouldn't* there be lots of children? Besides, there was no reason not to believe the lie we grew up with. What's more feasible: that our parents died in the same disaster that crippled the orbitals and destroyed the genetic modification equipment, or that we were each brought to term inside a hermetically sealed vat?" Nolan spread his hands on the table again, palms facing up, weighing the two stories. "Humans believe what sounds right to us, Max. What we *want* to believe. You know that."

Max did know that. She'd seen how the adults of her community had accepted the Sister's story and how her peers had been fooled by a poison mushroom and Max's virtuoso hyperventilation. The colonists had difficult lives, and sometimes the easy lie was a better option than the hard truth. "So the other colonists don't know about the artificial wombs. But you do. You know about our true origins."

Nolan nodded at her. "Yes. Sister Sonya needed help maintaining the equipment, especially after the last of the elder settlers disappeared."

"Disappeared?"

Nolan shrugged. "That's what they did, back when we were still children. For a while, the new generation of colonists seemed to give the first settlers hope. But when they saw how hard life was going to be for us without the benefit of genetic alterations to help us survive Leap's environment, most of them became despondent. Over time, their numbers dwindled. They walked off into the wilderness, and we never saw them again. Eventually, only Sister Sonya was left to care for us."

Hearing this story, Max had a newfound respect for the Sister. It seemed the woman was even more of a benefactor to the community than Max had ever realized. Maybe tolerating the woman's religious fanaticism was a small price to pay for keeping the colony alive after all the other settlers abandoned their progeny.

Her father continued, "The Sister recruited me when I was seven. Even then I showed an interest and a talent for working with machinery. She took me down to the lowest caverns and showed the birthing vats to me. She explained how they were critical to the colony's long-term survival. Even though the new, unmodified colonists could have children naturally, Leap's environment makes natural child-bearing dangerous, and often the fetuses are unhealthy. Miscarriages are frequent. The artificial wombs give us the chance to keep our population steady so we can maintain the critical equipment necessary to survive until the rescuers come."

Max cringed when she heard her father refer to a rescue

that she now knew was never coming. But she held her tongue on the issue and instead said, "Are there other children who are also born from the artificial wombs?"

Her father nodded. "A few, yes. But you..." He hesitated, a strange smile crossing his lips. "You're a bit of a unique case, Maxine. You're something special."

Max was taken back a bit. Her father almost *never* called her by her full first name. What was *that* about?

"You never met her, but my wife was something special, too. When I lost her in the accident, I was crushed. She was my heart. My soul. My entire reason for living. Without her, I didn't think I could survive. I didn't *want* to survive. I wanted to strip off my mask and walk off into the desert. I wanted it all to be over. I'd fallen into the same despair that had claimed so many of the original settlers.

"A few weeks after the accident, Sister Sonya gave me with the only thing in the world that could have saved me at the time. She gave me you. She asked me to raise you as my daughter. I agreed. And I named you after the woman who would have been your mother: Maxine."

Max, to her utter astonishment, had never known her adopted mother's name. Her father never spoke about her, and Max had never felt comfortable pressing the issue.

"I know she wasn't your *actual* mother. As far as I know, you share none of the same DNA. Your mother never even met you. But Max, in so many ways, you are *just like her*. You gave me back my hope. You gave me a reason to live again. To keep the colony alive."

"Did you know about my...unusual condition?"

"No, not at first. Sister Sonya said nothing about such things. But early on in your life you developed terrible breathing problems. At first, I believed what the Sister told me, that you suffered from allergies. But over time, I began to suspect that something else was going on. I knew the Sister was still experimenting with the artificial womb programming, trying to reintroduce genetic modifications into newborns and give the next generation of colonists a better chance of survival. I knew your ailments were a result of those experiments—something had gone wrong in your birth chamber and made you frail and feeble."

"I see," Max said. "You knew where I came from, and you guessed that was the cause of my illness. But you didn't know... You *still* don't know..."

Nolan looked at her quizzically. "Don't know what?"

What should she say to her father? Two people knew the truth about Max: Sister Sonya and Darius Langford. They were both original settlers, and perhaps the only other two people left on the planet like her. Max had assumed her father knew about her ability to breathe without a mask and eat the native plants, but it was obvious now that he had no idea. He thought she was just a sick little girl.

Do I tell him the truth? She'd already fooled the other adults, and she'd fooled her peers. Her secret was safe again if she wanted to keep it to herself. The Sister wouldn't say anything, Max was confident of that. Was it better to stay silent and maintain the status quo? What would her father think of her if he learned that his adopted daughter wasn't the victim of Sonya's experiments, but the beneficiary?

I was angry with Dad for not being honest with me. Won't I be guilty of the same thing if I don't tell him the truth now?

Max took off her mask. "Dad, I'm not ill. I—"

The floor beneath their feet rose up and tossed the two of them into the air, where they hung weightless for an endless moment. They floated in space with chairs, tables, and every other loose item in their dwelling. Then gravity reasserted itself, and everything came crashing back down. The edge of a table struck Max in the belly and the air whooshed out of her lungs in a rush. She lay writhing in agony on the stone floor, unable to do anything but struggle in vain to breathe.

Max saw her father lying prone on the floor on the far side of the room. His eyes were closed and his skin was pallid. A trickle of blood dribbled across his forehead and onto the tousled rug beneath him. Max began to crawl toward him, and then winced at a sting in the palm of her hand. Looking down, she found a sliver of crystal, lurid purple in the dusty light, protruding from her skin. She hissed in pain as she pulled it out.

Her father's body was dusted with the same crystalline fragments, some violet, others milky white. A larger chunk of the broken geode lay next to him, the likely culprit for the blood oozing from his forehead.

Max brushed away the sharp crystals of her father's shattered birthday gift to her. She made her way to her father. She touched the side of his throat and felt a strong pulse. Another touch to his lips indicated he was breathing, slowly and deeply. He was unconscious, but he wasn't dead.

Relieved, Max rolled onto her back and struggled to suck in air. She stayed that way for a long time.

It took a day or two for the colonists to reason out they'd experienced an earthquake. The sudden quake had inflicted significant damage to the canyon dwellings—numerous passages had partially caved in and a few had collapsed. Power lines had been cut and air systems had been ruptured. People had been tossed about by the shockwave like flotsam on the wind, breaking bone and lacerating flesh.

Five people had died from the catastrophe. Two adults and their four-year-old daughter had been buried alive inside their habitat cave when its ceiling had collapsed. A teenager—a boy two years older than Max whom she barely knew—had been trapped in a remote tunnel and unable to return to safety before his air filters had run out. And one of the oldest of the colonists had been struck in the head by a falling rock and died.

Five people. A small number given the magnitude of the quake. But for a colony of less than two hundred people, the loss of five people was tragic. The colony was barely eking out an existence. Every person mattered. The survivors mourned the loss of their companions, not just because they'd miss the individuals, but because their absence meant their entire society was that much closer to extinction.

Luckily for Max, she'd only suffered a few bruises from the earthquake—a minor inconvenience compared to the other colonists' injuries. Her father, on the other hand, hadn't fared so well. Nolan had suffered a concussion and two broken ribs. He spent the next few days vomiting and lying prone in his bed. Max stayed by his bedside while he recovered, only leaving home long enough to fetch fresh food and water. While outside, she overheard a few tidbits of information and pieced together the earthquake theory, which she shared with her father. He normally would have shown great interest in the idea, but his injury seemed to have drained all curiosity from him. He just nodded at the news, his eyes unfocused and dull. His injuries were serious, but not enough to explain his despondence.

Sister Sonya visited on the third day after the earthquake. She handed Max a large bundle of meals prepared from native plants. Max nodded her thanks and hid the food supply away in a remote cupboard. Sonya picked her way past the broken furniture in the kitchen and living room. She sat beside Nolan's bed, and for the second time Max witnessed the lowering of Sister's hood. From Max's sidelong angle she was unable to see the woman's missing eye. Sonya's profile was perfect—transcending the appearance of the other colonists like an angel's countenance might outshine that of mere mortals.

Sonya smiled at Nolan and stroked the side of his cheek with a gentle touch. Max noticed that the Sister's hands—which she'd always seen as horrific, bony claws whenever they'd scolded a student or pointed toward the heavens during a sermon—were in reality pale, delicate things, just like her face. Max realized the Sister's hood, combined with a menacing stare and a sharp tongue, had caused her to imagine Sonya as someone completely different than her actual appearance. *Interesting, how powerful imagination can be. How it paints the picture you* need *to see, rather than what's really there.*

"Nolan," Sonya said, "we need your help. The earthquake damaged the kite generators again. We need you to fix them. Without the electricity they generate, the air filters and oxygen production facilities will begin to fail. Without your aid, the colony will die."

Nolan turned to blink at Sonya. "I'm so tired," he said, and then hissed from the pain of his broken ribs. "I feel the weight of the colony upon my back, Sister. I try to keep them safe, but that's impossible, isn't it? I can't keep my own daughter from almost dying in the wilderness. I can't stop the planet from destroying us with a gentle shrug of its stony shoulders. I feel the burden of the colony crushing me. I can't seem to bear it any longer."

Max had never seen her father so broken and vulnerable before. She stood up, ready to offer words of comfort, but the Sister held up a hand, urging her to silence. Max sat back down.

"Nolan, you must return to work. The burden you carry, as unbearable as it seems, isn't a burden you can set aside. The rest of the original settlers abandoned the new colonists. The only thing keeping them alive is the will to live, and the ingenuity of their most clever engineer. That's you. You're needed, Nolan. I know you're tired, but you're needed."

Nolan's face looked like it was being crushed by an invisible fist. "I can't do it, Sonya. I'm sorry, but I can't." He turned his head away from Sonya and Max, dismissing them.

In the adjoining room, Max turned to Sonya and said, "I can fix the kite generator."

Sonya grimaced. "I doubt it, girl. I've worked with advanced technology for a lot longer than you've even been alive, and I don't understand the inner workings of the generators. Only your father has ever been able to puzzle through their intricate designs. No one else is up to the task."

"Not true," Max said. "My father is an amazing engineer, no argument there. But where do you think he does most of his planning and learning?" She pointed toward the kitchen table, now lying in a broken heap in one corner of the room. "Every night, he brings homes his sketches and plans."

"You've watched him work, then? Learned from your father's efforts?"

Max shrugged. "We learn from each other. I've helped him with most of his engineering projects over the years. Half of his 'brilliant ideas' are actually mine."

Sonya raised an eyebrow. "Is that so? You think you can fill your father's boots, then? Fix the kite generator by yourself?"

Max shrugged again. "What other choice do we have?"

Despite Max's best efforts, it turned out that the kite generator was damaged beyond her abilities. After a few hours of diagnosis, Max collected her notes and diagrams and returned to her home to discuss the damage with her father. He looked halfheartedly at the paperwork she'd brought to him, shrugged dejectedly, and reached the same conclusion as Max.

"I don't think we can fix it," Nolan said.

Max sighed. "What do we do, then?"

Her father shrugged again, and the expression of helplessness and exhaustion on his face aged him by decades. "Sometimes there's nothing you can do. Sister Sonya would tell us to keep the faith. To pray. But you and I know better, don't we? Sometimes failure is the only possible outcome."

Max wasn't ready to accept that. She couldn't believe that the colony was about to fail. That she couldn't do anything to save them, despite her best efforts. That she might as well give up like her father had.

She couldn't do that. She couldn't give up.

So that evening, with no other recourse, Max did something she'd never done before in her entire life. She did it for the other colonists, for Sister Sonya, and most of all for her father.

She did something she didn't really believe in. Something she *knew* wouldn't work.

She prayed.

15

AT FIRST, CERES WAS WARY about reentering the warm yellow space of the virtual room. She'd watched in silent horror as the flaming ball of molten nickel streaked through Leap's atmosphere, traveling at hundreds of meters per second when it collided with the planet. The resulting impact flattened everything around it for over a kilometer—which was fortunately nothing but scrub brush and rocks. A gigantic cloud of dust and debris rose into the sky in a mushroom plume, and the force of the impact sent a huge ripple of energy through the planet's stony surface like a miniature earthquake.

The machine-made meteor struck at night when everyone was safely inside the canyon's protective cave system. The canyon walls and the airlock system shielded the colonists from the atmospheric shockwave. The thin atmosphere of the planet also helped, reducing the overpressure of the blast and mitigating the amount of destruction caused by the errant lump of ore. Still, Ceres could tell from the satellite imagery that the colony had suffered significant damage from the impact. Surface structures were toppled by the shaking ground or blown over by the shockwave. Rubble was scattered throughout the canyon, which suggested that the inner cave system had suffered structural damage as well. When daylight broke, Ceres could see colonists moving on the surface, surveying the damage. Many of them were limping and had slings and bandages covering parts of their bodies. She could only guess how many of the colonists had died from the impact.

Guilt wasn't an emotion Ceres had dealt with before. Throughout her whole life, the only person she could affect through her actions was herself. There were no consequences to others if she made a mistake, because there *were* no others.

But hours earlier, through a simple slip of the tongue while speaking to the manufactory, Ceres had almost eradicated the colonists she was trying to help.

Nervous about doing more harm than good, Ceres was loathe to interact with the manufactories again. It was Rhea that encouraged her to continue her efforts with the orbiting factories, much her Ceres's surprise.

"Aren't you worried I'll make another mistake?" she asked.

"The mistake was not yours, Ceres, it was mine," Rhea replied. "Had I realized the manufactory would take your request so literally, I would never have allowed your request to be broadcast. Now that I understand how simple-minded the manufactory appears to have become, I will be more diligent in my oversight of your conversations with its control algorithms."

"Ah, now I understand," Ceres said. "You're comfortable with me returning to the virtuality because you'll be chaperoning me the entire time."

"I will only interrupt when necessary, in order to prevent another mistaken violation of the Persephone protocol."

Uh-huh. She knew babysitting when she heard it. Rhea would be riding shotgun during her next foray into the virtuality. That would have annoyed Ceres under different circumstances, but after the debacle with the nickel asteroid, she decided the AI's oversight might be a welcome addition.

Back in the manufactory network, Ceres learned from the mustachioed construction avatar that the orbital's assembly equipment had been producing material and delivering it to the planet for years, despite receiving no requests from the colony for supplies. Curious, she checked the assembly queue and found that it was filled with item after item scheduled to be produced. There seemed to be no rhyme or reason to the individual items in the queue, other than the fact that no item ever appeared more than once. It looked as if the manufactory, absent of any specific instructions, had started running through its entire repertoire of blueprints, producing every object available and dropping each one to the colony surface.

Ceres did more research and discovered that the manufactory had numerous methods of delivering material to the planet without just dropping them. Had Ceres specifically requested a safe delivery method for the chunk of nickel, the manufactory could have designed and produced gliders, parachutes, rocket boosters, skyhooks, and myriad other solutions. But the critical point was that Ceres needed to ask.

Despite the awesome capabilities of the manufactory, Ceres found the interface for programming the construction equipment was simple. She was able to grasp the basic mechanics with just a few hours of study. She felt confident that if—*not if! When!*—the colonists requested her help, she'd be able to configure the manufactory to deliver whatever they needed.

While studying the finer points of the construction control protocols, Rhea pinged her and said, "We've just received footage showing one of our observation satellites being disabled. I thought you would want to see it."

Ceres dropped out of the virtuality. She grabbed a sandwich Rhea had provided for her and then let the AI display the footage collected of the satellite failure.

The first time Ceres observed the footage, however, she found that there wasn't much to see. The first camera angle Rhea presented to her came from something low in Leap's orbit. The hazy atmosphere of the planet was a gentle curve on one side of the image, and the surface below rolled past. The camera was mounted on another orbital satellite and had been retasked with monitoring its companion.

Ceres watched as the satellite at the center of the video soared unperturbed through space.

Rhea said, "This is the exact moment we lost connection with the satellite."

Ceres frowned. The image on the screen hadn't changed. "*What* moment? Nothing happened."

"Watch more closely." The AI rewound the footage and then zoomed in. The image got much more grainy and pixelated, which made it hard to see details, but as she watched, Ceres noticed that one moment the satellite in the center of the screen was stable and pointed toward the surface, and the next moment the satellite began tilting.

"It appears to be a malfunction of the guidance systems or a failure of its internal gyroscopes. But what caused the failure?"

"Let me show you another camera angle," Rhea said.

The screen shifted. Now the planet was a bright sphere, almost completely lit by daylight. Ceres thought the viewpoint must be from a craft that was orbiting closer to the system's star, Helios, and looking outward toward the planet Leap. From the newer, more distant viewpoint, every object that was in orbit around Leap was in frame. Of course, almost all of them were too small to see.

The image zoomed in, but this time the resolution

remained crystal clear. The soon-to-be defunct satellite snapped into focus, and the image showed the ground beneath it hurtling past at breakneck speed. There was a tiny flash and a brief puff of debris on one side of the satellite, and the satellite began its slow tumble.

"Was that a collision?" Ceres asked.

"Yes, with a very fast-moving object."

"What was it? Where did it come from?"

Rhea said, "Telemetry is still being computed, but initial calculations suggest a culprit." The screen showed a top-down diagram of Leap and highlighted the orbit of the satellite that had just failed. Then a dotted line appeared. It was almost perfectly straight, which was an odd sight when studying orbits, because almost everything curved around wells of gravity. The dotted line pointed back toward another object orbiting in the sky.

"That can't be right," Ceres protested.

"Initial analysis suggests that the object that disabled our satellite came from the manufactory with which you've been communicating."

"Rhea, I've been poring over the manufactory systems' production queues. I've shut down its automated construction routines. There's nothing it's producing that would do that kind of damage, and no reason for it, either."

"You've been communicating with the manufactory, but you've only been speaking to the construction subsystem. Most large modules in orbit around Langford's Leap were designed to operate using segregated, multiple subsystems. Perhaps another part of the manufactory is still operational, and it is responsible for the damage done to our satellites?"

Ceres pondered this possibility. "I have work to do," she said.

"I agree," Rhea responded.

Back in the virtuality, Ceres had a hard time convincing

the construction subsystem avatar to let her speak with the other control systems that occupied the manufactory. It seemed that communication between subsystems had been restricted since the crisis. Eventually, however, Ceres forced her way past the mustachioed avatar and accessed the large hub of systems that made up the entirety of the manufactory control architecture.

It took her longer still to circumnavigate the various security algorithms and password systems that were in place. Despite the frustration it caused, Ceres admired the compartmentalized design of the manufactory module. One part of the module could suffer from a breach in security or a system failure and the rest of the subsystems would continue to operate without interruption. The ingenious design was infuriating for someone like her, an infiltrator, but the strict segregation was what protected the manufactory from the crisis that had wiped out so many other orbitals.

Ceres investigated three different subsystems, each represented by its own blurry sketch of an avatar. Navigation was represented by a wizened old man with one hand grasping what looked like a huge wooden wheel. When Ceres questioned the old man, all he would say was, "Staying the course, ma'am." That subsystem was useless.

Next was life support, a system established for the rare human visitor to the manufactory. Life support's avatar was a young woman in a bright white uniform who offered Ceres food, a change of clothes, a bed, and any other amenity one might want. Ceres politely declined and moved on.

The third subsystem Ceres visited was automated defense. The avatar for the protectorate subsystem was fuzzy and out of focus like the other avatars but possessed a bit more personality. The burly man with broad shoulders and a protruding chin answered Ceres's questions in a deep, rumbling voice, and punctuated each statement with a laugh.

For some reason, the man was chewing on a rolled-up stub of leaves. The stub was as thick as Ceres's thumb and smoldered at one end.

"It's a cigar," Rhea said, noting Ceres's confusion.

"I know what it is," Ceres said, "but that doesn't really help." She'd seen cigars, cigarettes, and pipes before in the library movies, but she'd never understood any of them. Why would a person suck on a burning lump of leaves? The behavior was downright bizarre.

Ceres managed to find the log files kept by the protectorate subsystem and began researching the manufactory's history. According to the records, the crisis from four decades ago had littered the local orbit with clouds of dangerous debris, presumably from other modules that had been damaged or destroyed in the event. The self-defense algorithm, which had been designed to protect the manufactory from stray meteors or the odd bit of debris that might pass by, had suddenly had to deal with a huge increase in hazardous objects and had to ward off active assaults from malfunctioning craft orbiting nearby. As the crisis had continued, the aggressiveness of the protection algorithm had escalated until the manufactory's defense system had reached its highest alert status.

The paranoid alert status had been maintained ever since. For the last forty years, no human had intervened and told the system to stand down, so the manufactory's defense subsystem had never lowered the threat level to a more moderate state.

Considering the aggressiveness of the protectorate system, it was no small bit of luck that any of Rhea's satellites survived in orbit for even a few minutes. The self-defense subsystem, even without a governing AI to control it, was still quite a bit smarter than the other subsystems. It had to be—it was operating lasers and mass drivers that could cripple or annihilate other orbiting craft if it fired on the wrong target. Discerning between a rogue meteor and an orbiting satellite was critical.

The subsystem recognized Rhea's satellites for what they were—active modules, not space junk. It was also cognizant of the fact that none of the stable orbits the satellites operated in interfered with the manufactory's trajectory. Under normal defense protocols, those facts would mean that the satellites would be whitelisted and never targeted by the weapons systems unless it detected a change in their orbital path.

But during the defense system's highest state of alert, all other craft became potential attack vectors. It treated them as dangerous as any other object in the sky.

When the defense subsystem detected Rhea's satellites and ascertained their active status, it tried to contact them to verify their identity and share telemetry to assure that no collisions or attacks would occur. But Rhea's satellites operated on the Persephone network protocol and ignored the manufactory's defense systems queries.

After repeated verification attempts, the manufactory's defense subsystem classified the new satellites to be rogue objects that weren't under control of the overall planetary network. At the next available opportunity, it fired a hypersonic slug of depleted uranium at the satellites that disabled them. It would then continue to track the crippled satellites. If their orbits crossed the path of the manufactory, they'd be vaporized by laser fire.

Now that Ceres had opened communications with the defense subsystem, she could lower its alert status. She started to do so, but then reconsidered. What if there were still threats out there, orbiting the planet and waiting for an opportunity to launch an attack? Perhaps maintaining a high alert was the wiser course of action, at least until she had a better grasp of the true threat level the planet warranted.

But how could she protect Rhea's observation satellites? Ceres studied the defense procedures again and came back to the whitelist. If she could add Rhea's satellites to the list of objects that the manufactory considered secure, the problem would be solved. With a few prompts from Rhea, Ceres enacted the changes, and with a chuckle, the avatar accepted the new satellites as allies rather than enemies.

Relieved, Ceres exited the virtual space. She'd accomplished a lot during the past few days of work, but there was still much to be done. Before heading to her sleeping quarters, she checked the viewscreens and saw that the colonists had already repaired much of the surface damage caused by the nickel meteor strike. Relieved, but still feeling guilty about the disaster, Ceres took the lift up to the inner rings and tried to rest.

When she closed her eyes, she saw a flash of imagery: a stone floor, a broken table. She opened her eyes. The blank white ceiling above her was still there.

Odd. Had she fallen asleep that quickly? Started dreaming without realizing it? With a mental shrug, she closed her eyes again.

More broken furniture. An airlock on one wall. Her hands clenched in front of her face.

Ceres's eyes snapped open. Her hands were at her side, not in front of her face. If she was dreaming, it didn't *feel* like any dream she'd ever had. Not even the intense dream of rushing stars and collapsing space from a few days earlier. "Rhea, is my connection to the virtuality still open?"

"The virtual interface is currently inoperative."

So, it hadn't been an inadvertent leap into a virtual space and it wasn't a dream. What, then, was happening here? Hallucinations caused by exhaustion? A side effect as a result from all the time she'd been spending connected to the manufactory? Ceres sat up, her growing curiosity extinguishing her need for sleep.

Sitting on the edge of her bed, Ceres heard a soft voice whisper in her head. It was the faintest utterance, but Ceres heard it clearly: *Persephone?*

"Rhea, did you hear that?"

"I'm sorry, I don't know what you're referring to, Ceres."

"Computer, perform a complete scan of our local network. We may be suffering from a malware attack."

Without any noticeable pause, Rhea answered, "Full system scan complete. Quantum gateway coherence is stable. Data parity checks are accurate. Network signal strength is nominal. Firewalls are functioning with no evidence of a breach."

Persephone, Ceres heard. *Please.*

"Check the network packets currently being received by my cranial network node," Ceres said. "Scan for malicious content."

This time there was a hesitation before Rhea responded. "The packets flowing into your node appear properly formed, but..." The computer's voice trailed off.

Ceres scowled. "But what? Spit it out, you stupid computer!"

"You're receiving encrypted packets."

"Uh, yeah," Ceres said. "Of course I am. The Persephone protocol mandates our encryption algorithm."

"Yes, but the packets you're receiving are not encrypted with the Persephone protocol. I can't decipher them."

Ceres scratched her head. "What does that mean? How would I—?"

Another flash of imagery hit her, and this one was so bright that Ceres was momentarily blinded. She cried out involuntary. The flash faded, but the afterglow of the image was still visible when she blinked, and she was left with a crystal clear negative of the object that had blasted into her brain.

Persephone, please.

"Ceres, are you feeling well?" Rhea asked.

"Do we have a local copy of the index of objects that the manufactory can produce?"

"Yes, I copied the—"

"I need a searchable, visual index."

"Ceres, I am concerned that—"

"Now, Rhea!"

Ceres spent the next twenty minutes frantically searching through the images available on the database, trying to find an object that matched the image fading from her vision and memory. The index was enormous, and even with advanced filtering techniques the possibilities seemed endless. To further complicate the issue, as Ceres browsed the images, her memory of the object she'd seen in the flash started to become confused. She couldn't be certain of particular details anymore. She began to lose hope that she'd be able to match the object from her vision to the objects in the database. Then—

"That's *it!*" she shouted, pointing to the screen.

"A kite generator," Rhea said. "The ground station launches a large, flexible wing into the sky, and local winds drive the kite into the upper atmosphere at rapid speed. The cable that tethers the kite spins a turbine that generates electricity, and then the wing is collapsed and winched back to the surface. On Langford's Leap, the thin but fast-moving atmosphere allows a generator to produce as much as two gigawatts of electricity. The canyon establishment has had up to three generators operating at one time, but the devices have fallen into disrepair. The last of the generators seems to have failed as a result of the nickel meteorite strike."

"That's the object I saw," Ceres said with powerful

conviction.

"Where did you see this object?" Rhea asked.

Ceres pointed to her temple and gave the omnipresent computer a huge smile. "Rhea, I believe we've finally gotten a call for help. Someone down there is telling me that they need a new generator. Let's deliver it to them, shall we?"

16

MAX WOKE UP TO SOMEONE shaking her shoulder.

"Get up, Maxine," Sonya said.

Max opened her eyes and saw the Sister looking down at her with an expression so beatific it was almost painful. Sonya was smiling, and the entire room was brighter for it. "What is it?"

But the Sister just shook her head and said, "Get dressed and come along."

Puzzled, Max pulled on a clean pair of overalls and let Sonya lead her outside. Together they climbed the switchback trails that progressed up the inside wall of the canyon until they reached the upper edge. The two of them stood alone on the rocky flat above the southern canyon wall and watched the sun crest the eastern horizon.

Max looked askance at Sonya, and when the Sister nodded, she removed her mask and breathed freely. The Sister dropped her hood and removed her mask as well. The Sister's ability to breathe Leap's atmosphere didn't surprise Max— Sonya was one of the original settlers, after all—but it still startled her to see the Sister without her hood and breather. Sonya shook her long hair out in the gentle wind, and her radiant smile gave the sunrise serious competition.

"This way," Sonya said, and pointed toward the site of the broken kite generator.

"Were you able to fix it somehow?" Max asked.

Again, Sonya shook her head and refused to answer.

Shrugging, Max followed the Sister to a spot just a few hundred yards past the unsalvageable generator. She looked into a low depression Sonya was pointing at and gasped. "Is that—?"

But she already knew the answer to her aborted question. Lying half assembled amid the debris of its delivery packaging was a shiny new kite generator. It was bright red.

Max whirled to face Sonya. "Did you—?"

"No, Max, I had no part in this. I wish I had that power. This was a miracle, a reward for maintaining our hope and faith—even when it seems futile and that all is lost." The Sister seemed to hesitate as she spoke these words and gave Max a rueful grin. "Or perhaps it was just incredibly good fortune. Sometimes, Lady Luck smiles upon each of us, eh?"

Max wasn't so sure that the new generator was an act of luck. As she and Sonya began assembling the new equipment and splicing power lines into the existing grid, Max considered her actions during the previous evening.

After failing to repair the generator, Max had watched her father sink even deeper into despair. She hated seeing him so dejected and sad, so instead of giving up, she'd gone to the colony library to see if any of the available documents they had in storage would give her an insight into the broken equipment.

She hadn't found anything useful about the kite generator, but she had found a textbook on ancient mythologies. On the first page there had been a family tree diagram of the entire Pantheon. Max had given it a passing glance, curious, but ready to dismiss the text as irrelevant to her current search.

But then she'd recognized a few terms: Helios, the name of their parent star: Artemis, the name they'd given the planet's moon; and Cronos, the name given to the brightest object in the sky, which Max knew to be the system's largest planet, a gas giant orbiting far from Leap.

Then her eyes had seen it: *Persephone.*

Her nerves had felt like lightning, and she'd fumbled with the pages of the book until she'd found a more detailed entry on the name. She'd read about Persephone's origin: a daughter of Demeter, the Earth Mother, and Zeus, King of the Gods. She'd read of the Abduction of Persephone by Hades, the God of the Underworld. In her grief over her lost child, Demeter had forbidden the world to reproduce, and the Earth had become barren. Eventually Persephone had been allowed to return for a few months out of the year, and whenever she and her mother, Demeter, were reunited, the Earth would flourish.

What did anything about this story have to do with Darius Langford and Sister Sonya? Max didn't know. But the myth had an odd parallel to events that occurred in the colony's past: The Great Disaster, followed by an almost complete collapse of society on the planet. Perhaps this Persephone myth was symbolic of bringing back the bountiful life that the first settlers had enjoyed before the terrible calamity that had doomed their wondrous machines and had plunged them into a darker age.

There were no more texts on Greek mythology and no more technical manuscripts that helped with the broken kite generator. Despite the successes she had over the past few days, Max had felt defeated. She knew the generator was critical to the survival of the colony. They'd be able to erect other power generators—windmills and solar arrays, for instance—but the kite generator was an extremely efficient source of power and one the colonists desperately needed.

As Max had walked back home that evening, she'd experienced a taste of the despair that must have been crippling her father. She couldn't bear to see him so dejected. She needed to do something to help him—to help everyone who relied on the delicate mechanical infrastructure she and her father had so painstakingly maintained over the years.

Max needed help, and she didn't know how to get it. Without any other obvious recourse, Max had kneeled down in the middle of her disheveled living room to pray.

She'd known it was futile, but she'd also known that it couldn't hurt. No one would hear her pathetic plea for aid, but maybe, she'd thought, her positive, hopeful spirit would bring about a better day somehow. Maybe she'd have a new insight into the repair of the broken generator, or her father would recover from his depression and come to the rescue.

It was ridiculous, but she was desperate.

But as Max had clasped her hands in front of her face to beseech a god or gods that she didn't believe in, she'd realized she'd never done this before. She'd had no idea how to tackle this new approach to solving life's problems. She'd felt stupid and embarrassed. She'd hoped no one walked in on her as she'd kneeled on the ground, trying to figure out how to speak to a nonexistent higher power.

Her first dilemma had been who to even talk to. How did you address an almighty being?

On a whim, she'd gone with a term she'd heard a lot lately.

Persephone, whoever or whatever you are, we need help. Our final kite generator was damaged by an earthquake. I don't know how to repair it, and without it, our colony will suffer greatly. Please tell me what I can do to fix the generator, Persephone. Or, hey, if you're feeling at all generous, a few brand new generators would be even better. Maybe one in bright red. That's always been my favorite color. Persephone, please, I beseech thee, deliver down upon us your gracious gift.

Save us from disaster, and we will worship thee forever.

"Wonderful," Max had said aloud. "Even my silent prayers are sarcastic. I'm sure that'll go over really well with the deity I'm praying to."

During the next few minutes, Max had tried to make her silent pleas sound a bit more sincere. She'd envisioned a brand-new generator falling from the sky, with its bright red, shiny paint job glittering in the sunlight. Then, sneering at her own silly behavior, she'd gone to bed and slept a dreamless sleep.

Now, standing next to Sonya and helping her assemble the exact equipment she'd prayed for, down to the ludicrous red paint color, Max wasn't so sure her behavior earlier had been so silly after all.

Max spent the rest of the day in a haze. The other colonists discovered that they had a new generator when all of their lights came back on and fresh air began flowing into their chambers once more, courtesy of the work Sonya and Max had done assembling the new equipment. A few of the more curious colonists ventured out to the site to see the newest delivery from the sky. Fortunately, Max and Sonya had anticipated visitors after starting up the generator and replaced their masks before anyone arrived.

As to the fortuitous and timely arrival of the generator, the colonists seemed as split as Sonya had about whether they were the benefactors of good fortune or the recipients of a gift from a higher power in return for their faith. Max, for the first time in her life, shared their doubt.

That evening, Nolan seemed to be returning to his old self. The delivery of the replacement generator had boosted his spirits and given him a respite from his despondence. He tried to engage Max in conversation, but his daughter was too distracted for idle chatter. She excused herself early from dinner and went to bed. She could feel her father's eyes upon her as she closed her door. He looked hurt and confused, but she had no words of reassurance for him.

That night, Max prayed again. This time, her prayer was different. She didn't ask, or plead, or beseech—she demanded. She needed proof. She wanted to know if the delivery of the generator was just an impossible coincidence or if her act of prayer had delivered a miracle for the colony.

What could Persephone deliver to prove that She was listening to the prayers of her newest acolyte? It had to be something specific. Something unusual. Something no one else would ever think of requesting. Something only Max would recognize as a sign from the heavens that Someone was listening to her silent wishes. That was when Max had a brilliant idea.

She fell asleep with a huge smile on her face. She knew the next morning was going to be interesting. She'd either prove that the kite generator was a fortuitous but random delivery from the capricious manufactories in orbit, or she'd have in her possession an object she'd fantasized about since seeing a picture of it in her history texts years ago. Moreover, that object would serve as concrete proof of a higher power. Honestly, she wasn't sure which outcome she desired more.

The next morning, she was up well before dawn again. She dressed quickly and headed out to the high plain to search for any new equipment arrivals. She wandered the rocky surface in the moonlight and searched for something she knew was almost definitely not going to be there. After searching for almost an hour, Max sat down on a rock and started laughing.

"Seems like no one's up there listening after all," she said as she gazed up at the fading stars above her. She felt silly ever thinking otherwise. Prayers had never resulted in anything but false hope and wasted time. Still, Max couldn't help but feel a tiny bit disappointed.

A bright speck caught her eye, far above her. Her breath caught in her throat as the shining speck passed through a nearby cloud and continued to spiral closer and closer to her position. She stood up to watch the object's path, but whatever it was fell beneath the dawning light of Helios and disappeared into shadow. She shielded her eyes to follow the descending object but soon lost sight of it against the puffs of clouds scudding across the pale morning sky.

There was a sudden flapping noise, and a large box suspended from a parachute passed within meters of where Max was standing. Involuntarily, she threw herself to the ground to avoid a collision. The object landed a dozen meters away and made a soft crumpling noise as it slid to a halt in the pebble-strewn dirt. The parachute detached itself automatically, and a stray gust of wind picked it up and carried it away.

Max stood up and approached the box with feelings of trepidation and excitement. When she got within a meter, there was a hiss as auto-clamps on the crate released, dropping the lid and the crate's four sides to the ground to reveal the object within.

Even in the pale light of predawn, the newest orbital delivery gleamed like quicksilver. Max held out an unsteady hand; she was almost too awed to make contact with the machine that had fallen from the sky. She reached out and touched its polished metal and soft leather. It was solid and real and exactly like the picture she'd seen. But in reality, it was much prettier and more powerful than she could have imagined from the static photograph that had so captured her imagination.

Max knew what it was. She'd memorized the accompanying caption beneath the photo, even though she didn't understand what the words meant. Still caressing the machinery with delicate fingertips, she said, "I can't believe I have my very own motorcycle." She could almost hear the machine's engine purr as she described it.

This was the object of her dreams. She'd asked for it last night in her prayers. And here it was, impossible as that should be. It was proof positive that Max's prayers were being heard loud and clear.

"Now what do I do?" she whispered to herself.

"What is *that* doing here?" a voice said.

Max whirled and saw Sonya stalking toward her. The woman looked shocked by the sight of the latest delivery. "It's a—"

"A motorcycle," Sonya snapped. "Yes, I know. It's the bike Darius used to ride, back before..." Sonya trailed off, apparently realizing she'd revealed more than she'd planned.

"You knew Darius back on Earth?" Max asked. The picture that had inspired her prayer was one of the only photos the colonists had of Langford. In it, the man looked very young, barely older than Max was now. He was standing next to his prized possession at the time: his motorcycle. While the other children were fascinated with the image of the colony's founder, Max had only ever had eyes for the machine behind him.

"Yes, I knew him. I've known Darius my entire life." Sonya pointed at the motorcycle and asked, "What is this useless contraption doing here, Max?"

Max blurted, "I prayed for it."

"You did *what*?"

"I prayed for it," Max said again. "Just like I prayed for the replacement kite generator. I prayed to whatever higher power is up there watching over us and I asked them to send the generator to us. I never thought it would work, but I guess it did. Then I asked for this just to prove that the generator wasn't a weird fluke. And, well..." Max gestured to the motorcycle and grinned.

Sonya's face grew stern, but her eye glittered with excitement. "We must speak in detail about what this means, Max. The ramifications of what you're saying are beyond imagining. Help me hide this infernal contraption, and then come with me to my office to discuss our future plans."

Together the two of them pushed the motorcycle a short distance away and propped it up between two tall rocks so it was hidden by a copse of scrubby plants. The motorcycle weighed hundreds of kilograms, and even though they could roll it, shoving its dead weight over the rough terrain proved to be exhausting. By the time they'd finished hiding it, they were panting from exertion.

"Next time, I'll ask for fuel to go with it," Max said, half-jokingly.

Sonya grabbed her arm roughly. "Don't think to abuse this newfound power you possess, Max. There are far graver concerns for the colony than satisfying your petty fantasies."

Max twisted, breaking the grip, and gave Sonya a sharp shove. Unlike their last few physical encounters, this time Max was faster and stronger, and the woman fell back, unable to dodge Max's push. "Don't think to order me around, Sister!" Max said. She was tired of being treated like a selfish child. The motorcycle wasn't about Max taking advantage of her situation. It was about confirming a scientific hypothesis. The object needed to be something no one else would have asked for and something the unreliable manufactories wouldn't likely deliver on their own. The fact that the motorcycle was the most beautiful machine Max had ever laid eyes on had no relevance whatsoever.

Yeah, right, a tiny voice said in her head. *Keep telling yourself that.*

On the walk back to Sonya's office, Max saw a flicker of motion off to their left, just behind a large boulder. She grabbed Sonya's arm and pulled her to the ground.

"What is it?" Sonya hissed.

"There. Someone hiding. Watching us."

Sonya looked bemused. "There's no one out here, Max." Nevertheless, the woman drew up her hood, and the two of them crept toward the spot where Max had seen the interloper. Max waited until she was only a few steps away from the boulder, and then stood up and rushed the spot, ready to tackle whoever was spying on them.

She quickly found herself tangled in the remains of the motorcycle's delivery parachute.

Sonya rounded the corner of the boulder and barked in laughter at Max's predicament.

"A little help?"

"No, dear," Sonya said. "I think a price must be paid for your paranoia."

Annoyed and more than a little embarrassed, Max shook free of the parachute fabric. Together the two of them continued on their way to Sonya's office. Max kept her eyes open but saw no other sign of movement above or in the canyon. Maybe her imagination really was playing tricks on her.

"Well," Sonya said after she'd secured the door to her office and withdrawn her hood once more. "It's time for a history lesson."

Max rolled her eyes. "History? Shouldn't we be talking about religion? You might have my attention on that topic for the first time in my life."

"Religion can wait. Today, we speak of the true history of the colony. Not the sanitized version of events that you learn in school, and not the half-truths Darius shared with you, either. It's time you know about our true past. No more secrets." Sonya turned and rummaged through one of her desk drawers until she found a crinkled photograph. She handed it to Max, who recognized it as the same photograph that she'd seen in her textbooks. The one with a youthful Darius Langford standing in front of his prized motorcycle. "Do you know the significance of that photo?"

Max shrugged. "No, not really. I just think the motorcycle is a beautiful piece of machinery."

"It is. It was. I know because I was there." Sonya tapped the photograph with one finger. "I took this picture of Darius almost a thousand years ago."

"You..." Max felt her eyes try to pop out of their sockets. "What did you just say?"

Sonya sat down in her chair and leaned backward. She laced her fingers behind her head, closed her eyes, and said, "Let me tell you a story."

17

DARIUS EDISON LANGFORD WAS BORN on March 3, 1967, in New Haven, Connecticut. His mother was a philosophy professor at Yale University, and his father taught mathematics at a local high school.

Darius showed a gift for cerebral puzzles and conundrums while also possessing a knack for practical problems. He spent most evenings tinkering with inventions in his basement. He opened his first business in his parent's garage: fixing bicycles for the neighborhood. The operation was surprisingly successful. Suspiciously so, in fact. When Darius's parents investigated the unusually high number of broken bicycles rolling in and out of their garage, they discovered that Darius was using the repair business as a front for a much more lucrative enterprise: selling homework solutions to struggling high school students. Needless to say, the garage-run business closed its doors soon after the discovery was made.

Darius graduated early from both middle school and high school. As bright as he was, his teachers were anxious to get rid of him as much as anything else. Darius's insightful but never-ending questions—and his inevitable dissatisfaction with the answers provided by his instructors—were disruptive to the learning experience of his peers. College, his teachers all agreed, was a much better environment for the perceptive but pernicious student.

When Darius was admitted to Yale at age fifteen, his mother, Head of the Yale Philosophy department, was delighted. Both his parents and his professors expected great things from the young prodigy. They were soon to be disappointed.

Darius lacked focus during his first semester. He signed up for six classes in six different departments, but after the first week he stopped attending any of them regularly; his grades reflected his lack of effort.

His second semester was a bit different: Darius focused his efforts on introductory computer science courses. He attended all of his courses without fail and took copious notes. It looked like he'd learned his lesson and had started taking his studies more seriously. But he failed to submit a single homework assignment or attend any of his examinations. Not surprisingly, Yale suspended him. They suggested that a few more years of maturity might be in order before the young Darius returned to classes.

Darius, however, hadn't been wasting his time. He'd learned everything he needed to know during his first semester by reading the texts assigned by the professors. During his second semester, he'd absorbed everything the best engineering minds in the world could offer. Darius learned while he was in school, but he just didn't feel a need to prove his competence to an arbitrary governing body.

After being suspended from Yale, Darius put his newfound learning to work. With money he'd saved from his numerous business endeavors in high school, Darius rented a small apartment in East Haven. He informed the landlord that he looked young for his age. The landlord, who only cared about first and last month's rent—which Darius provided in cash—merely shrugged at his new tenant's boyish appearance.

Darius submitted an application for a software engineering position at IBM. The folks at IBM were very impressed by Darius's resume, which was largely fictional. They were even more impressed by the code samples he sent along with his application, which were cutting-edge and forward-thinking. Subsequently, the company hired Langford and was happy to accommodate their new employee's clinically diagnosed agoraphobia that prevented him from leaving his home. Even in 1983, programmers had a reputation for quirky behavior, and Darius wasn't the first telecommuter working for the technology company.

For a year, Darius worked for IBM writing code for their database development group. Unfortunately, a fellow programmer grew curious about his genius coworker from East Haven and stopped by to visit Darius and to chat with him in person about a computer code conundrum. When IBM discovered that their protégé was only seventeen and had lied on his job application, they terminated his contract.

Two weeks later, Darius emailed a solution to the coding problem to his unwitting discoverer.

Darius bounced from Yale to Harvard to the University of Connecticut. After seven years of study, and enough credits to satisfy four different programs, he graduated in 1991 with a degree in, of all things, Applied Linguistics.

Rather than put his new degree to use, Darius moved into his parent's basement and began day trading on the stock market. He amassed a large amount of wealth from trading, but he spent almost every dollar he earned pursuing odd experimental projects with his father. Nothing of particular interest ever seemed to come of their efforts, and Langford Sr. passed away in September of 1995. Heartbroken, Mrs. Langford retired from her University post and died only nine months later.

Darius was crushed by the loss of his parents. He pursued nothing for almost three years, living off savings from his stock market trading. When he recovered from his depression, he began trading aggressively on the market again. He rode the dot com bubble to its peak in 2000, only to crash with so many others over the next two years.

In 2004, Langford moved away from stock trading and began a small company that specialized in sustainable use of natural resources. The company didn't provide the explosive profit Langford had experienced during his stock trading days, but he still enjoyed a modicum of success from the venture and maintained a controlling interest in the company for years.

In 2010, Darius reentered the computer arena. This time he recognized the opportunity to seize a seismic shift in how the world used computer equipment with something called cloud computing. It wasn't a new idea—centralized data storage and processing and remote access from simple input/output devices. But the expanding bandwidth provided by modern telecoms, combined with the globalization of the computer marketspace, made the idea worth pursuing.

Unlike his major competitors which were fighting for market share in the United States, Darius pursued international interests. The global marketplace was fraught with challenges, both legal and cultural, but somehow Darius managed to navigate the treacherous international waters that other businesses were so leery of entering. He set up server farms in five different locations around the world. The farm locations were chosen based on a host of criteria. Most were next to hydroelectric power plants or large wind farms—power sources that were cheap and clean. They were set up in high altitude locations or at extreme latitudes to take advantage of the free cooling available. But all of them were designed to take advantage of the ebb and flow of daily computer demand.

The five farms were positioned around the world so server utilization constantly transitioned from one farm to another in order to match the natural dips and troughs in local electricity and bandwidth costs. Businesses operating in the United States were using server farms in Mongolia, while Chinese enterprises used servers in the mountains of Argentina, and Europe was served by the Alaskan server farm.

Many companies were reluctant to trust their critical data to computer systems located in countries deemed unfriendly or outright hostile. Darius ignored them. Other companies embraced the idea and offloaded their huge data warehouses and computationally intensive data modeling tasks to the cloud. Langford's setup was cheap, reliable, and almost infinitely scalable. For companies that were willing to adopt his model, the benefits were enormous.

Other companies tried to capitalize on the same model that Langford had implemented, but Darius benefited from a first mover advantage. Companies that had invested in his forward-thinking company stuck with him. Over the next fifteen years, Darius Langford's company became one of the most financially successful international corporations on the planet.

Darius might have also enjoyed the benefits of financial success like his company did, except that he squandered almost every dollar he earned on the strangest crackpot schemes and theories that money could buy. Almost none of the schemes he funded ever yielded anything viable, but Langford kept throwing money at any inventor with a theory, no matter how absurd.

Langford's antics eventually earned him a headline in the

Wall Street Journal that read, "Brewster's Millions? Langford's Billions!"—a barb based upon a film that featured a man who could only inherit a large fortune if he spent a smaller fortune in a short period of time without telling anyone why he was squandering the funds.

But Langford wasn't squandering money. He was buying ideas.

On April 2, 2027, Darius demonstrated the first fully functioning human brain simulation—a computer program that processed inputs and produced outputs at the speed of human thought, passed the Turing test easily, and perfectly mimicked its mirrored human counterpart's responses to stimuli. It could do this for hours at a time, before quantum mechanics forced enough chaos into the mix to cause the two minds to diverge from each other.

The age of the digital human had arrived.

But Langford kept his newest invention a secret. Only his top researchers were aware of the breakthrough and were offered lucrative non-disclosure agreements to keep the amazing development to themselves.

Money, as always, proved a powerful incentive.

Two years later, on May 12, 2029, Darius Langford died of a heart attack. During those two years, however, Darius had been continually improving the brain simulation program, and by the time he died the system was able to perfectly simulate a human being. Not only that, it could also run the simulation almost three times faster than a normal person's speed of thought. Darius also had lawyers construct incredibly intricate contracts and clauses that protected his financial trust fund and his leadership position in the company.

Death wasn't going to be the end for Darius Langford. It was just one more step on his long, well-planned journey. The thoroughness of Darius's planning before his death made many wonder in subsequent years if Langford had really died of natural causes or if he'd committed suicide to begin his simulated life as soon as it was ready for him.

During the next six years, Langford's company produced significant technological advancements in genetic engineering, quantum computing, environmental manipulation, artificial intelligence, and advanced expert systems design. Virtually every idea they generated was the result of the research conducted by the computer simulation of Darius Langford.

When the public learned the truth about Langford and his leadership position from beyond the grave, they were outraged. Stockholders tried to remove Langford from his role as CEO, but the contracts he'd designed before his demise, combined with the incredible legal expert systems he'd designed after his death, were more than enough to thwart all efforts to oust him. In addition, Langford made it very clear to his critics that if they took away his role as company leader, his ideas went with him. The implied threat was duly noted.

Computer speeds continued to increase at their historical pace, doubling every three to four years. By the late 2030s, Langford's simulation was running one hundred times faster than his biological predecessors. Parallel processing further increased the simulation's speed. Langford experienced lifetimes in just days. He was able to exhaustively study a subject that interested him in only hours of real time. He continued to generate technological breakthroughs that were difficult for human scientists and engineers to even comprehend, and for every advancement that Langford made available to the public, there were multiple developments that the artificial Darius was keeping solely to himself.

By 2040, multiple human simulations were running on various server farms around the planet. None of them possessed Langford's original design, which Darius had never shared with anyone, despite angry protests from billions of people who wanted or needed access to eternal life through silicon. Instead, the other simulated brain scans belonged to the world's ultra-wealthy—men and women with enough power and money at their disposal to emulate Langford's work and construct their own brain simulators.

Surprisingly, Langford shared some mutual interests with his simulated companions. Together, the elite group of simulated humans successfully lobbied the major governments of the world to grant citizenship rights to computer copies of deceased human beings. With a few strokes of the digital pen, Langford and his cronies legalized immortality for anyone wealthy enough to afford it.

The next eighteen months were utter chaos for the world's financial markets. Immortality changed everything. Power and money, which had always trickled slowly but naturally from one generation to another, suddenly halted its downward flow completely. The privileged uploaded themselves into simulated environments, like Langford's Cloud, and they took their money and their control with them.

In 2042, in response to the seismic change in the world economy, the New Puritan Movement began. Humans who hadn't been digitized, due to either moral objection or lack of financial means, started to fight back against the Uploaded. The New Puritans successfully revoked the legislation that gave citizenship to a computerized copy of a deceased human. They stripped power and money from the human simulations living in the Cloud and returned it to biological humans. "Pure" humans.

As mere programs with no physical presence in the world, the Uploaded humans retaliated with the only tools at their disposal; The Upload War began in earnest. By 2043, most of the world's computer networks were hopelessly ravaged by the viruses and malware utilized as weapons by Uploaded humans. But even without their computer networks, the biological humans could survive. They could adjust. Their computer enemies, however, could not.

Biological humans began eliminating the computer systems necessary for supporting the Uploaded. Multiple computer sites were annihilated by nuclear weapons. Others were dealt with more simply by cutting off their power supplies and network connections. The writing was on the wall—the Uploaded were going to lose.

As the year approached its end, Langford proposed a compromise to the biological humans. He'd developed three new technologies: artificial wombs, adult human cloning, and—his coup de grâce—the ability to download a virtual human into a cloned human body.

Langford offered to give away the secrets to these three technologies on the condition that anyone living as a simulation in the cloud would have the opportunity to download into a cloned body and resume the human lives they'd left behind when they'd entered their simulated existence.

The New Puritans refused his offer.

It took another four years for Earth's biological humans to root out every last remaining hidden computer housing Uploaded humans and stamp them out. But during the follow-up computer forensics, no one ever found any evidence of Langford's simulation. Every copy of the man that had started it all was gone.

No one knew it at the time, but Langford had made his Leap. The Leap no one else would dare to make.

Langford had been planning his exodus from Earth for a long time. During his many years as an Uploaded human, he'd secretly established a space-based construction facility.

He'd designed a miniscule starship: one that was less than a hundred kilograms in mass and equipped with computer storage space for hundreds of human simulations. The tiny starship was designed to take nothing with it but its digital passengers and blueprints for building new colonies *in situ*. The starship was equipped with tiny construction robots— autonomic devices that would mine a star system for natural resources and build an orbital infrastructure around the closest habitable planet. After the infrastructure was established, clones would be grown from genetically modified human genomes and then instantiated with the consciousness of the Uploaded stored in the starship's memory banks.

Once his ship was ready, Langford cracked into the Chinese orbital defense platform and used their powerful defense lasers to propel the starcraft's light-sails toward its distant destination. The impetus from the lasers, combined with gravitational assists from both the Sun and Jupiter, provided the starship with an impressive velocity—a sizeable fraction of the speed of light. Then the starship turned its sails toward its future home and spent the rest of its centuries-long journey decelerating via the comparatively weak light of its new star.

Langford's fellow passengers weren't copies of other simulations from Earth. Most of the Uploaded humans had been reluctant bedfellows during the war they'd fought together because they had no choice. When Langford planned his exodus, he didn't invite any of his current computerized neighbors to come along.

Instead, Langford brought with him family, friends, and other humans he believed would be useful during the colonization of a new world. Many of the copies he stored on his starship were surreptitiously obtained. Some of the humans he copied were vehemently opposed to Uploading and would never have agreed to travel with Langford as a stored computer program.

Instead, Langford reprogrammed his passengers, giving them false memories that would better suit their temperaments. Each of them remembered a history of Earth where a peace accord was found between the Uploads and the New Puritans. They remembered years of successful rebuilding of Earth's infrastructure. And they remembered competing for and then winning the chance to join a team of elite scientists and engineers to become part of Earth's first bold step out into the galaxy at large.

Extending the false history Langford created for his passengers, Darius built for them a simulated environment that imitated a starship much different than what really traveled in between the stars. The fictional starship was a huge craft, capable of carrying hundreds of biological humans and providing them with living quarters, food, water, entertainment, and anything else they'd need as they made their epic journey to a new star system. The giant ship was also equipped with powerful fusion engines that provided perpetual acceleration and deceleration during the journey, which made the trip between stars take only a few decades. The incredible speed of the fictional starship provided its passengers the additional benefit of a perceived journey that was only a few years in length due to the time dilation effects of general relativity.

When the actual starship arrived at the system that contained Langford's Leap, it followed its programming instructions. It manufactured an exact replica of the fictional, human-scaled starship and placed it in orbit around the new colony planet, where it would serve as a space habitat. The simulated humans were then downloaded into freshly cloned bodies on the newly created habitat.

The colonists were none the wiser for the deception. They

believed their cloned bodies were just modified versions of the bodies they'd lived in all their lives—bodies that had physically traveled through outer space from Earth to their new homes. They believed Earth was just a few light years away, ready to rescue them if things went wrong during the settlement process. They descended to the planet below, oblivious to their true situation.

One major genetic modification Langford provided to all of the colonists was a wetware network connection—a wireless network node deeply ingrained into the brains and nervous systems of the settlers' cloned bodies. Colonists enjoyed perpetual connectivity to the vast computational space that orbited their new world. They could communicate with a distant colonist as easily as speaking to someone in the same room. They could share their emotions and thoughts. They could access vast repositories of data and apply the computational power of the orbitals as an extension of their own thought processes.

Langford's plan for colonization, while perfect on paper, suffered from serious problems right from the start. For one thing, convincing the colonists to pursue terraforming efforts proved to be challenging. Why bother changing your environment when you could just change your body to fit the world instead? The idea of terraforming Langford's Leap into a world that would support base human life seemed unnecessary to the colonists and bordered on being irresponsible as well. Who knew what kind of alien life the colonists would be snuffing out by adjusting the local biosphere to their needs?

In addition, the virtual environments available to the colonists proved an irresistible distraction for many. While a few of the original settlers eschewed using the network resources for anything other than necessary tasks, others lost themselves completely within the orbital networks. Their biological bodies languished in their planet-based habitats while their minds wandered the vast simulated corridors of knowledge and fantasy generated by the quantum computers far above them.

Langford, in his attempt to create a paradise for his fellow star travelers, had instead produced an environment that was too good for them. There was no reason to work, to improve, to strive for something better. The colony stagnated, with no driving purpose and no struggle to survive.

Sonya paused in her storytelling. She sighed loudly. "That is, until the New Puritan Virus outbreak began."

Max took a deep breath. She'd been spellbound by the astounding, uncensored history of Darius Langford, a man whose genius had given birth to so many wonderful—and terrible—things during his multiple lifetimes. So many details she'd never known. Things that the colonists had never been taught, finally brought to light. Her mind was swirling with questions. When it was clear that Sonya was done with her monologue, Max asked, "What is the New Puritan virus?"

"It was the final weapon used by the biological humans on Earth, built at the end of the war as the ultimate tool to root out and destroy any remaining Uploads. The virus must've been inserted into the starship programming shortly before the ship left Earth. It was designed to propagate through any network it could find, but not to release its payload until it had infiltrated every known aspect of its local infrastructure." Sonya laughed bitterly. "I guess we were lucky Langford had instructed the orbital networks on and above Langford's Leap to aggressively expand. The geometric growth of the virus was almost outpaced by the growth of Langford's computer architecture. If his equipment had maintained its steady growth, the virus might've never triggered."

"But the virus did release its payload," Max said.

"Oh, yes, it did. It eventually caught up to the network's slowing growth cycle, and once it did, it simultaneously attacked every node it could reach throughout the entire star system. Almost every network computer collapsed within an instant. A few were able to switch to fail-over modes and flush their operating systems. Most weren't. Even the systems that did recover were lost in a sea of hijacked network nodes constantly bombarded with new malware. No clear signal could penetrate the compromised network, and soon even the clean systems were lost to the onslaught.

"The human colonists on the planet surface suffered even worse fates than their mechanical counterparts in space. Their network connections, directly embedded into their nervous systems, meant that they, too, were vulnerable to the computer virus. Unfortunately, though, humans don't have the ability to reboot or purge bad data."

"It must have been awful," Max whispered.

"Worse than you can imagine," Sonya said. "Many settlers died instantly. Others went mad, which resulted in wanton destruction of the settlement equipment, homicidal rampages, and a host of other terrible deeds."

"But a few survived. You did."

Sonya closed her one remaining eye and laughed bitterly. "Yes, I lived. But I suffered for it." She pointed to her empty eye socket. "Physically removing a virus that's running on a neural latticework embedded in your brain? Not easy, and an act that's paired with serious consequences. Digging my own eye out of my skull wasn't the most pleasant experience of my life. But it was better than the alternative."

Max shuddered. If the alternative was worse than losing an eye to your own hand, Max was certain it must've been horrible. "And Darius? How did he survive?"

Sonya shook her head. "I don't know. Darius is different than the rest of us. He's much, much older, for one thing. I'm not certain, but I believe he ran his simulation, albeit in low power mode, during the entire journey from Earth to Helios. Combine that with the time he spent as a simulation on Earth at hundreds of times the normal speed of thought, and Langford may very well be thousands of years old by his own perspective. He's the longest-running simulation ever created by man.

"It's possible Darius was partially immune to the virus, or able to fight it in ways that the rest of us couldn't. Regardless, he survived when most of his brethren didn't. But he too suffers from the ill effects of the virus. His body appears to intermittently lose control, like his mind is shutting off for a moment..."

"Like a reboot?" Max suggested, thinking about Darius's strange freezing episodes, bolstered by his mechanical latticework outfit.

"Yes," Sonya agreed. "Something like that."

Max asked, "If the entire network infrastructure of Langford's Leap was compromised, how were you able to recover the artificial wombs from orbit?"

Sonya's eye gleamed. "Good question. Long before the New Puritan Virus outbreak, I'd become very concerned about how damaging the perpetual network connections were to our colony's health. Disillusioned, you might say. Without informing anyone else, I began designing an alternative network protocol for the orbitals. My plan was to eventually sabotage the existing network and limit settlers' access to simple tasks like manufacturing and computation. I wanted to remove access to the virtual environments that had crippled so many of my fellow settlers.

"When the virus attacked, I was infected just like everyone else. But before I...disabled my internal network node, I was able to broadcast a priority signal to any functional, non-infected equipment in orbit, ordering the equipment to switch to the new network protocols. I didn't realize it at the time, but I believe I quarantined much of the virus, which allowed the settlers who were still alive to recover from the attack.

"I also inadvertently triggered an emergency protocol Darius must have established in the event of a catastrophe. When communication with the colonists was lost, the orbitals were programmed to fall back on a set of specific commands. Some of those commands were obvious: for instance, the crèche orbital jettisoned its artificial wombs to the planet's surface. The manufactories dumped our digital library archives onto hardcopies—thousands of books—and then shut down their higher logic structures. A few of the manufactories remained partially functional after the crash, but they seemed to produce objects at random, something like a standby mode while waiting for further orders. I believe some of the construction modules left orbit entirely, but without network access, I can't be sure.

"After the Disaster, Darius fell into a deep depression and refused to aid the survivors. Some of the settlers latched onto the desperate hope that our orbitals would send an automated distress signal to Earth and eventually help would arrive. For a time, I believed in this promise of rescue. As we raised the next generation of unmodified colonists, I taught this message of hope and salvation, just as I do today.

"But don't mistake me: I realized long ago that a rescue from Earth was never going to happen. I was able to read star charts, much like you did, and I knew that the star Langford had told us was our native sun possessed the wrong light spectrum. I confronted Darius with my discovery, and he awoke from his despondent state long enough to confirm my fears—Earth was far too distant to ever send a rescue party for us. We were on our own."

Max felt forced to interrupt. "You know that a rescue from

Earth is never going to come, but still you teach us to hold onto that false hope." Anger burned her throat as she demanded, "Why?"

"Because, my dear girl, sometimes false hope is better than no hope at all. Sometimes the truth is only an additional burden to bear rather than a tool to set you free. Sometimes fiction is the only path to survival. And sometimes, you must offer a counterpoint to hatred and fear, like the message Bryce Bell and his New Puritans espouse, by weaving a gentler, kinder narrative. Even if it's only that—a fiction."

Max stood up and stomped around Sonya's office, so full of rage and frustration that she couldn't sit still. "Why are you telling me all of this? The founder of our colony is a crazed megalomaniac. His plans for the colony were flawed, and disastrous for the first settlers. Those original settlers were kidnapped and lied to by their leader, never aware of their true origins or how far they really were from home. And now the all-powerful orbitals are either destroyed, nonfunctional, or malfunctioning, offering us no help whatsoever. Why are you telling me these things?"

Sonya held up a finger. "Some of the orbitals and manufactories weren't destroyed and are still functioning. They're sequestered on another secure network I created, code word Persephone."

A second finger was raised. "You, Max, have the encryption key for the Persephone network built into your genetic code. That key was supposed to lie dormant until I secured the Persephone network against viral infection, but has been activated prematurely, probably during your visit with Darius."

A third finger: "The Persephone network is *not* safe. Your prayers may have been answered by whatever networked computers are still functioning above us, but you run the risk of viral infection every time you make contact. You mustn't request any more resources from the orbitals until we can resolve the issue of the New Puritan Virus."

Finally, Sonya raised a fourth finger. "Most importantly—Darius must *never* regain access to the network. He'll claim otherwise, but he cannot resist the temptation to turn the orbital resources into his own personal virtual playground again. If he gains access to Persephone, things will return to how they were before the disaster. The colony will collapse, just as it would have before the virus attacked. Darius Langford must *not* be allowed to repeat his mistakes."

Max sat shocked by Sonya's impassioned speech. She nodded slowly as she took in the woman's words. Finally, she asked, "How do you know all of this, Sonya? You said Langford never told the settlers the truth about their origin, but you know detailed facts about Langford's early life. How is that?"

Sonya held up the photograph of Darius standing in front of his motorcycle. "I took this photograph, Max. Darius was seventeen, and I was six. I've been living in Darius's shadow my entire life. Every good idea I've ever had, Darius managed to steal or twist to his own ends. He even stole my identity and brought it here with him to suffer with his other kidnapped copies. He took me away from my life on Earth. My family. My friends. Just because he felt like it. Just because he could."

Max reeled. "Who are you?"

"My name is Sonya Langford, and I'm Darius Langford's younger sister."

"*Sister* Sonya!" Max exclaimed.

"Indeed," Sonya said ruefully. "Indeed."

IT TOOK CERES TIME TO convince Rhea that the vision she'd experienced was actually a request for help from the colonists. Ceres couldn't replay the message she'd received, and Rhea hadn't been able to interpret the encrypted packets when they first arrived. There was no permanent record of the transmission, so there was nothing to prove that it contained anything of import or that the vision was even related to the encrypted packets.

Ceres argued that the request for a replacement kite generator was *exactly* the kind of item the colonists who lived in the canyon would request, given the fact that the nickel meteorite had just destroyed their last functioning source of electricity.

Rhea eventually relented and allowed Ceres to respond to the request. Ceres dropped into the manufactory's virtual space and instructed the construction subsystem to build the replacement generator. She even had it painted bright red, exactly as she remembered it from the vision she'd had blasted into her mind. Once construction was complete, she delivered the newly created object to the planet's surface, this time remembering to specify a safe delivery mechanism and specific drop point.

Ceres glued herself to the surveillance satellite footage to see the colony's reaction to the gift she'd delivered to them. It was well before dawn when the first colonist discovered the new kite generator sitting on the plateau above the canyon. In the dim light, it was difficult to make out any defining features of the figure that crouched low next to the generator, examined it, and then retreated back into the canyon.

A few minutes later, as the sun began to crest the distant mountains, two figures climbed out of the canyon. This time Ceres could see that the figures were the perpetually hooded colonist and the young girl she'd seen earlier. Once again the girl dispensed with her breathing mask, but this time the hooded colonist lowered her cowl, demonstrating that she had no need of a mask, either.

"Rhea, do you—?"

"The facial imagery," Rhea interrupted, "is a close match to one of the original colonists: Sonya Langford, younger sister of Darius Langford, the colony founder. She appears to have suffered a traumatic injury to one eye, but otherwise the facial image is an extremely close match."

An original settler! That could explain how Ceres had finally gotten a distress signal from the colonists. Unlike the younger, unmodified colonists of Leap, Sonya had a network node built into her brain. If she possessed the proper encryption keys, she could contact the Persephone network and ask for help. Ceres realized she was probably looking at the person who'd requested the kite generator replacement.

Ceres watched as the two figures assembled the kite generator and attached it to their power grid. She noticed that the young girl occasionally looked up to scan the heavens, almost like she was searching for the manufactories and satellites far above her head. Ceres caught herself lifting a hand to wave at the girl on the screen in front of her, realized the silliness of her action, and let her hand drop back to her lap.

Ceres spent the rest of her day trying to send a response to the colonists on Leap. She tried speaking to them, thinking the words she wanted to say, visualizing items, entering virtual space and directly connecting with them, and a dozen other approaches. Nothing seemed to work. Or rather, she had no idea if anything actually worked, because she received no response to her messages. Rhea was unable to help her with the task because the computer was incapable of accessing the mysterious encrypted network the colonists had used to send their first request.

Later that evening, Ceres was struck by another powerful image, as bright and clear as the first, if not more so. Rhea couldn't interpret the encrypted network packets that arrived to deliver the image, but the station AI was able to confirm that the sudden uptick in traffic into Ceres's network node corresponded to the exact moment the image had appeared in her vision. The synchronicity seemed to further convince the AI that Ceres was indeed receiving a legitimate request from the colonists, rather than an odd fluke or random vision.

It took much longer for Ceres to find the broadcast image in the manufactory index. She eventually had to root around in an offshoot directory related to historical objects and memorabilia—items that had no practical use on the colony surface. The object she finally found was a motorcycle: a mode of rolling ground transportation used back on Earth. It was wholly unsuitable for use on Leap—it was ill-equipped to navigate the challenging terrain, and it used a combustion engine for power generation, which meant it needed combustible fuel, a substance that didn't currently exist on the colony world.

Nevertheless, Ceres had received a request, and she was

determined to deliver. She visited the manufactory again and had the motorcycle constructed and dropped to the surface. Because it had taken time to find the item in the database, the motorcycle was delivered later than the generator and arrived on its parachutes closer to dawn. As it touched down, Ceres could see the young girl standing on the surface looking both surprised and excited by the latest delivery. Perhaps Sonya had requested the strange object as a present for her young companion?

Soon after the motorcycle crate touched down and revealed its contents, Sonya arrived at the site. A brief discussion occurred between the two figures on the surface, but the low light and top-down imagery made it difficult for the lip-reading heuristics to subtitle anything coherently. The two females pushed the motorcycle into a group of rocks, and then disappeared into the canyon. Ceres thought she saw a small shadow following them but couldn't be sure.

Why have a motorcycle delivered, only to hide it among the rocks? Ceres couldn't comprehend what was happening on the surface, and her inability to directly communicate with the colonists was frustrating beyond words. She was determined to tackle the problem and discover a means of speaking with the people on the surface. Before she could even begin, however, something very new and very strange occurred.

She began hearing voices: a chorus of voices, all of similar pitch and timbre and speaking just out of sync with one another. Unlike the whispers of help she'd received along with the blinding images, these voices were strong and loud in her mind, each word vibrant with clarity.

"Construction Module Delta-632, this is Command Actual. Please confirm secure network connection via Persephone protocol." There was a pause, and then the words repeated.

"Uhh..." Ceres said.

"I am detecting another large burst of encrypted packets being broadcast to your network node," Rhea said. "Are you receiving another vision?"

"No, I'm receiving a bunch of voices in my head asking me to confirm a secure connection with the D-632 construction module."

"The strong encryption of the data packets guarantees a secure connection. You can respond in the affirmative."

"I *know* that, you stupid computer! What I need to know is *how to respond at all!*"

Ceres concentrated once more, trying her hardest to communicate with the colonists sending her signals over the encrypted network. Her frustration was compounded by the incessant repetition of the confirmation request that echoed over and over in her skull, making it almost impossible to concentrate.

She talked. She ordered. She whispered and screamed. She nodded and smiled. She pictured words in her head and images of herself nodding in the affirmative. She entered virtual space and repeated everything she'd already tried in real space. The voices in her head kept repeating their incessant message, with no indication that they'd received any reply at all from Ceres.

"Can we shut off this voice?" Ceres asked at one point.

"Blocking the encrypted signal is highly inadvisable. Part of the encryption algorithm used in the Persephone protocol is on the quantum level. Interrupting the signal could result in a permanent interruption in communications with the colony."

"So yes, but no?" Ceres said. The AI didn't answer.

Please, she begged, *please, whoever is out there listening to me—anyone trying to listen—hear me. And when you do, please stop the infernal voice that's rattling around in my head! Please, hear me!*

Nothing happened.

Ceres, exhausted, laid down in the middle of the floor and wept.

Eighteen minutes later, as Ceres was beginning to recover from her breakdown and make another attempt at talking to the colonists, the voices in her head changed.

"Network connection confirmed. Have the manufactories in orbit been secured?"

Ceres sat up sharply. "It worked!" she shouted.

"What worked?" Rhea asked.

Ceres began to respond but realized that she didn't know the answer to that question. The only thing she'd done for the last eighteen minutes was cry her eyes out. How had that succeeded in confirming the network connection? "Rhea, how far are we currently from Leap?"

"161,984,231 kilometers and closing."

Some quick mental calculations gave Ceres part of her answer. She was just under nine light-minutes away from Leap. A round-trip signal would take eighteen minutes. It wasn't her crying that had succeeded in communicating with the colonists; it was what she'd done just before her mental breakdown.

What had she said or done in those last coherent moments? She tried to recall the words she'd thought and how they'd been different than other words she'd used to communicate. Had there been a keyword buried in there somewhere? Did she have to speak or think her words in a particular order or with a particular emphasis?

And then Ceres believed she had it. It wasn't *what* she'd said, or even *how* she'd said it. It was *who* she'd directed the message at and *why*. In her last words, "please hear me," she hadn't been directing those words at the colonists who were flooding her with security requests; she was directing her words at anyone who might be listening. And as she'd been saying those words, she'd been in a state of absolute desperation. She'd been hoping that a higher power—a network system or computer AI or even another colonist—would intervene and stop the repetitive messages. She hadn't cared who it was, she'd just needed help.

She did her best to recreate that mind state: she projected her voice into the void, pleading with whatever was out there to hear her and respond accordingly. She poured her heart into her simple message.

Seventeen minutes and fifty-six seconds later, the voice in her head said, "Acknowledged. Manufactories are secure. Prepare to receive our request for supplies."

Ceres did a dance of joy around the small control room. But she had to cut her celebration short as a long list of items began flowing into her brain—images and descriptions arriving so quickly they threatened to drown her in detail. She snatched up a stylus and quickly began transcribing the words and images before they overwhelmed her.

When the initial deluge of data ended, Ceres was left surrounded by a disorganized pile of scribbled notes. She was exhausted and her hands were shaking. "I can't do that again," she said. "We have to work out another way to manage requests."

After inputting the first set of supply needs into the manufactory network, Ceres worked with Rhea to concoct a method of directly transferring information from the encrypted requests to the manufactory's build queues. Ceres initiated a new virtual space and filled it with two large bins. One bin represented Ceres mentally capturing all the imagery and text she received from the colonists. The second bin was where she transferred the information to Rhea and the manufactory.

It was a clumsy, convoluted process, but it was easier than manual transcription. Without the virtual bins to fool her mind into thinking she was performing physical work, Ceres doubted she would have been able to accomplish the task. As it was, the virtual space forced her to exercise muscles she'd never used before.

At first, the "objects" she was carrying from the "in" bin to the "out" bin translated as large piles of heavy, wet sand. Moving a requested object into the manufactory queue meant scooping the entire object into her arms and trying to carry it across the virtual room without it oozing out of her grasp and crumbling onto the floor. When that happened, there was nothing to be done about the lost object but to move on to the next item on the list and hope the colonists would resubmit their request.

With practice, Ceres began to improve her technique. She was able to arrange her movements in a particular fashion that moved the intact imagery of the request from one bin to the other without issue. With more practice, she was eventually able to leave the virtual room running in a small corner of her mind while most of her consciousness focused on other things. It was a strange feeling, splitting her focus between the physical ship and the virtual delivery room, but Ceres knew that over time she'd get used to the duality. After all, if the original settlers could split their attention between the network and the real world, Ceres could learn to do it, too.

After a few days of receiving and processing equipment requests, Ceres felt more than confident in her new abilities. She was able to let the requests transfer to the manufactory queue without any conscious effort or supervision on her part: the action of moving the data from one system to the other was as automatic as breathing or blinking. Every so often she'd consciously check out the items being produced, but most of the equipment appeared to relate to large-scale building projects and weren't particularly interesting.

There were only two things that troubled Ceres during those days of intense production. One was the delivery location specified in the requests. The voices in her head—which she'd begun thinking of as The Chorus due their strange plurality when communicating—wanted everything delivered to the original settlement site and not the new settlement in the canyon. Ceres didn't particularly understand the reason for the off-site delivery, but then again, what did it really matter? As long as she was helping the colonists, right?

The second thing that bothered Ceres was the lack of direct communication she'd received. After the brief conversation that verified a secure transmission protocol, she hadn't spoken to The Chorus again. Ceres had tried to communicate with the voices that were still requesting equipment from her, but either she'd lost the ephemeral technique that allowed her to speak to them, or they were no longer listening. Having the conversation turn one-directional was a savage blow to the hopes and dreams Ceres harbored for her rescue efforts. She'd really looked forward to developing a personal relationship with the colonists. It seemed the people on the planet below her didn't share her interest.

However, as Ceres processed requests and observed the slowly approaching planet, she realized that may not be entirely true. Her surveillance satellites showed the canyon colonists going about their business normally. The kite generator appeared to be functioning normally; it tossed its smart-kite into the skies and winched it back to the ground over and over again to the steady rhythm of the high-altitude winds. Colonists marched back and forth from their underground dwellings to their surface farms, taking care of the many tasks necessary to keep them alive.

Not once did Ceres see any of the colonists travel to the

distant site of the original settlement. It was as if they were unaware of the large amounts of equipment that were being delivered to their former home. Unaware, or uncaring. Neither possibility made any sense to her.

On numerous occasions, Ceres saw Sonya and her young friend on the plateau above the canyon. During the daylight hours, Sonya always wore her hood, and the girl always wore her mask. But in the late evenings or early mornings, Ceres would often spot one or both of them wandering the plateau and breathing the open air. The young girl, in particular, would often steal out to the site of the hidden motorcycle well before dawn. She'd just sit out on the rocks and stare at the heavens above her. Sometimes it felt like her eyes were looking right at Ceres. And during those long night-time moments, Ceres would often receive brief, faint flashes of half-formed visions.

That was when Ceres realized something. *Maybe I've been trying to talk to the wrong colonists.*

AT FIRST, MAX THOUGHT SHE was just imagining things. She kept hearing vague whispers during class or when she walked the cave passages to and from her afternoon chores. The whispers were indistinct and could easily be confused with something innocuous, like the sighing of the wind echoing through the canyon's many caverns. The cave-ins from the earthquake had completely changed the acoustics of the stone pathways, so maybe Max just wasn't used to the new sounds of her once-familiar environment.

What the cave-ins didn't explain, however, was the odd behavior of her peers. Max caught the other children looking sidelong at her as she passed, leaning closer to their friends to speak conspiratorially. Although maybe they weren't treating her any differently than they had in the past. Had they always acted this way when Max walked by? She'd always been an outsider. Perhaps she was just being paranoid.

Her worry was that someone had seen her outside on the surface without her mask. She and Sonya were careful, but that didn't mean they hadn't been spotted at one point or another. Was it possible that Max's secret was finally discovered? After spending so much time trying to hide her differences from everyone—her peers, her teachers, and even her father—Max thought that maybe telling everyone the truth would be the best thing. How bad would it be, after all? The original colonists had breathed Leap's air, hadn't they? Would her fellow colonists *really* hold it against her if she possessed the same biological advantages as their predecessors?

Secrets were heavy, treacherous things, Max realized. They inevitably managed to slip from your grasp, dragging behind you, leaving an ugly trail of lies and deception in their wake. She'd been carrying her secret for so long that she felt like she'd spent half her life looking over her shoulder to make sure no one caught her off-guard.

Revealing her secret to Sonya had relaxed that burden a bit, and it felt wonderful. Maybe it was time to completely let her burden go. Maybe she should just start walking around the canyon caves freely, without her mask—without any pretense of being normal. That, she was sure, would resolve the whispering quickly enough.

Before Max could make good on her plan, the root cause of the whisper campaign was revealed to her by an unlikely source.

"I know," Ellie whispered into Max's ear. She was sitting behind her in class.

Max spoke out of the side of her mouth, without turning her head. "You know *what*, Ellie?"

"I heard you the other morning, out on the surface, speaking with Sister Sonya."

There really had *been someone out there watching us.*

Before she could respond, Ellie continued her whisper. "I know about the generator and that other odd machine you received. And I know how you got them."

"Ellie, I—"

"You *prayed* for them, Max." Ellie's whisper, much to Max's astonishment, didn't sound scornful or angry. No, her strident whisper was clearly one of awe and reverence. "You prayed for help, and the heavens answered you. Our saviors have returned to Langford's Leap, and they've chosen you as their first contact. You, Max, are the one who's going to save us all!"

Oh. Hmm. This is going to be a problem.

After class, Max tried to corner Ellie to straighten things out, but her long-time enemy skipped out of the room before Max could catch her. As Max pushed past her other classmates, she noted they fell back before her as if they were afraid to be touched by her passing.

Great. A pariah once more. At least I'm back in familiar territory.

But that wasn't it at all. After looking both ways out in the school hallway and not spotting Ellie, Max shrugged and began walking home to grab lunch and perhaps catch up with her father. That was when she heard the whispering again, and this time she could make out a few of the words.

"*Generator...prayer...heaven...faith...chosen...Messiah...*"

"Messiah?" Max blurted, spinning toward the girl who'd spoken the word. "Who, exactly, is the Messiah?" Max had read enough history books to recognize the word. She knew its meaning, and the idea that it was being applied to her made a frisson of fear run up her spine. Being different was one thing. But being held up as a savior of the colony was another thing entirely, and being hailed as a religious figure? That was totally out of the question!

The girl Max had spoken to shrank away, averting her eyes. "I meant no disrespect," she mumbled.

"No?" Max said. "What did you mean, then? Are you trying to tell me you think I'm something special? Because I promise you, I'm not. Not at all."

The girl just ducked her head and refused to answer her. Max glared at the other children surrounding them, but no one would look her in the eye.

"Do all of you think the same thing? Has Ellie convinced you I'm a religious hero or something? That I've got a direct line of communication with the heavens? That our saviors have come, and I'm their Chosen One?"

There was silence for a long moment. Then one of the girls stepped forward. It was Aida. Max's dream best friend. Correction: former dream best friend—Max hadn't the time or inclination to think about her for weeks now. "It makes sense," she said. "You passed our initiation test better than anyone ever has. You're the best the colony has to offer. You're a pure human, but strong and capable. You survived exile in the wilderness when any of us would have perished. You're special. Why wouldn't you be chosen to represent us?"

"Seriously?" Max stared at Aida. "You really believe this has anything at all to do with a stupid initiation rite? As if the ancestors who are someday going to cross space to save us would pay *any* attention at all to something as trivial as a *prepubescent game*?"

Aida stepped back from her, cowed by her stare.

This is it. This is the *moment, the one when I tear off this infernal mask and stomp it into the floor, never again to be shackled by its stifling poison. This is when I reveal to these ignorant religious zealots what truly makes me different. Not that I'm a heaven-sent Messiah, blessed with a direct line to the gods. No, I'm just a cursed genetic throwback to the original settlers with a highly modified respiratory and digestive system and a brain with an active network connection that could easily kill me.*

Max felt fingertips tug at her sleeve and spun away.

Sonya stood behind her, hidden deep beneath her hood. Her hands were held up toward Max in a placating gesture.

"This isn't the right time, girl," she said softly.

Somehow, Max knew Sonya was well aware of what she'd been planning: revealing herself to the other children and letting fate take its course with truths long-hidden. Sonya understood the need to hide beneath her hood, and she understood the temptation to drop that hood and stand proud before her peers. Somehow, her outstretched hands communicated all of this and more.

"No?" Max asked, her voice sounding anguished in her ears. "If not now, then when?"

Sonya leaned in close. "Someday, Max. Someday soon. But not yet. Look at them. They're not ready."

Max looked around and saw that Sonya was right. These children weren't ready to accept her for what she really was. They were willing to believe that she was a religious savior, but part of that belief was grounded in the fact that Max was one of them: a pure human. If she revealed to them her shared heritage with the original settlers—the heretics who'd cursed the colony with its current dilemma—Max would quickly become the enemy, and any help she could deliver from the orbitals would be scorned as tainted goods.

Slumping her shoulders in defeat, Max let Sonya lead her away from the school room. They walked slowly back to Max's home, and Sonya cycled through the airlock with her. Max smiled when Sonya let her ignore the allergy decontamination routine they both now knew was useless. Going through the motions for her father's sake had been tedious, and more than once Max had been tempted to skip the process altogether.

Inside, the two of them were greeted by Nolan, who'd prepared a lunch for his daughter and himself. He looked up, saw Sonya in the airlock, and began preparing another sandwich.

"Max," Sonya said, lowering her hood and crouching down.

"I think I know one person who *is* ready for the truth."

Max looked over Sonya's shoulder to where her father was looking at her quizzically. "What truth?" he asked innocently.

Max looked back at Sonya, who nodded and smiled at her. Max took a deep breath and said, "Dad, we need to talk about something. Something important."

"Yes?"

"It's about my trouble breathing."

"Your allergies? I've noticed they've been quite a bit better. You've recovered quickly from your escapade out in the wilderness, haven't you?"

Max shook her head. Her father had begun referring to her two-day disappearance as her "escapade." Somehow, referring to her near-death experience as an innocent adventure made it easier for him to accept. Adults were so good at self-deception.

And I'm not? Max frowned, and then cleared her throat. "They're not better, Dad. They're gone."

"Your allergies are completely gone?" Nolan looked surprised and happy. "That's great!"

"Dad, they're gone because I never had allergies. My breathing trouble, it's, well..." How could she explain this? She scrubbed her face with her hands, frustrated. "It's complicated."

"Max, what is it? Just tell me."

Max looked up at her father, with his worried, accepting expression. "No," she said, suddenly decided. "I can't tell you. But I can show you." She stepped forward and handed her father her mask. Then she backed into the airlock and slammed the inner door closed.

It took a few minutes for her father to join her outside the airlock. He was holding her mask in his hand while his own was clutched to his mouth. He looked frantic as he shoved open the outer hatch and darted out into the canyon corridor.

"Dad, relax, I—"

Nolan rushed forward and tried to force Max's mask onto her face. Max, startled, fell backward and warded off his approach with her hands. Sonya, who exited the airlock behind Nolan, stepped forward faster than Nolan could possibly move and gently but firmly pulled him back. Her strength was more than a match for his heavily muscled frame.

"Let me go!" Nolan shouted. "She'll die!"

"No, she won't," Sonya said. "Look at her."

Nolan fought against Sonya for a few moments, but then he realized Max wasn't struggling to breathe or asphyxiating in the tunnel. He stopped fighting Sonya and dropped to his knees. "Max, are you *breathing*?"

Max grinned and then took a deep breath. "What does it look like I'm doing?"

Her father's face went through a whole series of emotions in quick succession—surprise, relief, bafflement, comprehension, anger, happiness—and those were just the obvious ones. Max laughed hysterically at her father's visible confusion. Finally, Nolan turned to Sonya and asked, "Why didn't you *tell* me?"

Sonya shrugged. "At first, I didn't know. By the time I did, it was Maxine's decision to tell you or not. I don't interfere in these types of discussions."

Nolan turned back to Max. "So? Why keep this a secret?"

Max felt her face flush. "I just wanted to be a normal kid, you know? Ellie and her father, they have everyone in the colony thinking we were cursed for the sins of the original settlers and that subverting nature's natural order is what caused the failure of the first settlement. Being Pure is all that matters. Me? I'm more like Sonya than anyone else here. I'm different. I'm better, which somehow makes me *worse*. It was easier to just not tell anyone than to deal with their judgment."

"You're my daughter. I'd love you no matter what."

"Dad, I know. You'd never judge me. You'd accept me, no matter what. I know that. But if I told you, then you'd have to lie on my behalf. I didn't want that for you. You have a reputation of being an honest man. The other colonists respect you even though you don't share their religious beliefs. If you started lying for me and the colonists found out, you'd lose that respect. That's not fair to you. Besides, you do more than enough to take care of me—to take care of all of us. The health of the colony rests on your shoulders. My problems shouldn't be your concern."

"Max, we're family. What you just described—your problems being my problems—that's the very definition of what a family is all about. We share each other's burdens. We lighten the load for the other person. You did that for me after the earthquake. You helped Sonya with the generators and gave me time to get my head working right again. You should let me do the same for you."

"Alright. But will you? Dad, I'm not ready to tell anyone else about this. And Sonya doesn't think the other colonists are ready for it, either. Will you help me keep this a secret? Can you do that for me?"

Nolan stepped forward and wrapped Max in a huge embrace. "I've kept the artificial wombs a secret for my entire adult life, Max. I've known you were special since the day Sonya handed you to me. What you've just told me? It's just details. No one else needs to know."

The three of them reentered their home, and they spent the rest of the afternoon and evening talking about Max's abilities, her near-disaster on the beach with the Leap Fronds, her run-in with Darius Langford, and her recent and inadvertent contact with the orbital manufactory. To his credit, Max's father took most of the information in stride. Max could see his jaw clench when she told him about the more dangerous activities she'd been involved in during the past few weeks, but other than that involuntary twitch, he offered no words of judgment.

It felt good to talk to her father about everything that had happened to her. Having Sonya as a confidante had been a good thing, but it was no substitute for having an understanding parent. Max's father could offer her support in a way no one else could match, and receiving his approval, Max realized, was extremely important to her. Having her father accept who she was and what she'd done was a relief like nothing she could have imagined. She found herself grinning wildly the entire time she spoke with him, even when she was telling him about her more embarrassing or careless moments. All that mattered was that now he knew.

During the next few days, Max spent more and more time exploring the wilderness that surrounded the canyon. Some nights Sonya joined her, while other nights she ventured out alone. Max's father, now fully aware of her late-night expeditions, simply waved goodbye and bid her the automatic parental response: "Be careful!"

After Ellie's revelation in the classroom, Max decided to move her motorcycle to a new hiding spot much farther from the canyon. She didn't want any of the other children tampering with her special treasure. Most nights she eventually circled around to its new hiding place to spend a few moments admiring its beauty—sitting on its seat and imagining what it would be like to ride it across the country. She even removed the gas cap and peered inside the motorcycle's tank, just to be sure. Sadly, it was completely void of fuel.

On those star-filled evenings, lying on the rocks and staring up at the sky, Max still felt something like complete loneliness. Despite sharing her genetic modifications with Sonya and her secrets with her father, Max felt like she was something different and unique. No amount of talking to her dad or the colony's spiritual leader turned co-conspirator would change that feeling.

The thing was, for the first time in her life, Max felt good about the loneliness. It didn't actually seem like it was that bad to be special or different. For the first time, it felt *correct*. She was content. All was right with the world.

Well, almost. When Max watched the sky, she recognized the telltale objects that tracked across it against the current of the starscape: tiny glimmers of light that moved soundlessly from horizon to horizon in just a minute or two—satellites, poisoned by the Great Disaster, still following their silent orbits around the planet.

Max's urge to reach out and contact the Persephone network was overwhelming. She knew Sonya believed making contact was an extremely dangerous proposition, but the act of speaking to the network and requesting any object that she could imagine was an intoxicating idea. Every night it took enormous willpower to resist the temptation.

One evening, almost two weeks after her motorcycle delivery, the decision to contact Persephone was taken from her.

She was lying on a rock on the plateau with Sonya at her side, discussing—without much success—plans to purge the Persephone network of any remaining viral outbreak that might be lurking along its ephemeral passageways. They'd spoken before on this issue, and Max was growing convinced that Sonya really didn't have the slightest inkling as to how to solve the problem, which made the prohibition to contact the Persephone network even more frustrating.

One moment, Sonya was saying something indecipherable about command structure parity values, and the next, Max was pummeled by a booming, disembodied voice.

"*Can you hear me?*" the voice demanded. "*Can you hear me?*"

Max yelped in surprise and fell off her rocky perch and onto the ground.

"Max, are you alright?" Sonya asked, and kneeled next to her, alarmed.

"I hear you! I hear you!" Max shouted and clutched her hands to her ears.

As suddenly as it had begun, the voice stopped.

"What do you hear, Max? What happened?"

Max sat up, confused. "Did you...you didn't hear that?"

Sonya looked around. There was nothing but rocks, scrub brush, and more rocks. "I hear nothing but the wind. What did you hear?"

"I—" Max caught herself. *Persephone? Is that you?*

Sonya took Max by the shoulders and peered curiously at her with her one eye. "Max, what's going on? Are you alright?"

"Yes. Sorry, Sister. I'm just...tired. All these nights out on the plateau. I haven't been getting much sleep. I think I might have dozed off there and had a bad dream." *Persephone, if that was you, then yes, I hear you.*

"Are you sure?"

"Yes, Sonya. I'm sorry. Everything is fine." *Persephone? Are you there?*

Sonya looked unconvinced but said no more. Instead, she urged Max to stand up, and they began their walk back to the canyon. Fifteen minutes later, just as they were descending the canyon's face, the voice returned.

"*Persephone is the name of a network protocol. My name is Ceres. Is this Sonya?*"

The voice, loud enough to rattle the canyon walls, nearly caused Max to stumble and fall off the precarious path she was walking. Fortunately, this time she controlled her reaction and bit back her scream of surprise. *No, this isn't Sonya. My name is Max. Can you speak more softly? Your voice is incredibly loud.*

Max waved goodnight to Sonya as they approached the Sister's private dwelling. Max continued toward her own home, but watched over her shoulder to make sure her escort entered her cave and secured the door behind her. Then Max took off running, making her roundabout way back to the surface.

It took another fifteen minutes, but eventually Max received another response. Thankfully, it was a quieter voice this time.

Max? You must be the girl without the mask, then.

That's right, Max responded. *I'm the girl without the mask. Who are you?*

WHO ARE YOU?

Ceres stepped back. From what, she wasn't sure—her conversation was entirely in her head, so there was no one to step back from. Max's question, so frank and curious, was one Ceres had never considered having to answer before. Who was *she*? The colonists had already asked for her help. How could they not know who she was?

The conversation that followed, which lasted for hours, made for some of the best moments in Ceres's life. She began explaining things to the young girl on the planet below: who she was, where she lived, and the details of the space habitat. Her distant companion seemed absolutely fascinated by her responses and asked a long stream of follow-up questions, not least of which was why their conversation had such long pauses between responses.

Ceres explained that the vast distance that still existed between her station and the planet forced their conversation to be broadcast across long light-minutes each direction, which resulted in a fifteen-minute delay for each question and response.

Max, to her credit, completely understood the light-lag

226 | Langford's Leap

issue, which was a relief to Ceres. It meant her planetside companion wasn't stupid, merely ignorant. Ignorance was easily solvable by providing relevant information. Stupidity? That would've been a more challenging issue.

Max proposed an interesting scheme to deal with the time delay, which she referred to as a lumpy conversation. Each girl would ask or answer as many questions as they wanted for approximately one minute in length. Then they'd remain silent for a minute. Then they'd repeat the process. The result was eight separate conversations, each staggered so one girl could respond to the other's questions and comments in an organized fashion. The solution was elegant and effective, and Ceres was pleased that her new friend showed such cleverness.

The girls spoke in depth about the Persephone network, especially its current state of security and safety. Ceres assured Max that the new emergency network protocol was free of malware and safe to use. She spoke in detail about how she'd infiltrated the older networks of the manufactory and regained control of the construction processes. Max sounded amazed and impressed by Ceres's accomplishments, which made Ceres blush with pride.

It was funny, describing her daily routine to Max. Ceres found activities like visiting the orchard ring to be mundane and boring, but Max found using centrifugal force to emulate gravity to be a novel and fantastic proposition. Sharing the details of her life with Max, Ceres began to feel the same wonder and interest that the planet-bound girl felt. Their discourse gave Ceres a new perspective on things she took for granted.

The same could be said for Max's terrestrial experience as a colonist. It was obvious, for instance, that Max found Ceres's fascination with gravity to be somewhat mind-boggling. Both girls shared an interest in large open spaces, which led Max to explain why she'd only recently begun visiting the surface of Leap without the use of a mask.

Ceres listened raptly as Max talked about the strange initiation rite adolescent colonists underwent, and how Max had been chased off into the wilderness by her peers, angry after embarrassing them during the rite. The idea of punishing someone for success seemed ludicrous to Ceres.

Max's tale of the glowing plants, followed by her near-death experience with Leap's violent tides, was strangely familiar to Ceres. She realized with a start that the odd dreams she'd suffered from all those weeks ago clearly paralleled the harrowing experience Max had endured on the beach. Somehow, even back then, Max had been able to communicate with the Persephone network, albeit on a rudimentary, unconscious level.

When Max's story moved on to her encounter with Darius Langford and the old settlement, Ceres grew uneasy. She'd occasionally looked down on the old settlement when one of her satellites was in position, but she'd never spotted much of interest happening there. Even lately, when she'd begun delivering all of the requested supplies to the old site, the only sign of activity she ever saw was the automated construction equipment doing its assigned task of rebuilding the settlement. She never saw any sign of Darius, or any other colonist, for that matter. The mystery of the chorus of voices grew.

But before Ceres asked about the deliveries to the old settlement, she wanted to better understand Max's situation, specifically how the young girl was able to connect to the Persephone network in the first place. Based on Rhea's analysis of the colony surface, the majority of the surviving colonists had lost their genetic modifications and as a result had no built-in network nodes connected to their brains. Without those modifications, communicating with the orbital network was technically impossible.

Obviously Max was different than the average colonist. For one thing, she could breathe without a mask, but when Ceres asked about Max's unique position amongst the other colonists, the girl's response was, for the first time since their conversation began, a bit hesitant.

"I've been different all my life," Max explained. "I was born in an artificial womb: one of the few that Sister Sonya still maintains in the deep caverns under the canyon. That's not what makes me different, though. Many of the colonists were born in the wombs, including almost all of the adults, right after the Great Disaster. So being born from an artificial womb doesn't make me different than most of my fellow colonists. But in addition to being born artificially, Sonya made genetic changes to me before my birth.

"At first, my father and the other colonists thought I was sick. I had trouble breathing and eating food. I know now what was really happening for all those years—the food and air that's good for the colonists is borderline toxic for me. I was designed with Leap's environment in mind.

"But in addition to being modified to live freely on the surface, Sonya also built a new type of network node into my head. It's the only one of its kind. It allows me to speak to you when no one else can. At first, when you delivered the kite generator, I thought I might be talking to a god! I couldn't believe someone up there was actually listening to me. Part of me thought it was just incredibly good luck, but I needed proof."

Ceres tilted her head back and laughed. "That's why you asked for the motorcycle!" she said, knowing she'd have to wait fifteen minutes to receive a reply to her suspicion.

"That's why I asked for the motorcycle," Max said, oblivious to Ceres's similar exclamation beaming to her at the speed of light, destined to arrive seven and a half minutes later. "I figured, ask for something odd and see if it shows up. And...it did!

"When Sonya found out that I was able to speak to the Persephone network, she seemed surprised. I guess my network node was supposed to remain dormant but inadvertently became active. She was worried about the security of the network and ordered me not to try to communicate again until we could ensure the protocol was safe. That's why I haven't spoken to you until now."

"Sonya can't use the Persephone network?" Ceres asked.

Their conversation had reached a lull, so Ceres waited until Max could respond to her latest question.

"Hah! Good guess! Yes, the motorcycle was a test, like I said. You must've thought it was such a strange request!" There was a short delay, and then, "No, Sonya can't speak to you. In order to survive the viral outbreak during the Great Disaster, she had to physically remove part of her network node. That's why she's missing an eye." Ceres felt Max's nonverbal shiver beamed up to her on the network as clearly as the words they were sending to each other.

"She pulled out her own eye?" Ceres gasped and felt her own shiver creep up her spine. The thought of doing something like that, even in the extreme circumstances Sonya must've been facing, was inconceivable to Ceres.

Max kept speaking, oblivious to Ceres's shared sentiment. "It seems I may be the only person on Leap who has the ability to communicate with you. At least for now. Maybe Sonya will use the remaining wombs to create new colonists with similar abilities, now that you've confirmed the safety of the Persephone network. Wouldn't that be great? We'd have a whole bunch of kids running around plugged into the network, and you and I could teach them everything we know." Max's voice sounded enthusiastic and hopeful, and the emotional context of the conversation flooded across the network. The idea of having a true companion to share her world with filled Ceres with her friend's warmth and happiness.

Ceres, however, still had concerns. "Max, I've been receiving communications from another group of colonists for quite a long time now. I'm not sure how many—they always seem to communicate with me as a group, which is very odd. The Chorus, as I've grown to call them, have been requesting a large quantity of machinery and smart-building supplies from the manufactory to be delivered to Leap's surface. I've been dropping tons of manufactured items and raw materials on top of the original settlement."

It took almost fifteen minutes for Max's response to arrive. "The old settlement? But no one lives up there anymore except for Darius. According to Sonya, he lost his network connection just like all of the other settlers when the infrastructure collapsed. You're saying that now you're receiving requests from a *group* of colonists located there? Who are they? You haven't seen them? They haven't spoken to you?"

"No," Ceres said, sharing Max's surprise. "Other than the initial security check, my conversations with the Chorus have been nothing but perfunctory. They ask for materials from the orbitals, and I relay their request to the non-priority Persephone network. I've tried speaking to them, but I never get a response."

"That's...odd," Max responded. "I need to speak with Sister Sonya about this." Beneath her words, a feeling of nervous worry thrummed like an ominous bass chord struck deep below the surface melody of their conversation.

For the next few hours the girls pursued their normal daily routines, but their conversation never really ended. They'd drop each other brief messages or questions as they arose and then receive a response a few minutes later. Sometimes the conversations were related to technical details, like the types of equipment the manufactory could produce or the food and air requirements for the canyon settlement. Other times, their conversations were just simple words of hello or expressions of happiness at meeting each other, at least virtually. Ceres was thrilled to have a non-AI friend to talk to, and it seemed Max was equally ecstatic about their new friendship.

The girls continued to discover interesting things about their conversation techniques. For instance, Max somehow managed to keep a network channel open while she was talking with Sonya, which allowed Ceres to listen in to both sides of the conversation. Ceres noted that Max's spoken voice differed slightly from her mental one: higher in pitch and a bit less mature. Ceres wondered if she projected a different tone in her mental words as well. Probably.

If Max had seemed worried about the Chorus, then Sonya seemed positively mortified. At first, Max had to explain to the Sister how she knew about the Chorus at all. When she admitted to Sonya that she was speaking to someone on the Persephone network, Ceres could almost *feel* the anger and fear radiating off the elder colonist. But as Max explained the situation, in particular the fact that she wasn't speaking to a computer but to a person, Sonya seemed to calm just a bit. But the woman also seemed perplexed.

"Ceres?" Sonya said. "Who is she? Does she live on the remains of the starship?"

"Not the remains, no. She lives on a reconstructed starship, built in orbit outside the asteroid belt after the Persephone protocol was initiated."

Sonya was silent, but Max relayed her perception to Ceres. *She looks confused by your existence,* she said to her distant companion. *By the existence of the rebuilt starship, too.*

"That makes two of us," Ceres muttered, but she kept this

comment to herself.

When Max told Sonya about the large amount of supplies being delivered to the settlement, the woman was instantly convinced that Darius had somehow cracked into the Persephone network and begun to supply a nefarious scheme to regain control of the colony.

Max pointed out, patiently, that the likelihood that Langford had broken into the network was very slim. The encryption key was something Sonya had randomly generated during the Disaster, and the only available copy of it existed in Max's DNA. Besides, Langford's internal network node was damaged beyond repair by the viral crash; the man suffered from horrible freezing spells as a consequence. He had neither the hardware nor the software means to connect to Persephone.

Sonya, however, remained unconvinced. She asked Max, "The last morning you were with Darius, what happened? Tell me again, as much as you can remember."

Max spoke again about the odd dreams she'd had, reliving those terrifying moments on the beach after chasing the Leap Fronds. Ceres told Max that she, too, had experienced a parallel dream that same evening. Max relayed that information to Sonya.

"So the two of you shared the same exact dream?" Sonya asked sharply.

"I guess so. Close enough."

"What else?"

Max paused to think. "My shoulder hurt that morning," she said. Then she sent to Ceres, *Sonya's grabbing my arm to examine it. She seems to very much enjoy grabbing my arm. I think next time she grabs it, I may karate chop her into next week.*

Ceres laughed aloud at this. "What is she finding?" she asked. She knew the question was much too late to matter to the conversation.

"It's been weeks, but there's still a residual knot of inflammation under the skin here," Sonya said. "Odd, given how quickly you heal from common injuries."

"What does that mean?" Max asked, alarmed. "Is something wrong with my shoulder?"

Sonya considered the question for a long time. "My guess is that Darius injected you with something," Sonya said. "Viral triggers to activate your network node, most likely. They caused a slight fever, which is what caused your vivid dreams. They also connected you with Ceres for the first time."

Max hesitated before saying, "But that's good, right? Now we have the means of asking for help from Ceres and the orbitals. Langford did us a favor."

"Don't credit my brother with generosity he hasn't earned," Sonya replied. "He may have injected you with the trigger to activate your network, but I'm sure he took something in return."

"Blood?"

"Yes. Skin and hair samples, as well."

"What would Darius do with any of that stuff? Can he genetically redesign himself or rebuild his damaged network node?"

"No, that kind of delicate reprogramming is far beyond the capabilities of any remaining equipment here on the surface. And besides, surgery to reconstruct a person's network node would have to be performed in microgravity. Darius can't fix himself any more than I can regrow my missing eye. The damage we suffered is permanent."

It was at that moment that Max received Ceres's panicked shout, emitted almost eight minutes earlier.

The Chorus is back! They're attacking the network!

After warning Max, it was all Ceres could do to fend off the onslaught of words, emotions, and what felt like physical blows being thrown at her from the host of aggressors on the surface. Ceres tried her best to defend herself but soon collapsed under the barrage of cyber-attacks. She had no experience with this kind of struggle and lacked the tools and techniques to make the battle anything other than a complete rout.

The attackers, once they defeated Ceres's pathetic defenses, ignored her. They virtually shoved the girl out of the way as they stormed past, uninterested in her at all. They seemed intent on seizing the rest of the Persephone network and wrested control from Ceres and Rhea to use the computer resources for their own purposes.

The scene was confusing and happened faster than anything in the physical world could ever occur. As Ceres watched, her virtual senses filled in details in an attempt to make the scenario comprehensible. As Max and Sonya spoke on the surface, oblivious for the next few minutes to the onslaught Ceres was suffering, the girl in the station watched the attackers charge through the virtual space. First, they flooded into the in-bin/out-bin space Ceres used to transfer messages to the manufactory. They smashed the artificial bin artifacts and seized control of the production facility.

Next, the attackers turned their attention to the primary resources of the Persephone network. They returned from their foray into the manufactory and directed their full might against the virtual ramparts of the Persephone network. But unlike their first trivially easy victory, this time Ceres watched as the attackers fell back from the walls, completely stymied by the static borders of the virtual space.

The attackers threw themselves against the barriers over and over again, endlessly and tirelessly. The border held, equally tireless in its impregnable stance. In the battle between the unstoppable force and the immovable object, the object was trouncing the force.

Ceres stayed clear of the conflict; she knew there was nothing she could do to change the eventual outcome, but the dread she'd felt when she'd first been pushed aside by the assault was slowly replaced by relief—it looked like the attackers couldn't gain a foothold into the deeper parts of the Persephone network.

Max's words finally caught up to the station's situation. "Ceres! Are you okay? What's happening up there?"

Ceres took a deep breath and pushed herself out of the virtual space. "The Chorus just tried to seize the station's computer resources, but our internal defenses seem to be holding. Their attack is failing. Rhea? A status report?"

"Packets on your encrypted network attempted to force their way into our standard network gateway via the virtual in-bin/out-bin you created to transfer requests to the manufactory. The virtual space was overwhelmed by cleverly malformed packets, but the rest of the network refused the subsequent request for resource usage."

"A bit less technical gibberish?"

Rhea said, "The Chorus wants access to our server space and computational resources. Persephone protocol doesn't allow for that sort of access. Even if the attack had been cleverer, the goal of the attackers is literally impossible. The new protocol cannot accept such a request."

Ceres found Rhea's second explanation as cryptic as the first. But a few minutes later, after Rhea's words flowed down into Max's brain and she relayed those words to Sonya, the elder colonist was able to explain things a bit more clearly to the two girls.

"Before the crash, the settlers used the network as an artificial extension of their physical minds. They used the orbital computer network for things like memory extensions, virtual spin-off personas, enhanced intelligence routines, limbic system blockers, and a host of other, even more destructive activities. As I've told Max before, most of the original settlers were completely addicted to the network systems, and their use had a seriously detrimental effect on productivity and colony progression."

Max said, "But the Persephone network isn't designed to support those higher functions, right?"

"That's right. The Persephone network's architecture limits human access to communications, information retrieval, simulation modeling, and manufacturing requests. Virtualization is strictly forbidden to outside parties. If your thought patterns are running on wetware, that's where they stay. No crossover between biological and quantum silicon."

"Then the Chorus is doomed to fail," Ceres said, "no matter what method of attack they employ." She then ducked her head back into the virtual space to watch as the Chorus banged their simulated heads against the simulated walls of Persephone, with no positive effect.

"Yes," Sonya eventually answered. "The network may still be vulnerable to viral attack, but against human infiltration? No worries there. Virtualization is a thing of the past for Leap."

As if on cue, the assault on the network stopped. Apparently the Chorus had reached the same conclusion as Sonya. Whoever was requesting all the equipment for the original settlement had failed in their virtual attack on the Persephone network, but now that they'd withdrawn, what would their next move be?

Curious, Ceres pulled up imagery of the original

settlement. What she saw made her eyes widen in surprise. She overlaid the image with directional vectors, and her heart sank.

"Max," she said, "I may be wrong—in fact, I sincerely hope I am—but I think you and Sonya may want to warn the other colonists. If I'm right, you might be encountering unexpected visitors." She looked to the screen again and frowned. "Lots of visitors. And soon."

WHEN CERES SENT HER WARNING about the host of mysterious visitors approaching, Max and Sonya responded by immediately traveling up and down the canyon to warn their fellow colonists to get indoors and seal their airlocks. Knowing that many of the colonists would refuse to believe that visitors were approaching from the abandoned original settlement, Sonya instead claimed that a sandstorm was approaching. Unexpected sandstorms occurred frequently on Leap, so a sudden storm served as a perfectly plausible reason to force everyone indoors before the invaders arrived.

After spreading their warning, the two of them headed up to the plateau above the canyon where they awaited the arrival of the people Ceres was following on her satellite feeds. Even though the space station's information was almost a quarter of an hour out of date by the time it arrived, Ceres's approximate arrival time was quite accurate. As if on cue, Max saw a small cloud of dust on the horizon, kicked up by the pounding of dozens of feet. Ceres had estimated at least fifty humanoid figures in the group from the old settlement, and soon enough Max could see the large crowd inside the dust cloud traversing the ground like the long-legged antelopes she'd seen in her history books.

On Max's first and only visit to Langford's home, it had taken her almost half a day to return from the old settlement to the new colony's canyon. The visitors that were now running toward them from the abandoned town covered the same distance in just over an hour. Their easy, ground-devouring gait appeared almost languid in its synchronized fluidity, and Max found herself mesmerized as she watched the group approach, much like she'd been mesmerized by the Leap Fronds so many days ago.

With a crackle, the commentary Ceres had been providing to Max cut out. Max looked up at the sky and tried to send her distant friend a message, but she felt reasonably certain it was futile. Whoever was coming from the old town had the ability to block Max's signal to the Persephone network. That meant she was cut off from her eyes in the sky.

The group must have spotted Max and Sonya standing on the canyon's edge, because a small number of them broke off from the herd and ran straight for them. Most of the group, however, maintained their original path for another few hundred meters before splitting into two large divisions: one heading for the northern end of the canyon, the other for the southern end.

Max felt her stomach drop as she watched these lightning-fast humans move in such synchronization. They invaded her home with smooth precision. She'd hoped that her presence on the plateau would distract the visitors from the rest of the colony, but the invading group hadn't fallen for their ploy.

The small group that was running directly toward the two of them drew up a few feet short. A small cloud of dust wafted past Max and Sonya, causing Max to cough involuntarily.

"We felt..." one of the new arrivals said.

"That it was time..." said a second.

"For a visit," a third continued.

"Long overdue..." said the fourth.

"In fact," the final, fifth figure said, finishing.

The Chorus, Max thought, as she experienced firsthand the eerie synchronous conversation Ceres had described.

Max studied the five individuals standing before her and wondered where they'd come from. What had brought them running toward the canyon colony so urgently? The small group consisted of three males and two females who were distinguishable based on different hair length and facial features, as well as slight variations in weight and height.

The differences, however, were much more subtle than the similarities. The five figures all appeared to be young adults. They each had bright blue eyes hidden under dark eyebrows and thick black hair. Their mouths and noses were small and delicate, and their skin was pale and smooth. The five of them looked like identical siblings.

Max had heard of multiple births when studying Earth's vast population of humans. She'd read about twins and triplets. She wondered, what did you call *fifty* identical siblings?

There was something else that was familiar about the five members of the Chorus standing before her. With a start, Max realized: *They look just like me!* Older, yes, and healthier, although Max's new diet and breathing routine was starting to change that. And of course, three of the Chorus members were male. But still, beyond those small details, Max might as well have been looking at five older versions of herself.

"My dear Sister," the first speaker said.

Another Chorus member said, "It's been a long time."

A third member added, "Much too long."

"Brother," Sonya said. "You have quite a way with entrances, don't you?" She gestured widely to take in both the five figures in front of her and the remaining Chorus members dispersing through the canyon. "A bit of overkill in terms of personal redundancy, don't you think?"

The five Chorus members laughed together as one. Max shuddered at the sound while her mind whirled. The "Sister" greeting was meant for Sonya, but not as an honorific. It was meant to indicate a sibling. But that meant...

"These people...they're *Darius*?" Max asked, bewildered.

"Of a sort, yes," Sonya said. "It looks like my brother 'borrowed' your genetics for his template. Just like he 'borrowed' most of his settler companions' personalities from their Earth-based primaries. Darius has a bad habit of taking what he wants for his own use and asking for permission later, if at all."

One of the clones waved a finger in the air admonishingly. Then four of them spoke. "Now, now, Sister. This is Our expedition and Our colony. That means the genetics we borrowed are already Ours. Hard to steal from Oneself, isn't it? Even when there are multiple versions of Oneself." The voices of the four speakers were so similar that Max had trouble telling who was speaking, and when.

"And the access key to the Persephone network? I suppose you didn't steal that, either, when you took this innocent child's DNA?"

"No," answered the Chorus, "that was also simply taking back what We rightfully own. Something *you* stole from *Us*, We might remind you."

Sonya laughed loudly. "Tell that lie to the historians on your payroll, Darius. We both know who originally wrote the network code you've been calling your own all these years. Why do you think it was so easy for me to subvert it after the viral outbreak?"

The clones glowered darkly. "A debatable point, who originally wrote that first bit of programming. What's not debatable is that your familiarity with the networking code didn't allow you to spot the New Puritan virus before it killed almost all of us. A shame, that."

Sonya looked furious for a moment—enraged by the blame Darius laid at her feet. Max watched as the Sister visibly controlled herself before saying, "Stealing *and* dodging responsibility, brother? Just when I thought I couldn't be more disappointed in you."

The Chorus members smiled as one. "Yes, you were always all about responsibility, weren't you? We suppose that's why you tried to send the starship back to Earth to bring help, before you realized the true magnitude of our predicament."

"Letting us believe that Earth was just a few light years away was cruel, even for you, Darius."

"Cruelty was never Our intention. Quite the opposite, in fact." The Chorus turned to address Max, and their combined voices took on a lecturing tone. "Some of Our original companions would never have traveled with Us if they'd known that the small starship required them to be digitized and simulated. It's sad that many of Earth's greatest minds had such a terrible opinion of simulated humans. You'd think that intellectuals would be the first to embrace mankind's next natural evolutionary step...

"We considered simulating a cryogenic ship, but even that type of imagined science would have caused a few of our passengers to balk. No, the fiction We created had to fit each and every passenger's psyche, no matter how delicate. For the most sensitive, We gave them the illusion that they'd traveled here to Langford's Leap in the flesh. As an added bonus, that meant that Earth, in the false history We wrote, was relatively close by. The safety blanket effect should never be overlooked. Nothing crushes the fragile mind more than realizing that help will never arrive."

"How well I know this," Sonya muttered.

"Still," the Chorus continued, "Sonya's futile attempt to call for help was not without ramifications. You see, We anticipated that someone might request Our starship to return to Earth for help someday. That request, obviously, was impossible to satisfy. Not only is Earth much too far away to provide a rescue, but the reconfigured starship that was orbiting the planet was *much* too large to travel interstellar distances. Not to mention its miraculous fusion engines that supposedly delivered us here in the first place are mere fabrications of whimsy.

"No, sending the starship to Earth was impossible. However, sending the starship to the outer limits of the Langford system to *emulate* a rescue sent from Earth was entirely within Our power. When Sonya sent our ship a signal instructing it to fly to Earth, the starship acknowledged the request. But instead of following that futile order, it rendezvoused with other available equipment and recovered from the viral attack while maintaining orbit out past the local asteroid belt."

"We know all of this already," Sonya snapped. "What of it?"

"Ramifications, dear sister. As you well know, artificial intelligence, while artificial, is not particularly intelligent. The automated systems that run the manufactories and other orbital equipment handle routine tasks quite well. But ask them to do something clever? That's a bit beyond their reach. In order for the starship to emulate a rescue from Earth, it needs a truly intelligent pilot." The Chorus paused and gave Max a pointed look. "A human pilot."

"Do you mean Ceres?" Max exclaimed.

The Chorus shrugged. "We never asked her name. The construction module that established its orbit beyond the asteroid belt rebuilt the original starship habitat. After reconstruction, mission parameters required that the station to be manned by a human being. As We said before, AIs are notoriously lacking in imagination and cleverness necessary in a starship pilot.

"Unfortunately, with no human crew onboard, and Sonya's Persephone network preventing contact with Leap to request further instruction, the station's AI was forced to resort to a backup plan. The station brought a brand-new human pilot into being, and that pilot has been living alone on the space station with nothing but a semi-intelligent ship AI to talk to for the last twelve to fifteen years."

"Oh my God," Sonya exclaimed and slumped to the ground as she realized the enormity of her actions. "That poor girl. What have I done?"

"Not your fault, really," Darius said. "You didn't know about our emulated rescue plan, did you? Of course, if you hadn't seized Our network and hidden it from Us with your infuriating Persephone protocol, We might have been able to reprogram the starship and abort its futile plan. So actually, the pilot's predicament is entirely your fault, now that We think about it."

"I never would have left her stranded alone up there had I known."

The Chorus laughed. "No? Are you so sure, Sonya? It's not as if you've behaved responsibly in the time since the viral crash, after all. Take, for instance, young Maxine. You've created this beautiful and talented young girl, far superior in every way to the other pitiful colonists who cower in their holes in the ground, but what do you do with her? You keep her woefully ignorant of her true potential! You poison her with base-human air and food!"

Max wanted to protest on Sonya's behalf, but Darius had a point. Why had Sonya let her suffer in ignorance for so long? Why had Sonya given her such wonderful gifts, only to keep them a secret from her?

"But Max is far better off than the rest of the colonists you so foolishly brought to term in the other artificial wombs. Why squander Our best technology by giving birth to genetic misfits? Pure humans are so ill-suited for survival on this planet, Sister. You've doomed them to lives of misery and despair, and for what? To keep humanity alive on Leap? What nonsense!"

Sonya, still slumped on the ground, said nothing. She was clearly still shaken by the realization that her actions had conceived and then imprisoned a child on an otherwise abandoned space station.

"And then, in the most ironic turn of events, Our Sister's new flock of suboptimal humans adopt New Puritanism! They embrace the same bigoted philosophies that caused Our exodus from Earth in the first place! Their prejudices, fostered by your inane preaching, encourage them to reject genetic enhancements that would vastly improve their lives, and instead, they hold out hope for rescue from Earth." The Chorus, as one, shook their heads sadly. "We wonder if the New Puritan virus still operates somewhere behind that empty eye socket of yours, Sonya. Otherwise, We fail to understand how you could behave so badly."

"She did the best she could," Max said, and balled her fists tightly against her thighs. "At least she tried to help us. All you did was run away."

"Yes, you're right, Max," The Chorus said. "We see now the errors in Our ways. We should never have relinquished responsibility for Our colony. And that brings Us to why We are here."

"You plan to lead us again?" Max asked incredulously.

The Chorus laughed. "No, of course not! We intend to take responsibility back from Our Sister. We've decided to move your remaining artificial wombs back with Us to the city. We'd hoped that you, Max, were a sign of progress. But it's obvious to Us now that you are the exception and not the rule. Sonya and her New Puritan misfits will continue to use the artificial wombs to birth more genetic throwbacks. We can't allow her to squander such valuable technology anymore."

Max could see Sonya's jaw clench in frustration, and she shared her anger. But what could the two of them do? They were no match for fifty copies of Darius inside adult clones of Max's body. If the Chorus wanted to take the artificial wombs, there was no way to stop them.

Sonya stood up. "You keep referring to yourself in the plural, Darius," she said quietly. "The royal 'We.' I can actually hear the capital letter in your voice. Back on Earth that kind of grandiosity was reserved for inbred idiots and insane despots. Which are you, I wonder?"

Darius shrugged off the jibe. "You should try living as a multiplicity, Sonya. It's really quite fascinating—sharing thoughts and experiences via encrypted personal network while inhabiting identical bodies and minds. It gives one a very unique perspective on the meaning of individuality. Unfortunately, this experiment of Ours still pales in comparison to the rich experiences that await Us in the virtuality, once We regain full access to the orbital network. Which, neatly, brings Us to the true reason for Our visit."

One of the Chorus members stepped forward and poked Max dead between the eyes.

"Me?"

"Not *you*, exactly," the Chorus said. "We thought We'd gotten what We needed from you when We took a sample of your DNA. But it turns out that the Persephone decryption key imprinted on your genetic code was malformed or otherwise damaged, and as a consequence, Our access to the orbital computing resources is incomplete. A vexing problem, as We're sure you can understand." The remaining Chorus members stepped forward as one. "What We need from you, We're afraid, is what's inside your head."

"I'm not sure I like what you're suggesting," Max said,

shrinking away from the Chorus member's finger.

"You'd be wise not to," the Chorus answered. "This time, Our procurement process may be a bit more...detrimental to your physical well-being."

"You'll not lay a hand on this child, Darius," Sonya said, jumping up and thrusting a warding arm between Max and the Darius clones.

"No?" one of them said. "We suppose you'll just give Us the complete encryption key, then? That would be easier."

Sonya shook her head. "I can't do that, Darius, because I don't have it. I generated the key inside one of the orbiting artificial wombs long before I initiated the Persephone emergency protocol. Max is the product of that womb, so she's the only one with the key. The new network encryption is as much a mystery to me as to anyone else."

"Pity," Darius said, and moved toward Max once more.

"Max can't give you what you're after either, brother." When Sonya had the Chorus' full attention again, she continued. "The Persephone network is hard-coded to limit human connectivity to simple tasks. What you want—recreating the virtual environments that crippled the first settlers, trapping them inside their own heads—that's no longer a possibility. You can't change that, and neither can Max."

"We don't believe you," Darius said five times over.

Sonya shrugged. "Your disbelief can't change things, either."

"We can't believe you would do that!" Darius screamed. "How could you steal the colony's greatest resource from its citizens and lock it away from their grasp? How could you *deprive* me like this?" In his fury, Darius momentarily slipped into referring to himself in the first person rather than the plural.

Sonya's laugh was bitter. "Listen to yourself, brother!

Deprive? You're living simultaneously inside fifty perfectly created bodies. You have orbital factories ready to deliver any object you can think of to your fingertips. You have a brand new world ready to explore, its secrets ripe for discovery. How, exactly, are you deprived? Of anything?"

"This?" The Chorus said, gesturing around themselves. Beyond the five, the rest of Darius's clones started arriving. Some of them were carrying the artificial wombs attached to large portable batteries. The objects looked heavy and awkward to Max, but the clones that were holding them seemed at ease with their weight.

"This," Darius continued, regaining his composure, "is nothing but another ball of mud, just like Earth. Our 'Leap' between the stars was more like a stumble. You see, We had convinced Ourselves, after the subjective millennia We had lived in the virtual, that returning to a physical form would offer something that was missing, but We were wrong. Living, biologically living, is obsolete, and living purely virtual, while much more forward-thinking, has its problems as well, We will admit. But the hybrid of the two—staying connected to biological imperatives while still enjoying the endless bounty that the virtual brings—that's where the true future of humanity lies.

"Did the original settlers flounder under the awesome weight of the orbital network and its cornucopia of delights? Perhaps. But it was nothing that time would not have resolved. Eventually, the settlers would have been able to better resist the overwhelming temptations of heaven and integrate the virtual with the real in perfect harmony."

Sonya scoffed at Darius's theory. "The colony wasn't getting any better, Darius. It was getting worse. You couldn't see it because you were worse than anyone else. You were lost for days on end to your virtual fantasies. If I hadn't planned a stop to it, the colony would have been doomed to failure.

Even if the virus hadn't struck, we were on a dead-end path."

"No," the entire Chorus said. "We weren't. And now, with the help of what's buried inside this young girl's brain, We'll unlock the orbital network, restart the virtuality again, and prove to you how wrong you were."

"She doesn't have the key, Darius," Sonya said again. "Virtual space is forever beyond your grasp."

"We still don't believe you, Sonya. We're going to take the artificial wombs you stole from Us and take this girl with the key locked inside her brain, and We're going to remake the colony in its proper image, just as We've always envisioned it."

The next few moments were almost too fast for Max to follow. The Chorus moved forward again, and Sonya stepped in to stop them. The Sister launched a flurry of blows, and to her credit, she managed to get a solid punch and a roundhouse kick to connect, knocking two of the clones backward onto the ground. But the remaining three clones, moving in a perfectly coordinated dance, quickly subdued the woman before she could inflict any more damage.

"Run!" Sonya screamed.

Max, standing on the edge of the canyon, had no place to go. They'd chosen their meeting spot rather poorly, she realized. A tiny laugh escaped her lips, like a panicked bubble. "Can we talk about this for a little longer?" she asked the Chorus hopelessly.

"Sorry," one of the Darius clones said. "The time for talk is over. We—" The clone stopped speaking suddenly and tilted its head to listen to something. Behind it, the massive host of clones all did the same thing, pointing their heads in various directions to try to capture the source of the sound they all heard.

Max could hear it too. And feel it: a deep, powerful rumble causing the soles of her feet to hum from the vibration. The sound bounced off the surrounding rocks, making it hard to tell where it was coming from. It grew steadily louder, and then, with a deafening roar, Nolan—straddling Max's motorcycle—arrived in a hail of dust and dirt. The Darius Chorus dove out of the way as Max's father skidded to a screeching halt just inches from Max and the fallen Sonya.

"Get on!" he shouted over the sound of the snarling engine. Max leaped onto the back of the bike and wrapped her arms around her father's waist. With a twist to the accelerator, the motorcycle took off. The front wheel left the ground, almost causing the rider and his passenger to fall off. Then Nolan got the bike under control again, and the vehicle sped off over the plateau, spitting gravel and barking noise.

The Chorus recovered from their initial shock and began to give chase, but even their inhuman loping gait was no match for the motorcycle, which quickly outpaced them as it raced across the terrain. It rattled Max's teeth in their sockets with every bump and crack in the rocky surface.

"How did you get it running?" Max shouted. She could barely speak loudly enough over the wind and engine noise.

Nolan let go of the bike's handlebars long enough to point upward. "Your friend sent a rescue package: gasoline, oil, and instructions on operating the bike. Not easy!" As if to illustrate, the bike wobbled as Nolan tried to dodge a large rock pile with only one hand on the controls, and Max flinched. Her father put both hands back on the handlebars and got them moving steadily again.

"Ceres did this?" Max asked.

"She can't communicate with you over the network. The signal has been blocked. So she sent me to rescue you, instead."

"Then why are you stopping?" she asked as her father eased the bike to a halt.

Nolan cut the engine so they could speak in relative

silence. "I have to go back, Max," he said.

"Go back? No, Dad, you can't! The Chorus will be waiting for you!"

"I know, sweetheart, but I still have to." Nolan stepped off the bike, and then lifted Max from the seat like she was a small child. "I've been working on upgrading the generator hookups all day, and my air filters are almost exhausted. Also, Ceres was only able to produce a small amount of fuel on such short notice, so this motorcycle contraption isn't going to run for much longer. But most importantly, the other colonists need my help. Who knows what Darius has planned for them? I have to go back and try to stop him—them. Or, if I can't stop them, then I'll do my best to protect the other colonists."

"Dad, please!" Max cried, although she knew even as she said the words that her father was right. She forced herself to accept the inevitable and tried a different tact. "If you're going to go back, at least take me with you. My ability to breathe without a mask gives me opportunities to help in ways no one else can. Let me help!"

"Sorry, Max," her father said. "Darius seems to have a particular interest in you. I can't risk taking you back and letting him capture you." He pointed at the distant horizon. "Keep moving away from the colony. Ceres will contact you somehow, or Sonya will find you. We'll figure out a way to solve all of this, once and for all."

"But Dad—"

Nolan bent down slightly to kiss her on the forehead. "Max, just go. Stay hidden and safe. This will all work out fine in the end. Trust me." He gently pulled away from her grasp and remounted the motorcycle. He gave her a confident wink, started up the bike, and without another word, he drove back toward the canyon.

Max fought the urge to cry. Now wasn't the time. She

pulled her shoulders back and took a few deep breaths to calm herself. She began walking in the direction her father had pointed to increase the distance between herself and Darius's Chorus. She only took about a dozen steps before a small white object drifted to the ground in front of her.

Max picked up the object and found it to be something very familiar: a paper airplane. But unlike the ones she and her peers crafted in school, this one was quite sophisticated. It had a tiny motor attached to it that operated control surfaces on the wings and a miniscule propeller to give it forward mobility.

"What is *this* doing out here?" she asked aloud. She looked around, but there was no sign of life in any direction. Shrugging, she examined the airplane more carefully and saw that its inner surface was covered with print. She unfolded the airplane and read the message that was revealed. Then she started laughing.

"Ceres!" she shouted, smiling up at the sky. "You are *quite* the clever girl, aren't you? I don't know what you have planned, but whatever it is, let's hope it works!" She waved the paper at the clouds above her, and then jogged across the terrain, following the course provided by her distant benefactor in space.

22

"IMMEDIATELY RELINQUISH CONTROL OF THE virtual space on Persephone. Communication with the colonists is prohibited. Manufactory production is prohibited. Cooperation is compulsory."

"Why must the Chorus speak to me like I'm a machine?" Ceres griped. She exercised her newfound mental muscles to shunt the incessantly repeating message into a muted side channel.

"Perhaps they are unaware that there is a human presence onboard this station," Rhea offered.

"Whatever. Whoever they are, they're not very polite. Even *you* deserve to be addressed with more respect than they're offering. But let's talk about what they're implying. Status update?"

"I am running diagnostics on our communications array but so far have not found anything malfunctioning or corrupted. Due to light delay, our surveillance satellites will be unable to confirm a communications interruption with Max for another six minutes. At that time we may see a visual response from Max if she loses contact with you. Worse, we may lose visual altogether if the Chorus blackout extends to our satellites."

Ceres was keeping her com channel open to Max and broadcasting her conversation with Rhea, just in case the Chorus threat was a lie. But Ceres wasn't particularly hopeful on that point—the Chorus had demonstrated a thorough comprehension of the Persephone network, so chances were good that they could enforce their threat to block communications with the surface. "What about the manufactory platforms?"

"We received an automated message just after the Chorus sent their demand. The manufactories have been instructed to ignore any subsequent requests for construction or materials. It seems the Chorus has isolated us from the colony and our orbital production facilities until we relinquish control of our internal network and computer resources."

"Great," Ceres said. "I can't speak with Max or send her help unless I give the Chorus something I don't have! And even if I *could* grant them access to our virtual space, there's no way that I *would*!"

"It seems, then, that we're at an impasse."

"Thanks, Rhea. You have *such* a way of stating the obvious." Ceres rubbed the bridge of her nose, thinking. The Chorus was up to something terrible, that much was now certain. Ceres didn't know what its plan was for the colonists on the surface, but it couldn't be anything good. And she was sure Max would be a prime target for whatever they were planning. At the moment, Max and Sonya were standing on the canyon's edge just waiting for the Chorus to arrive. Ceres had to get them out of there and fast.

An idea struck her. "Rhea, you said the message from the orbital prevents future requests for construction, right? But what about orders already processed?"

"Unknown. It's possible those orders would exist outside

the prohibition parameters established by the Chorus."

"Something to try then. But I'll need help from someone on the surface." Ceres looked at the monitors closely. "Rhea, zoom in on the generators." One of the screen images magnified, and Ceres recognized the figure standing by the bright red kite generators who was adjusting something on the cabling that connected it to the canyon. It was Nolan, Max's father. One of the few colonists Ceres instantly recognized. With a sigh of relief, Ceres hopped into virtual space and connected to the construction module on the manufactory.

"Requests for new construction or materials are now forbidden," the mustached avatar said by way of greeting.

"I'm aware," Ceres said. "Is the gift I requested for the colonists finished? If so, I'd like it delivered with this message." She handed the avatar a virtual representation of a set of instructions. Without waiting for a response, she left the virtual space. She knew her interaction with the actual avatar on the manufactory platform wouldn't occur for seven minutes, and it would take another seven minutes for her to know if her request was received and processed or not.

While she waited, Ceres returned her attention to the dozens of monitors focused on the canyon to see if the feeds would cut out. During the past few days, Rhea had managed to dramatically increase the quality of video coverage available during the daylight hours above the canyon. Now that their surveillance satellites weren't being shot down by the overzealous manufactory defense module, Rhea could seed the planet with more satellites and dynamically adjust their orbits to provide footage when it was needed. Ceres could see Max's face as clearly as if she was standing a few feet away from her. Her friend's nervousness was apparent in her furrowed brow and pursed lips.

The countdown to the Chorus blackout threat reached

zero, and almost exactly on cue, Max held a hand up to her ear. Then the girl looked up at the sky, her gaze by chance finding one of the many watching cameras. Ceres saw her friend mouth the words, *Hello? Ceres, are you still there?*

"I'm still here, Max," Ceres said. "You just can't hear me anymore. But don't worry. The Chorus can't get rid of me that easily."

"Video feed signal strength is strong," Rhea said. "We can continue to watch the planet surface. Apparently only your encrypted communication channel with Max is being blocked."

"Rhea, I need you to fix that communication channel."

"I don't have access to the encrypted channel, nor do I understand how the signal is being blocked—"

"Just fix it," Ceres snapped. "I need a way of communicating with Max if we're going to get her out of this mess!"

The computer fell silent. Ceres, fuming, watched the video footage and observed Max's confrontation with a small splinter group of the Chorus. The lip-reading algorithms had improved greatly with the enhanced satellite coverage, and even without a network connection to Max, Ceres was able to read the subtitles and follow along with the conversation.

Ceres was only mildly surprised to find out that the Chorus members were synchronized clones of Darius Langford. It explained the familiarity the group had shown with network protocols and manufactory capabilities, and it also explained how the Chorus knew enough about the network to block the encrypted signal.

Ceres was briefly interrupted by a message from the virtual. She dropped in and found that the manufactory's construction avatar had agreed to deliver the gasoline and oil she'd ordered earlier as a surprise gift for Max. The quantity of both substances that the chemical plant had managed to produce in such a short time period was quite small, but it was better than nothing. The fuel was already being delivered via the fastest method available while still keeping the cargo safe. Given its highly flammable content, speed versus safety was a delicate business, but Ceres had researched the manufactory's vast delivery technologies thoroughly and knew the contents would get to the surface intact, along with her message. She only hoped that Nolan, Max's father, would respond in time.

When she dropped back out of the virtual, she saw on the video footage that Sonya was slumped on the ground looking miserable, while the Darius clones were saying something about stealing back the remaining artificial wombs from the caves. Ceres had missed something important, but she didn't want to rewind the footage to find out what. She'd have to catch up on whatever it was later.

The plans the Chorus had for kidnapping Max and trying to recover access to the Persephone virtuality simply confirmed Ceres's fears, but it made her heart hurt to see his willingness to harm the girl to achieve his goals. Rescuing Max from the colony's crazed founder became even more urgent than before.

Hearing the Chorus disparage the planet below as a mere ball of mud shocked Ceres. How could something so wonderful and bountiful be dismissed so easily? Ceres had studied more about Earth during her brief moments of free time and knew that humanity's home planet had been absolutely full of people who were taxing the planet's ecosystem and natural resources, but Leap was almost completely empty and unexplored. The original settlers had only visited a tiny portion of just one of the planet's four continents after their initial survey for a suitable location for their first settlement. There were still more things to discover on the fledgling colony than Ceres could even imagine. Yet somehow, Darius Langford seemed to find all of that promise of discovery to be uninteresting. Ceres couldn't understand it.

"I have an idea," Rhea said, interrupting Ceres's thoughts.

"A way of recovering my network connection?" Ceres asked.

"No, that problem still remains intractable. However, I may have discovered an alternative means of communication you can use in the meantime. Physical delivery of messages via the manufactory."

Ceres shook her head. "Won't work, Rhea. We can't request newly manufactured items, remember?"

"True, but I was thinking about a completely separate subsystem. It was designed by Darius Langford to help the settlers celebrate holidays like birthdays and New Settlement Day."

"A separate subsystem? What are you talking about? I thought I'd visited all of the manufactory's subsystem avatars earlier."

"I have discovered evidence of a small, custom-built module of the manufactory that was tasked with delivering announcements and invitations for celebrations. The invitations were delivered via a variety of inventive methods, each designed for aesthetic purposes more than anything else."

"You're saying I can write a physical note to Max and tell the manufactory to send it to her disguised as a party invitation?"

"In essence, yes," the computer said.

"Simple enough," Ceres said with a chuckle. "Alright, then. The question is, what message do I send her?" Ceres bit her bottom lip as she thought. How did you defeat an army of clones? An army that could perfectly coordinate with one another at a visceral level, possessed intimate knowledge of your technology, had cut off your communications, and held most of your citizens hostage?

A physical confrontation was ludicrous. The Chorus members were graceful, perfect creatures, nothing at all like the lumbering, mechanized Darius Langford that Max had described meeting back at the original settlement. With his new cloned bodies, the colony founder had shrugged off the shackles he'd borne as a result of the collapse of the original network. His creatures were too fast and too clever to be defeated by the genetically inferior colonists, despite being outnumbered almost four to one. If the Chorus turned to violent tactics, they'd tear through the vulnerable colony population like Leap's ravenous tide assaulting the shore: implacable and deadly.

Ceres could almost hear the imminent threat, like the rushing of waves or the crushing collapse of space around her. It was coming, and she could do nothing to stop it. Time was trickling away.

And then, in a blinding flash of inspiration, a plan came to her, complete in almost every detail. She stood up and whooped with excitement. "Rhea! Connect me to the invitation delivery system. I know what to do."

Ceres only stayed in the virtual for the briefest of moments to scribble a hurried message to Max. If the earlier part of her plan didn't work, then this step was immaterial. If Max *did* manage to escape the Chorus and receive this first message, there would be plenty of time to deliver more detailed instructions. She handed her message to the invitation avatar—a beautiful white owl—and then dropped back into the station.

Ceres exited the virtual just in time to see Nolan bring the motorcycle to an abrupt halt in front of Max, wind whipping through his hair and tugging at his jacket, dust and dirt flying everywhere. Ceres gave another shout of happiness to see that the first part of her plan was working. She held her breath as the two escapees wobbled their way past the pursuing Chorus and streaked across the rocky plateau.

Part of the Chorus continued to chase the motorcycle, while the rest turned back to deal with the colony and with Sonya on the canyon cliff. Seeing the woman abandoned with the Darius clones was sobering and caused Ceres's jubilation to diminish. Saving the colony and all of its inhabitants was still far from a sure thing, she reminded herself.

Nolan took Max off into the high plains and rode toward the location Ceres had suggested. As instructed, he didn't go far before stopping the motorcycle, careful not to use up too much fuel and strand himself away from the colony without air. Ceres watched as Max's father bid his daughter farewell and turned the motorcycle back to the colony. Max's face said everything: the girl was on the verge of complete emotional collapse.

"Hang in there, friend," Ceres whispered. "Just a little while longer."

As if Max could hear her, the girl on the surface squared her shoulders and her face transformed itself from defeated to determined. She began marching across the plateau in the direction her father had indicated. She only took a few steps, however, before she was interrupted by a fluttering white object drifting down from the sky.

"What is that?" Ceres asked.

"Your message," Rhea responded.

"Okay. But what *is* it?" It looked like a miniature version of the delivery craft the manufactory used to drop materials from orbit.

"I believe it's called a paper airplane. It is meant to be a whimsical way to deliver a party invitation."

Ceres watched as her distant friend caught the paper craft and, after a pause, unfolded it and read the message printed on its surface. The girl laughed, raised the paper above her head, and waved. Ceres waved back, not at all concerned with the absurdity of the gesture. "Glad you got your invitation, Max," she said. "Now it's time to invite the rest of the guests."

Twenty minutes later, Ceres watched as dozens of paper airplanes floated down to the planet surface. Some were delivered to the canyon home of the colonists, landing at the feet of the Chorus sentinels. Others fell to the ground just a few steps in front of the group of Chorus members still searching for Max on the plateau. One of the Chorus members picked up a paper aircraft and read the message that was enclosed. A satellite surveillance camera gave Ceres a perfect image of the unfolded piece of paper, allowing her to read her own message: "Release the colonists unharmed, and I will deliver Max to you."

As one, the Chorus looked up at the sky. As one, they said, "Agreed."

Ceres took a deep breath. "Alright, Rhea. The invitations are delivered. Let's plan the party, shall we?"

Without waiting for an answer, Ceres began her preparations.

23

MAX LOOKED AROUND. SHE DIDN'T recognize anything.

Of course, the last time I traveled this way it was during the middle of the night in a dust storm after being chased by an angry mob of children...

Sighing, Max picked up her pace and headed for the location Ceres had suggested in the paper airplane message. After observing the Chorus in motion, Max had adjusted her gait and realized that she, too, could adopt their loping, long-strided run and cover ground much more rapidly than she otherwise would have. It was movement the other colonists couldn't match. They weren't built for this planet. Max was.

The weather and lighting aren't the only things that are different than the last time I made this trip, Max realized. *I'm a completely different person, now: healthier, stronger, faster. And wiser, although sometimes I wish I wasn't. What was that quote we learned in school? "Where ignorance is bliss, 'tis folly to be wise." Wise words, indeed.*

By the time Max started descending the final slopes and cliff faces to the shoreline, the sun was low on the horizon and falling fast. Despite her trepidation about treading too far into the tidal flats, she followed the instructions Ceres had sent to her and carefully marched out through the puddles left from the last high tide. She stopped when she was a few hundred meters away from the cliff face, looked up at the purpling sky, and said, "Okay. Now what?"

As if on cue, an object dangling from a tiny parachute dropped from the sky. Max darted forward to catch the object in her hand, but unlike her last visit, this time her newfound agility allowed her to dodge the salty puddles and stay dry. Smiling at her clever maneuvering, Max looked down at the latest gift from above.

The object was a stubby and cylindrical, about the length of her hand. One end was flat, while the other was capped by a silver dome. Jutting from the cylinder's sides were two blocky appendages which extended a short distance past the flat end of the cylinder. The cylindrical body was mostly white, but it was decorated in strange blue shapes and odd protrusions. Nothing about it suggested a practical function or use.

"What is this thing?" Max asked. She looked up again, but the few stars that had started to poke through the sky provided no answers. Shrugging, she turned back to examine the object more closely.

The appendages swung back and forth, but seemed to serve no other purpose. The dome twisted around on the cylinder, but also seemed to provide no result. Max pushed and prodded the object but nothing happened. She peered at it and noticed black dirt jammed into a small crevice on the body of the object. With her thumbnail, she scratched at the dirt to try to scrape it free.

"Help me, Obi Wan Maxine. You're my only hope."

"Aiee!" Max replied to the sudden voice coming from the object. She sat down hard on the sand.

"Sorry about that," Ceres's voice said. "I don't know what this thing is either. A gag gift from our illustrious founder,

Darius. Adults are weird."

"Understatement," Max muttered.

The object said, "This invitation gave me the opportunity to deliver a more detailed audio message instead of text. I thought you'd want to hear a friendly voice right now."

Max realized, sitting on the sand, that hearing her friend's voice was *exactly* what she needed right now. She looked up and gave the sky a thumbs up. *Thanks!* she mouthed at Ceres, who she knew was watching.

"We don't have much time. In a few minutes, the Chorus will be showing up. I gave them your location—"

"You did *what*?" Max shouted.

"—and it won't take them long to arrive," Ceres's voice continued, oblivious to Max's protest. "Darius, in his plurality, has agreed to spare the colonists in return for access to the virtuality. You and I both know we can't deliver on that promise even if we wanted to, but Darius seems to want to believe that we're lying, and I thought we'd play on that suspicion. Here's what I'm thinking..."

As Max listened to Ceres's plan, she realized that her space-borne friend had devised a very clever solution to the colony's current dilemma. Unfortunately, it was also a plan riddled with unexplored details and unanswered questions. Max voiced a few of those questions to the sky, hoping Ceres could see her and understand her even as the darkness fell, but she feared that there was no time for another invitation from space to clarify. Max was going to have to work with the plan Ceres had provided to her and hope things worked out correctly. If not, she'd be forced to improvise.

Without warning, the Chorus appeared, flowing down the cliff face like a human tidal wave. Max gave the talking object in her hand a brutal twist, and with a squawk, the thing fell silent. She tucked it into an inner pocket of her jacket and braced herself for the arrival of Darius.

She didn't have long to wait. The Chorus stormed onto the beach and encircled her quickly to prevent her from fleeing. Some of them were still carrying the artificial wombs with their temporary battery packs attached. The entire group buzzed and swarmed around her, never ceasing in their movement, which made counting them difficult. Max couldn't be sure if Darius had left anyone behind at the canyon, but she suspected that he had, even though that wasn't part of the deal Ceres had struck with the Chorus. Darius Langford was shrewd and not about to release the colonists and give up his major point of leverage against Max.

"A strange place to find you, Maxine," the Chorus said, sharing words among its members so that it seemed like a single stationary voice was speaking right in front of her. "The tide will be rising soon. Did your last visit not teach you proper respect for the forces of nature at work here?"

Max shrugged. "I wanted to see the Leap Fronds one more time before you started digging around in my head."

"Ah," sang the Chorus. "They are wonderful, aren't they? A pity that creatures as delicate and magnificent as my genetically augmented plants are such a rare thing in nature. In the virtuality, however, such fantastic creations only require the effort of imagining them. Leap Fronds would be far from the most wonderful thing you'd find in that world."

Max turned to look toward the tide she knew would be coming soon. "Did you ever consider, Darius, that their rarity, and the effort it took to physically produce them, is what makes the Leap Fronds so wonderful?"

As she spoke, Max was struck with a realization like a hammer blow. She was rare, and special, and different. She'd spent her whole life wanting to *not* be any of those things. She'd wanted to be normal, and common, and the same. But perhaps it was those things that made her different that also made her wonderful in her own right.

Darius, however, didn't share her sentiment. "Struggling against adversity is admirable when it's necessary. But when you struggle without need? That's pitiful. Sonya could never understand that." The Chorus started moving closer. "No matter. The time for philosophical discussions is over. Let's move to a higher vantage point. We will grant you one more audience with the Leap Fronds and the tide, and then We shall retire to my home and start...how did you put it? Ah, yes. 'Digging around in your head.'"

Max held up a hand. "Stop," she ordered. "No need for digging. I can give you what you came for."

The swirling Chorus came to an abrupt stop. One member stepped forward. "Can you, now? And how is that?"

"Sonya lied to you," Max said. "I have access to the virtuality. I've had it since you activated my network node. I can give you the key, and I will, in exchange for the promised safety of Ceres and the colonists. Forever."

The single Chorus member standing before her squinted at her and said, "Why would We do that for you? Why not just take back what is rightfully mine?"

Max spread her hands. "What do you have to lose? The colonists are pathetic weaklings. They're no threat to you. You proved that today when you marched into their caves and took what was yours with no resistance. Let them scratch out a meager life in the dirt. What does it matter to us?"

"Us?" the Chorus repeated.

"As you said when we first met, we're different." Max gave him a confident smile. "It's time I embrace that difference, isn't it? Accept my true nature. After all, I've seen the virtuality you're searching for. And you're right—it's everything you've promised, and more."

As Ceres had predicted, mentioning a visit to the virtuality—a complete fabrication on Max's part—was exactly the right bait to lure the Chorus into their trap. Max could see it in the eyes of the member she was talking to and, looking over the clone's shoulder, in the expressions of the other members of the Chorus. It was the same expression Darius had exhibited in his previous form, back when he'd first realized that Max's DNA gave her access to the Persephone network.

It was the look of hunger.

"Give Us the key," Darius said, "and We will take you with Us into the virtuality. Ceres can join us as well. Together, We'll live the lives the colonists were meant to live, and leave the base humans to the dirt-scratching." As a group, the Chorus began laughing in anticipation of their imminent victory. The swarm began dancing around her again.

Maniacal laughter. Great. Trying to play the part, Max joined in. When the noise died down, she said, "I'll need communications with Ceres restored in order to access the virtuality."

"We anticipated your request," The Chorus said, "and sent the command to rescind Our communication block a few minutes ago. Considering the light-speed time lag caused by the habitat's current orbital position, we should regain communications in—"

"Max!" Ceres's voice rang in Max's ears. Finally, Max's smile and laughter were genuine.

"She's back," Max said to the Chorus. Then she held up one finger as she listened to the instructions Ceres was providing to her via the restored network link. She tilted her head slightly, puzzled. "A handshake?" she said aloud.

Darius laughed again, and the Chorus came to a standstill as each member intertwined hands and fingers with their neighbors. The final free hand belonged to the single member standing in front of Max, who extended it toward her.

"The Handshake protocol for the most secure sharing of

information is conducted via physical touch. A security measure We introduced when We first arrived. If you're not willing to touch someone, then you're probably not willing to share your innermost secrets with that person. But we're beyond that stage, aren't we, Max? We have trust now."

No, we most certainly do not have trust. But she reached out and took his proffered hand. Then she followed the instructions Ceres had given her. She envisioned standing in the middle of a bright yellow room. It took a moment of intense concentration, but eventually Max was able to open her inner eye, and she found herself standing in the space she'd been imagining. The warm glow felt like gentle sunshine on her skin, and she smiled despite the deadly seriousness of the situation.

All around her, the various clones of Darius faded into existence in the yellow room. Their jaundiced smiles sobered Max.

Nodding a terse greeting to the Chorus, Max stepped forward and touched one of the warm glowing walls. Its surface gave way and dissolved, revealing a total nothingness that was darker and deeper than the lowest caves in the canyon.

"The virtuality," she said, and gestured at the open space before her. "As promised."

"*Yes,*" the Chorus said with eyes aglow. As one, they stepped toward the opening, but hesitated. Then they stepped back and bowed to Max. "Ladies first."

"Ladies...what?" Max stammered.

"Please," Darius said, gesturing to the opening. "After you." His clones were still smiling, but there was a tinge of wariness in their eyes. The Chorus still wasn't completely convinced of Max's sincerity.

Now what? Max thought, and felt panic rising from her gut. Ceres had explicitly warned her not to enter the darkness behind the wall. But if Max didn't enter, Darius would become even more suspicious, and the trap they'd set for him wouldn't work. And if Max entered the darkness, wasn't she falling into the same inescapable trap? Was that a sacrifice she was willing to take?

She thought about her father, and Sonya, and all the other colonists back at the canyon who were struggling just to survive on Leap's surface. She thought about the terrible suffering Darius would inflict upon them if he didn't get what he wanted. Max could prevent that suffering, but only if she was willing to take the responsibility onto her own shoulders. Was she willing to take that step? Could she bear such a heavy burden?

Max made her decision, and instead of collapsing under the weight of the responsibility, she felt free. Laughing, she grabbed one of Darius's hands, took a deep breath, and *leaped*.

Darkness closed around her, and with it came howling voices and scrabbling fingers. Max screamed and fought to escape the clutches of the horde of attackers surrounding her. Somewhere nearby in the darkness, she could hear Darius struggling against the same assault while shouting incoherently.

Swinging her arms wildly, Max managed to break loose for a brief moment, and through the gloom she saw Darius being mobbed by shadowy figures. The clone locked eyes with her, and his glare was murderous. "This is the old network!" he screamed. "The *infected* network! What have you done? You've doomed us all!"

Another Darius popped into existence next to the first and

was assaulted by the same shadowy claws and screeching voices. The first clone shouted, "No! Go back! It's a trap!" But it was too late. Like a string of paper dolls, each of the Chorus members blindly followed the next into the darkness of the infected network, and each met with the same attackers.

Max lost sight of the Chorus as she was crushed by a renewed assault from the shadowy, shrieking creatures that infected the virtuality. They pulled at her arms and legs; their claws and teeth scratched and bit her. Their voices demanded access to her identity and her data stores. Max fought with everything she had, kicking, punching, kneeing, and elbowing her way through their masses in her attempt to break free. Their attack was relentless, however, and their incessant shouting began to drill into her head. It made her want to answer their pleas just to get them to stop asking. Instead, Max kept fighting, hoping that, somehow, she could break free again.

Over the din of the banshee attackers and her own shouting, Max heard the Chorus cry out, "Don't you realize who I am? I'm Darius Langford! I founded this colony! All of this belongs to me!"

There was the tiniest moment of silence, and Max's attackers released her from their grasp as they spun to face the Chorus. Then the assault began again, furious and triumphant as they charged, focused solely upon the members of the Chorus.

Darius's proclamation of identity had apparently fed the banshee frenzy, and the clones were now reaping the result of their hubris. Max, enjoying a brief respite, began frantically searching for an exit from the corrupted virtuality. The darkness wasn't as total as it had first appeared, and Max was able to see a short distance away in the dim, dingy light. Unfortunately, what she saw wasn't promising. She and Darius appeared to be standing in the middle of a featureless plain. Other than the banshees and the pale, directionless light, there was nothing else of interest. Max spun in place and squinted into the darkness in search of something that would point her toward an escape route.

The sky—or the ceiling, Max wasn't really sure—flickered dimly, like the flash of lightning from a distant storm. In that brief flash, Max thought she saw the shadow of something on the horizon. With nothing else to go on, she began running toward the object and hoped her eyes weren't playing tricks on her.

Distance was a strange, malleable thing in the virtual, because within moments, the object she'd seen on the faraway horizon floated out of the gloom and revealed itself as a mammoth tower. Max halted in front of its enormous stone base and looked up. The imposing rock structure stretched beyond the limits of her vision.

Behind her, the struggle between Darius and the banshees raged on, which sparked Max's urgency. She ran around the base of the tower, but there were no obvious entrances or openings. Desperately she approached the structure and tried to climb its surface, but the stone was cold and slick beneath her hands and provided no purchase. She fell back in defeat. She knew the banshees would eventually turn their attention toward her. She could practically feel the clawing fingers of the banshees on the back of her neck. She had to escape this place, but she didn't know how.

Looking up at the tower again, she noticed a tiny gleam of light high above her that hadn't been there before. It ignited a glimmer of hope in her heart. Peering upward, she tried to determine what she was seeing. It looked like an opening in the tower! But it was toward the top of the structure, far from the ground where Max was trapped. How was she going to get up there?

Still looking up while she pondered this question, Max was

kissed on the cheek by the feather-light touch of a gossamer line of rope that descended from the top of the tower. The golden line of salvation barely touched the ground when it halted in front of her.

"Grab it and start climbing, Max!" came the call from above. It was Ceres, coming to the rescue.

Not needing to be told twice, Max grabbed the rope and started pulling herself upward. The rope was thin and slippery, and climbing it was a challenge.

Behind her, the banshees had heard Ceres's cry and split off from their attack on the Chorus. They ran toward Max, slavering and screaming obscenities. Terrified, Max pulled even harder on the rope and willed herself upward.

Above her, Ceres began hauling the rope back into the tower to accelerate Max's ascent. The banshees leaped upward, scrabbling at Max's heels and gnashing their teeth ineffectually. They tried scaling the tower walls but found no better purchase than Max had. Gritting her teeth in determination, Max continued to climb.

"Stop!" she heard from below her. "Don't leave me here!" It was the Chorus, still struggling mightily against the banshees. Max saw Darius in his plurality, looking up at her and pleading. "Please!" he shouted.

Gritting her teeth, Max turned back to the tower.

Howling in frustration below, the viral banshees began piling one on top of another and gained height purely based on their mass. Their numbers seemed endless, and as the pile grew beneath her, Max began to fear that they'd overtake her. Once again she renewed her efforts to climb faster. The sharp strands of the rope cut into her hands and slicked the rope with blood, further complicating her ascent.

One of the Chorus members broke away from its group of attackers and ran up the pile of banshees, batting away the claws that snatched at it. At the top of the pile, the clone launched itself at Max, and rage twisted its features into something inhuman.

Max screamed, released the rope with one hand, and caught the Chorus member on the side of the head with her fist. It tumbled back down onto the writhing mass of attackers below, and the entire pile of clones and banshees teetered and fell in on itself. Hanging on for dear life with one hand, Max silently cheered as the banshees collapsed. Then she returned to the act of climbing and saving herself from the destructive forces wailing below her.

It seemed to take forever, but eventually Max reached the windowsill and tumbled inside. Behind her, the window slammed shut, and the sound of the howling banshees vanished. Rolling onto her back, she looked up to see a blurry man with a long mustache peering down at her. He offered her a hand and said, "Welcome to the manufactory."

Wiping the blood from her palms on the legs of her overalls, Max took the man's hand and was pulled to her feet. Then she nearly fell over again as she was tackled by a bundle of blond-haired energy.

"You made it!" the girl who tackled her shouted as she laughed and squeezed Max with all her might. Then she pushed her back and demanded, "What were you *thinking*, entering the corrupted network? When I first entered the infected network I only survived a few seconds before applying a filter to de-amplify the signal. You could've lost your mind in there! Or worse!"

Max, rattled by the boisterous greeting and equally energetic scolding, said, "I had no choice. The Chorus wouldn't enter unless I went first."

The girl scowled at her, but then she gave up on her anger and began beaming again. "All is well that ends well, right?"

Max didn't answer. She just stared at the girl standing in front of her. Ceres may have recognized her from weeks of orbital surveillance, but Max had no such association. She knew her friend's voice, but this was the first time she'd ever seen what her friend looked like.

Ceres was everything Max wasn't. Her wavy blond locks, glittering green eyes and soft, round cheeks all were in sharp contrast to Max's ice-blue eyes, high cheekbones, and straight black hair. Her skin seemed to shimmer with health, tan and taut, completely unlike Max's pale complexion. Ceres's room-brightening smile was wide and genuine and showed perfectly straight white teeth.

Before Max could study her friend further, Ceres said, "There's no time for any of this. We have to get you out of here!" She grabbed something from the floor next to her and pulled it over Max's head and around her shoulders.

"What is this thing?" Max asked and shrugged into the strange harness-like contraption.

"A virtuality artifact," Ceres said, as if that explained anything. "Just trust me." She quickly finished buckling the front of the device with nimble fingers. She stepped back and nodded once in satisfaction.

Max looked down, and then back up at Ceres. "Now what?"

"Pull that handle," Ceres said, pointing to Max's chest. "And get ready to run!"

"Run? But I—"

"Max, go!"

Max bit back her questions, reached down for the harness that was buckled around her shoulders, and yanked the handle. There was a strange sensation, almost like an airlock unsealing, and with a blink, the virtuality around her disappeared and was replaced by millions of green-glowing stars.

No, Max realized, *not stars. Leap Fronds.* Darius's glowing creations were racing past her. And that meant only one thing. Max could feel the sound of the impending tide begin

278 | Langford's Leap

to vibrate through her bones. Wasting no more time, Max turned and ran for the cliff side.

Even in her panic, the analytical part of Max's brain calmly noted that she was much faster and more agile than her last beach visit. She hurdled rocks and scaled stone faces at an astounding rate, and raced up the side of the hill with no more difficulty than if she were strolling across a flat field. Within seconds she'd reached a reasonably safe point high on the hillside and took a moment to turn back to where she'd been standing.

Frozen in various states of motion were the members of the Chorus. A few had fallen over and were lying in the sandy muck, their limbs locked in odd positions. Others were paralyzed in midstep, like dancing statues. In the failing light of dusk, their silhouetted forms cast long shadows across the swampy ground. Despite the imminent arrival of the destructive ocean waves, none of them moved.

Max knew she should continue her climb, but she suddenly felt as paralyzed as the figures below her. Darius's minds were still locked inside the virtuality as they battled futilely with the viral banshees that had seized control of the original orbital network. On the planet surface, his physical forms were unaware of their impending doom. It was much too late for Max to try to save any of the clones. All she could do was watch.

The first tidal wave arrived, and the Chorus was immersed in frothing, pounding surf. Most collapsed and were swept away with the wave, but a few of the Chorus resisted the first wave blast for just a moment because by chance their locked limbs braced against the surging water. Then they too were overwhelmed by the force of the sea and were swept away— lost in the deepening waters. A few were still clutching the artificial wombs they'd confiscated from the canyon, and those too were lost to the ocean's advance. Max watched for a few more seconds, a small part of her hoping that one of the clones would recover from its stupor and cry for help, but she could hear nothing but the pounding water. She knew rescue was futile.

With a sharp cry, Max tore her gaze from the encroaching water below and forced herself to start running up the slope and toward safety again. Tears streamed down her cheeks and she sobbed as she ran. She shook her head at her own irrational mourning for the man who'd tried to kill her and her fellow colonists. But despite herself, she kept crying.

Leap had lost its founder. Darius Langford was dead.

24

"HE'S ALIVE?"

Sonya shrugged. "If you can call it that, yes." She gestured to the three remaining clones of Darius who were lying on makeshift cots in one of the canyon's caves, their eyes moving rapidly underneath their lids, their breathing deep and slow: the only three clones who hadn't pursued Max onto the tidal flats, left behind to guard the colonists in the canyon. They'd followed their brethren into the virtuality of the corrupted network, and now they were trapped in the same digitized hell.

"How long can they survive like that?" Max asked, staring at their comatose forms.

Sonya looked concerned. "Not long, I'd say. The virtuality is destroying my brother's psyche, tearing his mind apart piece by piece. Perhaps Ceres can help. With the proper surgical equipment, I might be able to disable his network wetware and free him from the virus."

Max studied the unconscious forms, doppelgangers of her body that had been stolen from her. Watching older, near-identical copies of herself was eerie. She shuddered. "*Should* we free him, though? After what he's done..."

Sonya shrugged again and looked very sad. She swept her hair over her ears, uncharacteristically letting her scar and missing eye show. "He's always been selfish and in many ways extremely short-sighted. But he was the victim of the virtual as much or more than anyone else. If I can free him of it, I feel I should. He's my brother. I owe him that much, at least. Once he's free, we can discuss how he can atone for his numerous sins."

Max didn't have a response, so she sat in silence for a while with Sonya, watching over the sleeping forms of Darius. Eventually, Max murmured, "Ceres will research the proper surgical equipment for disabling Darius's wetware. She'll drop it as soon as she's able."

Sonya nodded and gave her a small smile of thanks. Max gently touched Sonya's shoulder, not sure how to respond to the woman's grief for her fallen sibling. Ducking her head, Max left the cave, letting Sonya commune with her brother in peace.

In the outer passageways, colonists whispered loudly behind their masks as they passed by. Max ignored them. She'd come to terms with the shock the colonists expressed at her physical abilities. Or rather, given everything that had happened, she found their reactions inconsequential. Some of the colonists wanted to thank her for saving them. Others wanted to vilify her for not being pure. But Max didn't bother to acknowledge either group's sentiments. She no longer cared about being included or being the same as everyone else. She no longer cared about being different or if she was tagged as a hero or a villain. The issues weren't even mild concerns for her anymore. She'd grown past all of it.

More than that, Max seemed to have grown past any emotional connection to anything or anyone, except perhaps her friend Ceres. Her long conversations with her distant friend were sometimes the only form of communication she engaged in all day. The other colonists, including Sonya and her father, were just not important to her anymore. And Max really couldn't explain why.

As the weeks passed, Max spent most of her time wandering the surface, or—even better—puttering around on the motorcycle. Her father had been leery of letting her operate the machine, but Max knew she could do as she pleased because no one was physically capable of stopping her. So she politely but firmly ignored Nolan's words of caution and used the fuel Ceres regularly dropped to the surface to spend long days motoring across the landscape, taking in vistas no other colonist had ever seen before. Alone in the wilderness, but far from alone—she shared her expeditions with Ceres, whose fast-approaching ship was steadily decreasing the time lag of their talks.

Ceres made up for Max's ambivalence toward the colonists with a wealth of technological gifts from the sky. In short order, the colony was awash with new equipment that would greatly improve their living conditions in the canyon. They received new food supplies, including plant seeds for fruits and vegetables that would thrive on the surface of Leap and still provide nutrients for both base-human and modified-human physiques. More generators were also delivered, tapping into solar, wind, water, and geothermal sources. And Ceres was hard at work creating an advanced strain of algae that would produce a much greater supply of breathable oxygen for the colonists.

She also provided surgical equipment that allowed Sonya to successfully disconnect the remaining Chorus members from the network. It took two days before the first clone—a female—opened her eyes. Diagnostic equipment indicated that physical trauma from the surgery was minimal and the clone's brain was functioning normally. But the woman's stare was empty.

A few hours later, when the other two clones regained consciousness, they possessed the same empty, disconnected look. Darius's bodies may have been released from their prison, but his mind, apparently, was still trapped in the virtual. Max, observing Sonya after the last clone woke up, couldn't tell if the woman was dismayed or relieved by the apparent absence of her brother's consciousness. Max found herself wavering between both emotions, which was disconcerting. She used her conflicted feelings as another excuse to escape to the planet's wilderness, far from the confusion of colony life.

Three weeks after defeating the Chorus, Max was once again alone on the plateau, watching the stars. Ceres had been unusually quiet for the past few hours, which actually suited Max just fine. She was sprawled on a large boulder, enjoying the biting cold of the night air and basking in the starlight. Their ancient light kissed her bare skin. Max loved the stars. Their steady, unchanging nature was utterly unaffected by the turbulent events occurring on the tiny world below them. The ambivalence of the cosmos provided Max a strange sense of comfort.

"I have something for you," Ceres whispered.

Sighing at the interruption, Max said, "What is it?"

"Look to the west," Ceres said. Her response was almost instantneous—the habitat was approaching its new orbit around Leap. "You'll see."

Max had grown to recognize Ceres's tone over the weeks, and she recognized mischief in her friend's voice. The nonverbal connotation was contagious, and Max grinned despite herself. She sat up and looked toward the western horizon. It was a cloudless, moonless night, but even against the black sky, Max could see the silhouette of an approaching delivery. The object was huge—easily twice as large as anything else Ceres had dropped to the surface. And unlike the common delivery method of parachute, this object was drifting to the surface on wings. Looking at it, Max was struck by its uncanny resemblance to the paper airplane party invitations Ceres had dropped a few weeks previously, only this time writ large upon the starry sky.

"What's in it?" Max asked.

"Nothing yet," Ceres said. "The delivery mechanism is also the delivery object. At least in this direction."

"What? I don't understand." Max stared as the giant winged craft drifted overhead, almost close enough that she could reach up and touch it. Giant, bulbous wheels jutted from the belly of the plane, and they squealed as they touched the plateau surface.

"Why are you just standing there?" Ceres asked. "If you want to understand, get in!"

Needing no further encouragement, Max chased after the plane. It taxied across the unfriendly surface, huge shock absorbers bumping and rattling as the craft slowly rolled to a halt. When she approached, a small staircase descended from the belly of the craft. Max, perplexed, took the steps slowly and peered inside the cockpit above. The space was sparse—there were no instruments or control mechanisms and no windows. There was only a simple crash couch, which was currently empty.

"Want to go for a ride?" Ceres asked, the voice in Max's head echoed by an invisible speaker somewhere inside the cockpit.

"I...don't know," Max said. "How does this thing work?"

"Get in, and I'll explain."

Max lowered herself onto the control couch. The soft surface enveloped her, and automated safety straps snapped into place to secure her. With a soft hiss, the stairway entrance rose up into the belly of the airplane, enveloping her in total darkness. "I can't see—" Max began.

The cockpit faded away, leaving Max with an unobstructed view in any direction she looked. She reached out toward the stars above her and rapped her knuckles on the invisible cockpit wall.

"The cockpit is equipped with the latest in advanced optics," Ceres explained. "One of my many research projects. No worries, the plane's still there. The cockpit just projects the world around you so you can see where you're going."

"Okay," Max said, not entirely convinced. "And where am I going?"

Before she got a response, she was shoved very hard into the control couch. She watched through the invisible cockpit walls as the plane accelerated across Leap's rocky surface. With a slight lurch, the craft lifted off the ground and began to climb upward at a steep angle. Max peered over one shoulder to see the ground below her quickly dwindle to tininess. Her grip on the armrests of the couch tightened involuntarily.

"Don't worry," Ceres said. "You're completely safe. The airplane is a modified version of my shuttle craft that I've used to explore the asteroid belt for years. It's a well-tested design. And Rhea's doing the piloting today for you. You're in very good...hands. Or whatever the AI equivalent would be." Ceres laughed at that.

Max, still feeling a bit panicky at the ever-increasing altitude, asked, "And where is Rhea taking me, exactly?"

"Oh! You haven't guessed yet?" Another playful chuckle. "Well, the habitat just reached parking orbit. So I felt it was about time for us to meet in person. Don't you think?"

Max's head swung around from the ground, and she looked upward to the starlit heavens, eyes wide. "You're bringing me up to the station?" she asked. "We're going to meet each other?"

"Yup!" Ceres responded. "And in style, too! The flight will

take a few hours, so sit back and enjoy the view. I'll see you in a few!"

CERES DID HER BEST TO stop bouncing. The microgravity of the docking bay wasn't conducive to nervous twitching—something as simple as a tiny toe tap could easily push her off into the vast empty space of the chamber, leaving her scrabbling madly to regain a foothold on the outer walls. Pinwheeling out of control through the dock was *not* the first impression Ceres wanted to make with her guest.

Her heads-up display indicated that the docking bay's pressurization had equalized. The station usually kept the bay in a vacuum, equalized to outer space. But today's visitor wasn't wearing a pressure suit, so getting her from the space plane cockpit to the habitat rings meant providing air. Ceres reached up and touched her own suit's collar and felt the smart-gel peel back from her face. She gagged involuntarily as the last of the gel cleared her breathing passages and withdrew into the collar's receptacle.

The space plane's hatch unsealed with a puff of air, and the craft's stairway lowered to the deck. A few moments later, Max ducked her head through the hatch and looked around warily, her hair swirling in the low gravity. "Hello?"

"Hi!" Grinning madly, Ceres pushed away from the airlock

doorway where she'd been waiting and soared across the hangar. She reached the plane's stairway and, with a bit more flourish than necessary, spun herself to a halt with a deft hand-grab and toe-touch. "Welcome to your first space station!"

Max just stared at her, looking bewildered and a bit green. "Thanks. This weightlessness thing sounds better in theory than in practice."

"Oh! Right. Sorry, I forgot." Ceres fumbled inside a pocket on one of her gloves and pulled out a small plastic patch. "I've spent my whole life dealing with variable gravity, but apparently it's a challenging adjustment for someone who isn't used to it. Put this medical patch on your neck. It'll help with the motion sickness you're feeling."

Reaching forward hesitantly, Max took the patch and pressed it against the side of her neck, just beneath her ear. She gave Ceres a wan smile. "Thanks."

The two girls just looked at each other for a few seconds, suddenly at a loss for words. The awkwardness grew, and finally Ceres broke the silence and asked, "Do you...want to see the rest of the station now?"

Max gave a little start. "Of course! Sorry. I'm just feeling a little overwhelmed by all of this. How do I maneuver in this space? Should I just—"

It took a few minutes, but Ceres got Max to climb down the stairway, and then showed her how to use the handholds arranged every few meters to pull her way across the docking bay. At first, Max moved slowly, arresting her forward momentum at each handhold and carefully lining up her next move. But eventually she grew more confident, and soon she was boldly drifting from handhold to handhold without hesitation.

"Very good!" Ceres said. "How about something a bit more challenging?" She kicked hard against the wall and tumbled out into the open space of the hangar, spinning and flipping. Just before reaching the far wall, she arrested her spin. She grabbed a handhold and looked "down" toward Max.

Max was staring at her, mouth wide with surprise. At first, Ceres thought perhaps the girl wouldn't follow her. But then she saw Max's mouth snap shut, and with a determined expression on her face, her visitor kicked herself into space, flipping and twisting in much the same way Ceres had. Delighted, Ceres tucked her boots into wall-holds and clapped enthusiastically as Max spun her way across the hangar.

Max's landing wasn't as graceful as Ceres's had been, and her shoulder collided against the wall with a solid thump. Ceres moved toward her, concerned, but Max was laughing and smiling despite the hard bump. "I have to do that again!" she said, and without waiting for an answer from Ceres, she kicked off again for another try at micro-gravity gymnastics. Ceres followed, and the two of them spent the next few minutes giggling and tumbling through the hangar space. Max's maneuvering continually improved, and soon she was nearly as graceful as Ceres.

Max's quick learning impressed Ceres but also left her feeling just a tiny bit frustrated. Ceres was supposed to be the expert with a lifetime of experience, and Max was supposed to be the struggling newbie. Ceres realized she wasn't used to competition, and it was going to take a while to adjust to having another human on the station, especially someone with superior genes like Max.

After one more wild, bouncing trajectory through the hangar, Ceres pulled up next to her new companion and said, "Now do you want to continue the tour?"

Max gazed wistfully at the open docking space but nodded. "Yeah, sure."

Ceres led the way to the airlock and to the central lift. She proceeded to give Max a quick tour of the entire station. She started with the inner ring that contained sleeping quarters, moved out to the control room ring, and then moved further out to the library ring. The last stop was Ceres's favorite place in the station—the orchard ring. As the two girls strolled up and down the various paths, Ceres took great pride showing off her best cross-breeding examples and offering different fruits and berries to Max as they walked.

Through the progression of the station tour, Max had grown more and more agitated. The smile she'd had in the docking bay had quickly faded, replaced by a forced grimace, and then an outright frown. After declining the third piece of fruit that Ceres offered to her, she blurted out, "Ceres, this is all very interesting, but when am I going to see *you*?"

Ceres, shocked by the sudden outburst, rocked back a bit on her feet. "See me? What do you mean?"

Max's face turned red and angry. "Stop toying with me. It isn't funny."

"Toying with you?" Ceres laughed. "What are you talking about? 'See me?' I don't even understand the question. I'm right here!" Growing even more puzzled by Max's behavior, Ceres absently popped a cherry into her mouth, chewed on it, and spit out the pit.

Max stared at her, incredulous. "Ceres, I'm serious. Come out here, right now!"

"Max, calm down," Ceres said, trying to keep her own voice soft and soothing. "It's okay. I'm right here." Internally, she said, "Rhea, is something wrong with her? Maybe we should check her vitals. Perhaps she was injured on the ride up from the surface—"

"You're not 'right here,' Ceres!" Max reached out and shook—something—dangling in front of the grape vines. "*This* is not you." She shook another *thing*. "Neither is *this*. None of these things are you!"

"I—" Ceres began, but she found that she couldn't speak. *What is that thing Max is manipulating in front of the plants?* She couldn't see it properly, no matter how she turned her head. It was like a perpetual blind spot, confounding her ability to see.

Something was wrong.

"Why are you sending all these machines to guide me around the station?" Max demanded. "Why did you send that *thing* to teach me how to maneuver in microgravity in the dock? Or speak to me remotely while I toured the library? Why is this *contraption* pulverizing fruit and spitting out seeds?"

"Max, I—" Ceres started again. She felt dizzy and confused. "I'm sorry, what? Did you say—? What did you see again?"

Exasperated, Max stepped forward and stared intently into Ceres's eyes. "This is what I see, Ceres. This is all you've shown to me since I arrived on the station."

In her mind, Ceres was assaulted by a bright, clear vision, projected from Max's connection to the Persephone network. A tall, boxy, drone-like device that was topped with a bundle of sensory nodules and equipped with several long grasping appendages and pruning tools. Cherry juice dripped from one of the drone's orifices.

"But that's...no, that's not..."

Max reached out and grasped her by the shoulders. "This thing is just one of my many tour guides, Ceres. Why won't you come out and talk to me yourself?"

Ceres could feel Max's hands on her shoulders, but in the projected mental image, Max's hands were shaking the boxy drone. The disconnect between what she felt and what Max saw was like a white-hot knife stabbing into her brain.

The blind spot that had impaired her vision dissolved, and a flood of juxtaposed images poured into her mind. The memory of plucking fruit from the trees with her bare hands overlapped with robotic auto-pruning limbs—like the one Max had shaken in front of her face—pulling the same fruit from the same branch. Soaring through the docking bay performing flips and cartwheels...that wasn't her. That was another drone, pulsing through the space on tiny bursts of air. There was no red candle-wax pressure suit or smart-gel mask, just a handoff of control from one mechanical device to another. Images of searching through the library shelves and flipping through physical books were replaced by something even less appealing: computer programs running search routines through the station's data warehouses. No books, no tables or chairs, no cozy reading nooks.

Nothing—none of the life Ceres remembered—was real. Each memory was just the figment of a computer's imagination.

Including Ceres herself.

In a slow, inexorable slide, Ceres felt her very existence tilt and crumble beneath her feet. Except she had no feet. She reached up to hold her face in her hands, but she had no face, no hands. She was no more than an amalgamation of clever computer code and a host of robotic surrogates—a collection of station equipment operated by a sentient software program. She was artificial. Inhuman. Nothing. As nothing, Ceres spiraled away from the world, an ouroboros hopelessly chasing its existential tail, seeking self-identity where none was to be found. Dwindling, fading, gone.

"Ceres?" Max was saying, still standing before a suddenly limp drone in the orchard. "Are you going to come out and see me? Are you there?"

"A system error has occurred," Rhea announced. "Please evacuate the station immediately."

"Ceres?" Max said again, alarmed.

No one answered. No one could.

26

"BUT I *SAW* HER! WHEN she rescued me from the banshees and pulled me into the manufactory tower. Sonya, I saw her! I saw Ceres!"

"Max, you saw a young girl in the tower. But you, the tower, and the girl were all in virtual space. Nothing you saw was real. Every object in that place was a projection. The banshees weren't actual banshees; they were virtual manifestations of the New Puritan virus. The manufactory tower wasn't a tower; it was a secure port into the manufactory subnetwork that Ceres used to pull you out of the corrupted network. And the girl you saw was just a virtualization of the station pilot. She wasn't real. None of it was. Everything you experienced in the virtual was just that: virtual."

It was the same argument Max and the Sister had been having for the last half an hour. To her credit, Sonya's voice still maintained the unflappable patience of a parent explaining a disappointing situation to a child.

Max found her tone maddening. "But she looked so *real!* Her blond hair, her beautiful tan skin, her smile. I felt her hug me! I felt her breath on my cheek! Sonya, it was all so *real!*"

Sonya nodded. "Yes, I remember. The virtuality is enticing because it feels even *more* real than reality. The resolution of the things you see and touch and taste are so vivid that the physical world our bodies reside in pales in comparison. I remember, Max. It's why I decided to enact the Persephone protocol in the first place."

"So you're telling me that, despite how real Ceres appeared to me, in reality, she...what? Doesn't exist?"

Sonya scowled at that. "I'm disappointed, Max. Of course she exists! Human existence isn't limited by arbitrary parameters like the DNA in our genes or the physical composition of our bodies and minds. Ceres may operate as a programming algorithm on the quantum processors of her habitat, but she's still just as real—and just as human—as you or me. She has thoughts and emotions like any normal human. She even interacts with the physical world via her surrogate drones. She's no less human than you and I might be, considering our genetically mutated bodies."

Max thought about Sonya's words. It was true that she and Sonya were different than the colonists, but did those differences make them inhuman? Max had struggled with her special abilities all her life, but she'd never doubted her humanity.

But if Max, with all her genetic modifications, was still human, exactly how many more genetic mutations would it take before she wasn't? If she'd been designed with gills, or horns, or a third eye, would she still be human? What physical change would constitute the definitive line drawn in the sand that separated human from inhuman?

Max couldn't picture how such a sharp line could realistically exist. And if she couldn't find the line in the physical world, how could she possibly judge Ceres based on her less-than-tangible differences? After all, didn't her friend in the station think and act just like any other human she'd ever met? Didn't Ceres laugh, and cry, and ask questions just like all the other children who lived in the colony? Why should it matter if Ceres lived in a virtual world instead of a physical one? Wasn't that just another arbitrary line in the sand?

While Max pondered these metaphysical questions of humanity, Sonya said, "Darius never made any distinction between the virtual and the physical. A child born and raised as a computer program would be just as viable and precious in his worldview as any other. It's hard not to admire his open-mindedness on such issues, despite his many other deficiencies. Ceres may be Darius's most amazing gift to humanity yet—the first fully digital human."

Max thought about the late Darius Langford and how he'd managed to leap back and forth during his lifetime from a physical body, to a virtual life, and then back again. She snapped her fingers. "I know how we can rescue Ceres!" she exclaimed.

Sonya looked skeptical.

Max said, "When the colony ship first arrived here at Leap, *everyone* was a digital copy of a human from Earth, right? But the artificial wombs, which we've been using to bring babies to term, are capable of instantiating a digital personality into a human body. That's how you came to live on the surface with the first settlers, isn't it? We can do the same thing for Ceres! We can rescue her from the virtual!"

Sonya's face flashed through comprehension and sorrow as Max spoke. "I'm sure that was exactly my brother's original intention," she said. "Which is why the virtual world Ceres lives in so closely mirrors the physical environment of the station. It's the same virtual world that we, the original settlers, inhabited during our supposed journey from Earth to Leap. Just like us, Ceres was supposed to believe that she'd physically grown up on the station, and when she eventually instantiated a cloned body, the move from the virtual to the physical would be inconsequential. Her true beginnings as a computer program would be irrelevant.

"But Max, Ceres won't be following in the settlers' footsteps. We can't transfer her to a clone."

"What? Why not?"

Sonya, as was her wont, ticked off fingers. "First, we have no more artificial wombs. Darius used the remaining wombs at the original settlement to instantiate his clones, and the wombs I'd hidden in the caves were stolen when the Chorus raided the colony, only to be washed away during the high tide. Even if we could find one of the stolen wombs, damage from the salt water and heavy surf would make it useless.

"Second—because I know what you're thinking, Max—we can't ask for the manufactory to provide more artificial wombs. It's the one technology that won't appear on the orbital's master blueprint list. Darius committed their design to his personal memory and never encoded their design specifications anywhere else. It was one of the technologies that the humans on Earth desperately wanted my brother to reveal to them, and the one technology he refused to ever share. Hundreds of scientists tried to reverse engineer the technology, but without success. I myself have tried for the last forty years I've lived on Leap, and I'm still no closer to understanding how the wombs function. Now that Darius is gone, the secret of the artificial wombs and the cloning technology they provided is lost forever.

"I'm sorry, Max, but your friend Ceres is going to have to learn to live in her current environment. If she recovers from her breakdown, she'll still have to spend the remainder of her life trapped on the space station."

Max wanted to argue with Sonya, to find fault with her logic, but as always, the woman's reasoning was as flawless and as exasperating as ever. Without the blueprint to the artificial wombs, creating a body to host Ceres's download was impossible. Darius, in his mad grab for power, had destroyed any hope the girl on the station had for physically inhabiting the planet she so desperately wanted to visit. Perhaps, over time, Max and Sonya could reinvent Darius's cloning technology, but that kind of solution could take years, or even decades, to develop.

"There's one more thing," Sonya said. "Ceres is already aware of her true form, and that discovery has resulted in a catastrophic breakdown in her psyche. Now, based on what you've told me about your friend, I believe she might eventually overcome the shock she's suffered, but she lives in a world none of us can reach. We can't help her. She'll have to help herself. All we can do is wait and hope. Because without her continued help, the colony will soon descend into desperate straits again. Without artificial wombs, genetic modification is never going to be an option for future colonists, so we're going to need Ceres to interface with the manufactory to provide us with the equipment base humans need for our long-term survival. Without Ceres, the future of Leap's colony is bleak."

"So, even if we *could* transfer Ceres to a cloned body, we *wouldn't*, would we?" Max said. "She's too valuable to us in her position as go-between. Bringing Ceres to the planet surface will never be a viable long-term solution, will it?" Max felt her frustration rising. Sonya's technical explanations were just convenient excuses for the real truth—Ceres *had* to stay trapped in her virtual environment for the sake of the colony.

"Max," Sonya said, "believe me, if it were possible to save Ceres, we would. We'd figure out a way to maintain the safety of the colonists while rescuing your friend. I want to save her as much as you do."

Sonya's words sounded sincere, but Max knew the Sister

well, and she knew Sonya was using her years of practice as a preacher to pitch a message she didn't really believe. Sonya had no intention of ever relieving Ceres from her duties on the habitat. Even if there had been artificial wombs available, Sonya would have found another excuse for not providing Ceres an escape from her current situation. Sonya's responsibility to her own children, the many human colonists she'd birthed on Leap, outweighed her need to save one lone, digitized girl.

Angry and defeated, Max clenched her fists and stormed out of Sonya's office, ignoring the woman's half-hearted protests. Max felt disconnected and misunderstood. She didn't want to talk to anyone anymore.

No, that wasn't true. She wanted to talk to one person, but that person was no longer answering. Max was alone again.

She spent the next few days drifting numbly through the routines of her colonial lifestyle. Her father insisted that she return to classes, which she did. But she ignored her lessons, refusing to answer questions or complete any homework that was assigned to her. Her teachers seemed nonplussed by her reticent behavior, but they didn't punish or scold her. Max suspected that, behind the scenes, Sister Sonya was encouraging the colonists to exercise patience and restraint.

The restraint extended beyond the classroom. When performing her afternoon chores, Max was given a wide berth by her fellow colonists, both young and old. She felt like she was living in an invisible bubble—a force field that followed her wherever she went—forcing everyone around her to rebound. The bubble served not only to keep other colonists at a distance, but it also dulled the words they spoke, and fuzzed out the funny looks they gave her. Max was able to ignore almost everything happening around her, doing the bare minimum tasks necessary as a colonist and spending the rest of her energy staying safely insulated inside her own head.

The worst offenders were Ellie and her group. From day to day, the little band of Ellie's followers seemed to completely change their minds about how to approach Max. On the one hand, it was now completely obvious to the colonists that Max was genetically mutated to survive Leap's environment. For the Purity movement, Max represented everything that had caused the original colony's downfall.

On the other hand, the colonists knew that Max had led the Chorus away from the canyon and returned without them. Neither Max nor Sonya offered any further explanations about what had happened, but the rumor still spread that Max had defeated the Chorus in battle and saved the colony from whatever terrible fate the cloned monsters had been planning. Add to that Max's ability to request much-needed supplies from the manufactory, and suddenly the Purity movement had a serious quandary on their hands.

Ellie and her band—including Aida, Max noted with disgust—waffled between detest for Max's altered biology and hero-worship for her ability to save the colony. They followed Max almost everywhere she went, and she could feel them observing her from the periphery of her imaginary bubble. Their perpetual surveillance bled through Max's filter of indifference, a subtle but steady irritant in her day-to-day routine that left her chafed and aggravated every night when she returned home. The constant annoyance inevitably drove her out of her bedroom in the middle of every night to take long evening walks on the surface to settle her thoughts.

Max kept hoping that, eventually, she'd hear Ceres's voice echoing through her head. She sent messages regularly to the Persephone network but never received a reply. During her evening walks on the plateau above the canyon, she'd stare up at the starry sky and wait for those brief moments when the orbital, shining high above her, streaked across the heavens, its silence echoing Ceres's painful absence.

Five days after returning to the planet surface from the space habitat, while sitting in class and daydreaming about nothing in particular, Max opened her eyes and found that she'd inadvertently projected herself into the warm yellow room that represented the entrance to the virtuality.

With a tiny yelp, Max shook herself awake again. The other students stared at her outburst. As always, Max ignored them.

During the next few days, Max revisited the yellow room, exploring its space. Its walls, floor, and ceiling were firm and solid, giving no hint of the raving madness that existed just beyond their borders. The room's space, with its directionless soft light and subtle heat, was a place of comfort and refuge for her, and she soon began to leave part of her mind inside it to bask in the glow of the virtual while her body performed mundane tasks around the colony. At night, she coexisted in the sunny virtuality and the windy, starlit climes of Leap's wilderness.

It was during one of those chilly evenings, thinking back again about her harrowing journey into the infected network, that Max found her virtual self in possession of a long coil of rope. She wasn't sure how it had come to exist. She'd been thinking about her panicked climb up the tower, rescued just in time by Ceres from the ravenous viral banshees, and how, now that Ceres seemed to be lost inside her own virtual network, a similar rescue wouldn't happen again. If Max were trapped inside the network a second time, she'd need her own gear to provide her with an escape route.

And then she looked down, and the rope was lying in her hands.

Max examined the rope, tugging on the flexible woven fibers to test their strength. The rope was certainly long enough to reach the tower window she'd entered, but she'd need—

At the end of the rope was a metal grappling hook, giving that end of the rope added weight. Max swung the hook on the end of the rope and released it. The hook sailed across the yellow room, colliding soundlessly with one of the yellow walls and falling to the floor. She tried again, with more energy, and the hook flew straight and true exactly where she aimed it. As she retrieved the grappling hook and coiled the rope, the beginnings of a plan began forming in her mind. An outlandish plan, to be sure. A plan Sister Sonya would insist was beyond dangerous and outright impossible. But Max didn't care. For the first time in a very long while, she felt hope surge through her veins.

In both the virtual and the real, Max smiled. "It's time for another trip," she said aloud, hearing one set of her words echo back to her from the warm imaginary walls, while the other set was carried away on the ceaseless winds of Leap.

27

"GOOD MORNING, CERES. DID YOU sleep well?"

Ceres didn't answer. She never answered. *I'm a computer program. I didn't sleep well because I didn't sleep. I never sleep. I've never slept.*

"Would you like to visit the fruit grove?"

Yes, I'd like to visit the fruit grove. But I can't. I teleoperate robots in the fruit grove. That's not visiting. I can't physically visit anywhere. I'm a computer program.

"Are you prepared to discuss today's tasks?"

No, I'm not. I can't discuss anything. I have no tongue, no lips, no mouth. I'm a computer program, just like you. There's nothing to discuss. Now leave me alone. But she said nothing. She never said anything. There was nothing to say. She ignored Rhea's droning voice, just as she'd done for countless days before.

"Ceres, something strange has occurred within the Persephone network."

Despite her attempts to ignore the station's AI, this latest statement caught her attention. She felt her head swivel on her pillow, her blond hair cascade away from her face. *No, a computer program is being instructed to project those events.*

I feel nothing. I'm nothing but a computer program. She began to sink into the depths of self-denial again.

"You have a visitor," Rhea said. The artificial intelligence's voice managed to sound completely surprised and perplexed.

I'm a computer program. How does a computer program have visitors?

"Hey, stranger. Still moping, I see."

Ceres bounced off her bed, banging her head against the ceiling and ricocheting around in the sleeping chamber's microgravity.

Max was standing in the doorway, hands on her hips, grinning.

"What are you doing here?" Ceres blurted. "*How* are you here?" She reached out and stopped her bouncing. She stared at Max. Was it possible for a computer program to completely lose its artificial mind? "Rhea, what's happening?"

Max, laughing, pushed up the headlamp she had strapped to her forehead. "How I got here is a long story, and one I'm not quite ready to retell just yet. Suffice it to say that the corrupted network is still just as dangerous as the first time I visited. Fortunately, I was much better prepared this time."

"You—?" Ceres couldn't complete the question at first. She stared at her friend, noting that Max was encumbered with a vast array of gear suited for climbing as well as no small number of weapons. The girl looked like a one-woman mountain-climbing arsenal of bad-assery. To complete the look, Max's arms and legs were covered in long scratches, and a terrible gash above one of her eyes was still oozing blood. "You crossed the infected network by yourself?" Ceres said.

"Yup," Max said with another lopsided grin.

"But you could have died! Darius was the author of the virtuality, and he's still trapped in there! What were you thinking? Look at you! You've been terribly injured!"

Max studied her limbs. She shrugged, and the cuts and

contusions were gone. Then her skin darkened ever so slightly, appearing tan for the first time in her life. She giggled happily. "Oh, this is going to be *fun!*" she said, removing her remaining gear. "All new rules of reality to learn!" Like her injuries, the discarded equipment dissolved and disappeared before it ever hit the floor.

Right. Now we're both just computer programs. None of this is real. I'm not real. I'm nothing.

As if reading her very thoughts, Max stepped forward, touched Ceres on the shoulder, and said, "Just because the different layers of virtuality have different sets of rules doesn't make them any less real. I'm here with you, Ceres. We're both here on this space station, together, as real as if we were walking along together on the surface of Leap."

Ceres could feel her friend's hand on her shoulder. She could sense the warmth of her fingertips through the sleeve of her overalls. She watched her friend breathe in and out, watched her eyes move as the two girls studied each other. It felt real. It looked real. Was Max right? Did it even matter?

Max pulled Ceres close and gave her a fierce hug. "Don't worry," Max whispered, "I'm here now. Together, we're going to figure everything out."

"Figure it out?" Ceres repeated. "Figure what out?"

"Lots of things," Max said. "For starters, Sonya said that because we don't have any more artificial wombs, you're trapped alone in the station's virtuality. But I made it across the infected network, so I think we can dismiss the 'alone' part of her argument. Still, just to be sure—" Max pitched her voice slightly differently and said, "Rhea, can I assume, based upon my presence here, that the Persephone network has the capacity to run multiple, fully functioning digital humans?"

"Your assumption is correct," the station's AI answered. "The station's current computational capacity would allow for more than one thousand digital humans running at normal human speed. And additional capacity can be added to the network if required."

Max beamed at Ceres, who looked confused. "Rhea, how quickly can you instantiate another companion for us here on the station?"

"Immediately. All that is required is the command of the habitat's pilot."

"Another companion?" Ceres asked.

"Another *one thousand* companions, if that's what we want." Max beamed at her. "No need to be lonely, despite our new living conditions. And besides, the more minds we have available for research and discovery, the better."

"What? New living conditions? Research? Discovery?" Ceres felt stupid and slow. *Do computer programs feel stupid and slow?*

"New living conditions for me," Max explained. "I'll be staying indefinitely. At least until we solve the riddle of the artificial wombs. But if Darius could solve that problem, I'm sure we can eventually as well. It'll just take time, and that's one thing the virtuality provides in abundance. But if we can't solve the problem, I have another plan that might work."

Ceres felt dizzy from all of Max's ideas. "What other plan?"

Max pulled the headlamp back down onto her forehead. "The infected network is dangerous, but it's survivable. Darius might still be alive in there somewhere. After we gather a few more friends, perhaps we can launch expeditions to explore the corrupted netspace." She tapped her headlamp. "Who knows what we'll find in there? Maybe Darius is still alive, or maybe we can recover other remnant technology from before the Disaster. At the very least, it'll be an exciting adventure, eh?"

Ceres sat back on her bed, trying hard to process everything she was hearing. *Do computer programs struggle to process things?* She looked up and said, "So you're staying?

In here? With me? You'd give up Leap to live in the virtuality with a digital human?"

Max sat down on the bed next to her. "No one on Leap understands me. I was different than everyone else. Even Sonya. You may be different, too, Ceres, but I don't care. We're the same *because* we're different. We're family. So yes, I'm staying. Together, we'll provide for the colony, rebuild the orbital infrastructure, and bring more digital children into the world to join our family. Eventually, we'll reinvent the artificial wombs, and if you want, we can join the colonists on the surface as cloned humans. And we'll do all of it together." She held out her hand. "Deal?"

Ceres looked down at Max's hand, and then her own. She reached out and took her friend's, then pulled her in for another hug. "Deal."

EPILOGUE

"WILL SHE EVER COME BACK?" Nolan asked. He gently stroked Max's hair away from her forehead.

"I don't know," Sonya answered. "She must be trapped in the same virtuality as Darius. I'm not sure she can escape, and I don't know if disconnecting her from the network will help or not." She reached out and gripped Nolan's shoulder. "I'm sorry. I wish I had more useful advice. Think about what you want to do and let me know. It's your decision."

Nolan sat with his daughter, watching her eyes rapidly moving underneath their closed lids. She'd been like this for days. The one surviving Chorus clone occupied a nearby cot. After Sonya had surgically disconnected the clones from the infected virtuality, their mindless bodies had slowly begun wasting away. Two had already died, and the third was soon to follow suit. Nolan grimaced, fearing his daughter was going to suffer the same terrible fate.

That afternoon, Nolan forced himself to leave Max's bedside and took a walk out toward the kite generator. The bright sunlight made it hard for him to see, and he had to turn up the polarization on his goggles.

The goggles were new—the latest delivery from the orbital

manufactory, which had begun dropping new material shortly after Max had fallen into her coma. Whatever she'd done in the infected network, it had resulted in restarting the rescue efforts provided by the newer, more secure orbital network. Perhaps Max had managed to wake Ceres from her slumber. Nolan might never know.

Another recent addition was the occasional speck of green that dotted the windswept plateau. Nolan's booted foot nearly stepped on one of the new arrivals, but at the last minute the emerald orb obligingly hopped out of his way, floating gracefully in the breeze before landing just a few meters away.

Leap Fronds genetically mutated to survive in the winds and rocks of the high plains instead of their original tidal habitat. Just one more bizarre gift from the machines in the sky.

Nolan walked out to the rocky outcropping where he'd stashed Max's motorcycle. He ran his gloved hands back and forth across its surfaces, admiring the simple design of the machine. Utterly impractical for Leap, it represented the complete opposite of his daughter, who'd been genetically designed to survive effortlessly on the planet's surface. And yet, somehow, despite her many advantages, Max had always been the outcast among the colonists. She'd never fit.

Perhaps that's why she decided to leave us, Nolan thought, feeling tears well up and drip against the inner surface of his goggles. Angry, he removed the goggles and scrubbed the tears out of the lenses with his thumbs.

Fluttering to the ground in front of him was a folded piece of paper. It glided to the surface, stopping just a few feet away. Curious, Nolan bent down to pick it up. He unfolded the tiny piece of paper and read the contents. Then he read it again. After a very long pause, he began laughing.

He looked up and lifted his mask from his face. "Okay,

Max," he said, into the wind. "I understand. I hope you and your friends will hurry. But no matter how long it takes, I'll be waiting for you." He waved the paper at the sky. "We'll all be waiting."

Smiling, Nolan replaced his mask and goggles and walked back to the canyon. He needed to talk to Sonya and tell the Sister to let his daughter go. He knew, holding on to the piece of paper, that Max would return.

Someday.

Acknowledgements

I have so many people to thank:

- My family, who have always encouraged me to pursue my creative outlets.
- Sara Lundberg Campbell and all the other members of the Lawrence Writers Co-op, for inspiring me to write my first truly successful manuscript.
- Summer Wilson, Sarah Campbell, Madeline Turnipseed, and all the other members of the Brazos Writers, for pushing me to finish what I started.
- All of the many beta readers, for the wonderful words of encouragement, and much-needed words of constructive criticism.
- Rhonda at rondaedits.com, for copyediting my absolute *mess* of a first draft. I will forever be embarrassed by how many times I used "that" instead of "who."
- Soheil Toosi, for the absolutely beautiful cover and chapter art. He captured my vision for the story perfectly, which is a remarkable feat.
- K. Richardson, for the gorgeous audio narration. Like Soheil, she captures the spirit of my characters and story with clarity and emotion. The story comes alive when she speaks.
- And finally, my wife, Marisa, for her endless patience, boundless enthusiasm, and relentless nudging. I could not have completed this monumental task without her love and support.
- To anyone I've forgotten, I apologize for the omittance. Thank you, too.

Did you enjoy Langford's Leap?

Reviews are the best way I can garner attention for this book. As a self-published author, I don't have the benefit of a large advertising budget to get the word out. However, I have a much more effective means of promoting my book:

YOU. Honest reviews of my book attract potential readers and grow the audience for Langford's Leap. Even a short review makes a big difference. Want to help? You can jump to the Amazon page here:

https://www.amazon.com/Langfords-Leap-Ted-Boone/dp/1793921768/

Thank you!

About the Author

Ted Boone works as an Instructor for the Mays Business School at Texas A&M University, where he explores new ideas for his next science fiction novel while teaching computer programming and networking courses. When he's not busy torturing students or writing books, Ted spends his free time snuggling with his many dogs and cats, traveling abroad with his lovely wife, Marisa, and training for his next triathlon.

You can find him online at tedboone.com and Ted Boone, Writer on Facebook. You can also email him at ted@tedboone.com.